Cranks and Revolutions

Cranks and Revolutions

101 demonstrations
that might have changed the world

A Novel

Mark Gold

GREEN PRINT

© Mark Gold, 2008

First published 2008 by Green Print
an imprint of
The Merlin Press
6 Crane Street Chambers
Crane Street
Pontypool
NP4 6ND
Wales

www.merlinpress.co.uk

ISBN. 978-1-85425-097-1

The author has asserted his right under the
Copyright, Designs and Patents Act 1988
to be identified as the author of this work.

British Library Cataloguing in Publication data
is available from the British Library.

All rights reserved. No part of this publication may be
reproduced, stored in a retrieval system, or transmitted,
in any form or by any means, electronic, mechanical,
photocopying, recording or otherwise, without the prior
permission of the publisher.

Printed in the UK by Imprint Digital, Exeter

Contents

Introduction – An area the size of Belgium   7

Part One – The times they are a changin'   13

Part Two – Corruptible seed   104

Part Three – This place don't make sense to me no more   156

Part Four – The hour that the ship comes in   195

Appendix – Writer's note   222

'Never doubt that a small group of thoughtful, committed citizens can change the world. Indeed, it's the only thing that ever does.'
Margaret Mead

'You're better off laughing than crying.'
Lennie Mitchell

Introduction
An area the size of Belgium

'So finally', began the interviewer, 'how much of the Amazonian rainforest would you say has been destroyed in the last year?'

As he asked the question, he looked not at his guest, but at the large clock on the studio wall, calculating the number of seconds before he was required to play a radio station jingle and move on to the next item. Tom Moore realised from the frantic hand gestures and the exaggerated grimace from the producer sat on the other side of the glass barrier that his answer had to be quick and concise. Focusing upon the tips he had been taught many years previously at the media training course (LAWW was the message the instructor had hammered home – lively, assured, with warmth), he offered his snappy reply:

'It has been estimated that an area roughly the size of Belgium was destroyed last year alone – most of it to clear land for the cultivation of animal feed.'

'That's real food for thought', responded the presenter with what he evidently thought was startling originality, sounding fascinated yet already adjusting his notes in preparation for the next news piece. 'Tom Moore, thank you so much for coming in and taking the time to talk to us this afternoon'.

Interviewer and interviewee both took off their headphones. The former offered his thanks again, and, pointing to the studio door, checked that Tom could find his way out of the building unaccompanied before hastily replacing his headphones in time to meet his cue for the following item.

Although he had visited this and many other local radio stations numerous times before, Tom Moore was so busy beating himself up over his last contribution that he briefly took a wrong turn while making his way through the narrow corridors towards the exit. How could he have said that? For God's sake, he was over fifty years of age and had been doing this sort of thing regularly for nearly thirty years. Why on earth was he trotting out just the kind of cliché he had criticised so many others for using? What area of a country is affected by some brutal civil war? How much rainforest has been destroyed to graze cattle for the burger industry? How far has famine and disease spread during some environmental catastrophe? If you laid out the bodies of all those Africans who have died from AIDS, how far would they stretch? Whichever desperate catastrophe they were trying to publicise – and there were always plenty to choose from – campaigners like him inevitably seemed to end up comparing its scale to an area the size of Belgium.

By the time he had completed the ten-minute walk back down the hill from the radio station into the city centre, self-admonishment had given way to reflection. Why did everyone pick on Belgium as an indicator of death and destruction, he wondered? It was one thing to mock a country for producing nothing more famous than a fictional detective with the unlikely name of Hercule Poirot, but what had the inoffensive Flemish nation ever done to become a standard measure of the world's misery and degradation? For while it was true that he'd recently heard one or two maverick interviewees liken the scale of some emergency or other to an area the size of Wales, or even in one case to Bulgaria, it had become impossible for any upstart country to imitate the full, doom-laden force of the original.

It had been Tom Moore's experience that not everybody was as interested as he was in finding immediate solutions to problems as big as Belgium. Politicians, he had found, tended towards a much more cautious approach – even though they often expressed great concern over the issues Tom raised with them. Typically, their response was to adopt a sombre tone and to suggest – sometimes a bit patronisingly in his view – that 'the salami approach' would be more appropriate. Accompanied by weighty hand gestures to indicate a sharp implement cutting through imaginary sausage, they would recommend that the best way to tackle the stated problem would be slice by slice. One step at a time. The art of the possible. Nothing ruled in, nothing ruled out.

Let's face it, Tom thought, protestors and politicians are normally entirely different beings, conditioned to react differently. On the one hand, it was impossible to envisage government ministers announcing immediate allocation of unlimited funds for public transport or an outright ban on gas-guzzling vehicles. They just didn't work that way. First there would be a focus group or two and then a committee. This would be followed by the formation of several sub-committees. Reports would be initiated and consultation papers endlessly discussed. Perhaps a quango would then be set up to oversee possible implications.

By contrast, you could hardly imagine protestors marching through the streets chanting

'What do we want?'

'Signs of steady progress towards a just solution!'

'When do we want it?'

'Within the lifetime of the next parliament, provided that economic conditions meet the indicators laid down in part one of the government's White Paper and referred to by the Chancellor of the Exchequer in his pre-budget speech of November 2007!'

All Tom knew was that he hated the slice-by-slice approach. He had always wanted to demand the impossible now. He was the type of troublemaker who politicians and businesspeople dismissed as 'out of touch with the complexities of the real world'. He had never felt much attraction for their real world. And what he particularly resented were those grave hand gestures, since he wasn't deaf and didn't need sign language to assist his understanding. He may have been a vegan, but he was perfectly capable of following how to cut a lump of sausage into slices without visual aids.

Tom Moore had been an animal rights campaigner – not to mention every other kind of do-gooder – for as long as he could remember. Protest and thrive – that had been his motto. Road expansion programmes, nuclear weapons, war, racism, cancellation of Third World debt, hunting with hounds, fairtrade, seal culling – you name it, if a 'green' cause had been around to get involved with, he'd been there and worn the T-shirt. And not just the T-shirt either: other fashion accessories had included red noses, pink and purple ribbons, white poppies and campaigning wristbands – not to mention a bewildering array of badges and stickers. In service to the activist cause he had dressed up at demonstrations in a fetching array of costumes, including mad scientist, grim reaper, undertaker, politicians of various persuasions, the devil, a dalek and miscellaneous animals including a farting cow. Then there was that huge 'citizen's survival bag' he had worn over his head to ridicule government instructions on what to do in the event of a nuclear missile attack. Over the years, he had resisted few indignities, though thankfully he had at least spared the world the sight of his tackle in 'I'd rather go naked' protests. Less self-conscious colleagues, however, had embraced the fashion with relish, discarding their clothes for a plethora of good causes. They would rather go naked than wear fur or leather; they would rather go naked than eat meat, shoot or hunt; they would rather go naked than wear clothes made by slave labour, build roads that destroy the countryside or drive cars that pollute the atmosphere. He sometimes wondered if the real message was that some would rather go naked. Full stop.

In retrospect, Tom wondered whether any of his creative

attempts at fancy dress had had much influence on the world, even though many photographs of his weird and wonderful guises had found their way to the far side of the globe. Unfortunately, this had mostly been achieved via the coachloads of Japanese visitors who had insisted on having their pictures taken – one by one – alongside Ronald the Rabbit or Pippa the Panda, rather than frenzied interest from the paparazzi. In recent times, the tourists had been joined almost as enthusiastically by gaggles of young teenage girls.

'Oh my God. There's like a...giant *panda*?' one approaching youngster would exclaim, deep in phone conversation with a friend. Minutes later, she would reappear, friend and the rest of the giggling gang in tow, their mobiles poised for the impending photo-shoot.

Over the years Tom had put up with a fair amount of mockery. Acquaintances good-naturedly poked fun at him with nicknames ranging from 'bunny hugger' to 'eco-warrior' and 'wishy-washy, bleeding-heart liberal'. And that was just the light-hearted stuff. Why didn't he grow up? Why didn't he get a proper job? Why was he always trying to make people feel miserable about everything they enjoy? It's true that there were those who expressed a grudging admiration for his enduring service to the world of dissent, but there were also plenty who dismissed him as a misfit or waster. Others called him sentimental, paranoid or humourless. Clearly the kind to seek out at the local dating agency then!

It was stereotyping like this that really got up Tom's nose. 'Many of us may be a bit odd – even a little bit bonkers in some way or another', he admitted whenever a detractor drew attention to some apparent folly or nastiness committed by a fellow "protestor type". 'But when it comes to it, who is there in this big wide world without a loose screw or two? You shouldn't lump us all so easily together.' When it came to protest, his experience had been that there was rich and infinite variety out there. Indeed, if you placed all the diverse characters together, they would extend a long, long way in many different directions. Quite possibly they might encompass an area roughly the size of Belgium.

Part One –
The times they are a-changin'

1

A neighbour named Chris once gave him a lift home from a concert. While he was hardly a close friend and nearer in age to his older brother, Tom Moore had known the driver for several years and was aware that he had suffered a prolonged period of debilitating depression before recently converting to an evangelical form of Christianity. Tom felt compelled to enquire what had led to his new faith.

'By a set of circumstances that could easily be construed as a miracle,' answered Chris, intriguingly.

Tom was anxious to hear more and his chauffeur was only too glad to relate the mysterious circumstances. It turned out that, throughout his troubled and relatively solitary youth, one of Chris's greatest sources of consolation had been the songs of Bob Dylan. He was one of those passionate devotees – not uncommon during the period – who considered Dylan a prophet and treasured every word. He could recite most of the lyrics word for word, even learning to accompany them rather badly on a cheap second-hand guitar purchased specifically for the purpose. Not only did he sing Dylan's songs, he performed them in his inspiration's own voice – or at least as near as he could get to a nasal drawl complete with mid-west American accent.

From his idol, Chris also adopted a set of beliefs that included deep scepticism about orthodox religion. The anti-war ballad

With God on our Side was a particular favourite, his version including a particularly heartfelt rendition of the pivotal ironic line, 'you don't count the dead when God's on your side'. Chris's earnest execution of this lengthy old number was legendary at local folk clubs, though not entirely for positive reasons. Invariably the audience's overwhelming reaction was one of relief at the conclusion rather than admiration of the deeply felt interpretation. When asked what his songs were about, Dylan once famously remarked that some were about three minutes and some were about six. In Chris's hands, they might seem to last about as long as any winter's night in Siberia.

Years passed without much discernible change in Chris's troubled outlook. Then, out of the blue, Dylan re-invented himself as the voice of born-again Christianity rather than a champion of rebellious youth. Humanity would have to make a simple choice, he sang, between the Devil and the Lord. Chris heard the Word of Bob Dylan in his twenty-eighth year and decided to serve the Almighty. And that was the full extent of the miracle.

Like many children of the sixties, Bob Dylan played a significant part in Tom Moore's development too – though he had never considered there to be anything particularly miraculous about it. His admiration for the singer had been more an inheritance than a discovery. The circumstances were these. Tom had been brought up in a fairly large – if a little neglected – Edwardian detached house on the edge of a comfortable market town in Somerset. His parents were ex-Cambridge intellectuals with impeccable liberal and radical credentials. His father, a greatly admired university lecturer, was engaged particularly in promoting the Arts and their role in humane education. He had written three successful books on educational matters and published regular articles in academic journals. His mother taught with energy and dedication at a nearby primary school. Tom also had a big brother, Rob – more than six years his senior – whom he worshipped.

Through the mid 1960s, the older Moore child enjoyed a mostly contented school life at a single-sex grammar school with a reputation for academic achievement and traditional values. He had a lot going for him. He was clever, athletic, easy-going, witty and popular with his peers; a bit of a natural leader, too. Rob seemed to take everything easily in his stride – daring and rebellious enough to impress his colleagues, yet sensible enough not to go too far and invite hostility from the conservative teaching establishment. On the rare occasions when he did overstep the mark, he had the happy knack of avoiding detection. The only near exception had been that worrying incident in his third year, when the text of an article in the school magazine entitled *The Thrill of Drag Racing* had been altered to create a crude and smutty adolescent piece called *The Fill of Shag Racing*. The doctored copy had accidentally fallen into the hands of Deputy Headmaster Mr Wragg, resulting in an investigation of near-fanatical proportions by that menacing black-gowned enforcer of the school's prized ethos. Wragg's dedication to his role was unstinting. He circled around class 3A like a vulture waiting to pounce on his prey, causing Rob to go home from school in terror on three consecutive afternoons. A public caning would inevitably follow any establishment of guilt and anticipation of the pain and humiliation was almost unbearable. Yet despite the terrible pressure that 'old dish Wragg' managed to exert – including a series of detentions for the whole form – none of his colleagues had betrayed him. The exasperated inquisitor played his final card, peering threateningly over his spectacles and handing every pupil in class 3A a piece of paper on which they could write down in complete confidence any information that might lead to the culprit's apprehension. Once this shabby tactic had been defied, Rob knew that he was safe. The matter was reluctantly dropped and his only close call with corporal punishment had passed.

As they approached their senior years at grammar school, Rob and his friends came to consider themselves an elite crowd, gurus of good taste and culture. Women, politics, music and art were among the issues that most engaged their teenage minds, and they entertained no doubts as to their own exquisite taste. Some weekends this privileged and mostly carefree bunch would gather in Rob's large attic bedroom at the front of the Moore residence – a room that fully reflected the refinement of its occupant. Adorning the walls were posters of Brigitte Bardot, Marilyn Monroe, Van Gogh's Sunflower, Che Guevara and the inevitable Bob Dylan. Saturday night entertainment was regularly enhanced by the illicit purchase from the local off-licence of a large bottle of cheap Woodpecker cider, the wearing of Rob's fashionable little square-shaped sunglasses, expressions of outrage against 'the system' for a wide range of perceived injustices, the ending of most sentences with the word 'man' and a portable gramophone dominated by the music of Dylan. The Beatles had only recently emerged from their simple pop song period and were still considered too much part of the detested system. The Rolling Stones were more cutting-edge, yet still bore the unforgivable stigma of regular appearances on that fortress of the establishment, *Top of the Pops*. The enigmatic Dylan, on the other hand, presented the perfect role model for this self-consciously arty and alternative set. They emblazoned his name large upon their school rucksacks to demonstrate to the world their superiority and sophistication.

Tom was normally excluded from the gatherings of wisdom and learning in Rob's bedroom, but occasionally filial affection would get the better of his big brother and the youngster's presence would be tolerated. And since the big boys championed Dylan so passionately, he quickly learnt to do the same. By the time he reached the age of eleven, Tom Moore knew all the words to those angry protest songs – from *Masters of War* to *Desolation Row*. He could rage against war, racism, impending nuclear disaster, religion and reactionary authority as passionately as the most fervent teenage rebel. The only difficulty was that he had very little outlet for his revolt. His parents were dedicated to liberal enlightenment, so there was really little point in telling them 'not to criticise what they don't understand', nor that their 'sons and their daughters are beyond their command'. Indeed, both of them positively welcomed signs of a dissenting streak in their children. How could they not, when John Moore's teaching and writing had been ruled by a belief that the Arts should be a tool to develop a questioning instinct against authority and orthodoxy?

The parents had met during their second year as Cambridge University students in the mid 1930s, part of that significant minority of left-wing intellectuals who sympathised resolutely with communism and Soviet Russia in particular. They were inspired by what they read about reforms there since the revolution – equal rights for women, universal education and rapid strides in the fight against hunger and extreme poverty. They compared reports of Soviet energy and idealism with what they saw as their own inequality-ridden world, wracked by social injustice and obnoxious class prejudice. Above all, they saw in Stalin and the communist state the only principled opposition to Nazism, contrasting it with the tacit approval of Hitler in influential areas of the British establishment. And so it was that this passionately idealistic young couple spent many of their university days under the wings of the Communist Party, spreading the anti-fascist message as far and wide as they could.

Soon after the end of the war – which he managed to sail through by getting himself a position in a 'protected occupation', managing a department within a factory producing nuts and bolts for ammunition – John Moore had seen and heard enough of the Soviet regime to realise that it was not quite as admirable as he had once believed. Nevertheless, when the scale of atrocities was reported in more detail after Stalin's death in 1953, he found some of his youthful enthusiasms difficult to revise. He read about the reign of terror, the arrest of an estimated twelve million 'enemies of socialism' and the million deaths by state executions or as a result of the harsh regimes in the Soviet prison camps – and chose to be sceptical of every word. This denial was not, as it might seem, a result of unshakeable left-wing values or the continued belief that Marxist doctrine was a panacea for all human injustice. Neither was he in complete denial about atrocities that had taken place. It was more a matter of scale. Tales linking Stalin with persecution and genocide were exaggerated. Russia was a vast country in chaos both before and after the war, so the leader of such a nation could not be expected to be aware of everything that had occurred. The presentation of Stalin as a monster of Hitler-like proportions was a propaganda exercise fuelled by US paranoia about the dangers of communism. How could you possibly be convinced by reports originating from a nation that was still conducting vicious witch-hunts against left-wing sympathisers? And while anti-Russian sentiment might not be so extreme over here in the UK, our media also had a Cold War agenda and could not be trusted either. No, Stalin might be flawed like every other human being, but he was no evil monster. He had modernised feudal Russia and – despite the unfortunate brief alliance with Hitler – forcefully opposed fascism. Nobody could deny that.

Ever since his rejection of communism in his late twenties, John had in fact developed a deep cynicism about political solutions – or indeed any solutions – to the darker forces of human nature. His only real enduring faith was in teaching. Art, he believed, represented the best that humans could think and feel. Helping others to appreciate its power and wisdom was to open a window upon civilising forces. Literature could encourage empathy and understanding. This was his doctrine. It was not altogether surprising therefore that it took a work of fiction to change his opinion of Stalin where politicians and journalists had previously failed. It was in the first few days of 1964 that he picked up Alexander Solzhenitsyn's *One Day in the Life of Ivan Denisovich*. A translated version had recently been published to great critical acclaim and Margaret had given the hardback edition to her husband as a Christmas gift. John felt sceptical about the enterprise, assuming it to be more American inspired anti-Soviet propaganda, but the quality of the narrative soon convinced him otherwise. This was persuasive, great literature and the tale must be trusted. He sat by the glowing coal fire with the slim volume open on his lap. Outside the snow was falling again on an already hard frozen ground. The afternoon light was fading fast and the trees appeared ghostly white and gloomily beautiful. On the arm of his comfy, cat-clawed armchair sat a steaming mug of tea and a large chunk of homemade cake. As he followed the story of the starving prisoner, aching with cold and hunger inside the heartless Siberian labour camp, he visualised the frost-bitten hero, worked half to death and savouring every last crumb of his meagre daily ration of soggy black bread. The extent of his own misjudgement hit him hard. It made him feel uneasy about his own comfortable existence. John looked across at his two young boys, both of whom had spent the afternoon frolicking in the snow and were now sprawled out across the floor in dry clothes, warming themselves in front of the fire and contentedly playing with Christmas presents. Rob was reading a sport annual and doing his best to ignore Tom, who was involved in an intense game of traffic jams that featured his loud range of car and bus noises.

'Mmmmmmmmm, urhhh,' young Tom yelled, the sudden change to a piercing 'urhhh' indicating an emergency that demanded urgent application of brakes.

The father smiled indulgently, yet gripped by the angst of parenthood. Pangs of protective love mingled with fear for the future. What did the world have in store for his children? More injustice and war? Nuclear annihilation? Political corruption? And what did his long denial of the depth of Stalin's betrayal tell him about his own powers of discrimination? How could he – who prided himself above all else on his fine intellect – have admired a man responsible for so much suffering and brutality? Who had he been kidding with his assertions about the enlightening qualities of literature and art? It all seemed so pie-in-the-sky when human beings were capable of such horror. What did it matter that Solzenitzyn's tale was of heroic endurance and stoicism in the face of vicious persecution, if that was the best that could be hoped for? Was there more to endure than to enjoy – was that all there was in life?

Although John Moore was not given to self-dramatisation, a physical sensation in his gut made him question whether things could ever quite be the same for him again. As hard as he might struggle to remain optimistic and angry in the face of injustice and inequality, he was weighed down by a gnawing sense of disillusionment. Yes, he would go on earning his daily bread by extolling the civilising values of humane education, but in his heart he no longer truly believed in human progress, let alone greatness.

Or perhaps, as he approached his fiftieth birthday, he was just growing old and grumpy.

Throughout childhood, their parents were forever wheeling out the Moore boys on some protest or other. Outside school assemblies it was the nearest thing in their lives to religious ritual and they mostly went along with it unquestioningly. For the younger Moore child, sitting in his pushchair in the middle of the huge, noisy crowd on an Aldermaston to London anti-nuclear march was amongst his strongest early memories. It must have been the end of the 1950s. Rob's recollections of these annual events were much more vivid, of course, the procession being associated with the Easter bank holiday as surely as chocolate eggs. The whole event fascinated him. Brought up as he was in an atheist household, it was a teenage girl limping along the procession barefoot, her feet bloody with blisters, that provided a far more haunting Good Friday symbol of human suffering than the death of Christ. He could also remember the excitement of the day out – the early morning start, the café where the family always stopped on the way home for tea and cakes, the friendly strangers who gave him and his brother sweets, the awe-inspiring size of the march and his weariness at the end of the walk. Although the family only joined the procession for the same four miles along the route each year, it felt like a long, long way for a nine or ten-year-old and he was proud of the achievement. He could recall, too, jazz bands with their joyful versions of *Down by The Riverside* and *When The Saints Go Marching In* and the heartfelt singing of the protestors – particularly the conviction with which his mother joined in on *We Shall Overcome*. Her soaring soprano voice sounded as if she really believed they would. The highlight of these outings, however, was always meeting up with his Aunt Helen, who had a toddler, Sophie, of roughly Tom's age and an even smaller baby girl, both of whom were pushed along on the same section of the march as the younger Moore child.

Helen Newton was a family friend rather than a blood relation – one of a number of his father's ex-students who had become part of the Moore social circle and to some extent disciples of their teacher. She had that generous, unpatronising charm that some adults instinctively possess with children and the young boy was enchanted by her white blonde hair, warm blue eyes and infectious smile. She always found time to take Rob aside for a chat and he had an innocent crush on her.

Unlike John Moore or most of his former pupil friends, Helen's pivotal interest was politics rather than art or literature. If there was a radical cause to be supported, she would find it. She was at the forefront of local CND activities and – amongst other things – a leading light in the UK Communist Party, a vegetarian and the leader of a support group for Castro's Cuban revolution. In contrast to her mentor, she possessed an immovable belief in the potential of humanity to share and improve. If communism had failed in the Soviet Republic or elsewhere – and she was perfectly willing to accept that it had – it was simply down to the frailty of the ruling elite. Next time it would be different. The fact that every attempt at socialist political solutions had thus far failed to live up to her hopes and expectations could do nothing to diminish her faith. She dismissed the achievements of Atlee's post-war Labour government because it hadn't been radical enough. In Russia and the rest of Eastern Europe, the problem was that Stalin and Khrushchev were inherently corrupt, not that the core ideology was suspect.

If these views and such political fervour suggest a rather fierce and uncompromising personality, then nothing could be further from the truth. Helen Newton oozed kindness and gentleness. In her personal relations she was as trusting as in her revolutionary sentiments. She would help anybody, and if or when they let her down she seemed to show no bitterness, nor behave any more guardedly next time around. It was nobody's fault. Shortcomings in individuals were simply the result of deficiencies in the political and educational process. It was all down to nurture.

Her optimism was currently invested in Cuba. She dismissed any negative press coverage as capitalist propaganda.

'This time it's really happening. Giant US companies are being dispossessed without compensation and all the large estates are being turned into state farms. The land is being redistributed to small farmers, who are forming co-operatives. Castro has declared that half of casino profits will go to help the poor. It'll be an example that will change the world.'

As fond as he was of her, John Moore found such unstinting enthusiasm a bit much to take. It was still a few years before the Solznitzyn book and the full depth of his disillusionment with the Soviet Russian regime, but he had already seen enough of the world's ways to judge Helen's optimism as absurdly naïve. More than this, her belief in some socialist utopia irritated him more than he could understand. It made him chronically aware of how completely his own youthful zeal had faded.

As the sixties progressed, the Moore family kept the flame of protest burning bright. Every so often Tom would volunteer for the equivalent of a lent period, encouraged by his mother to give up sweets in solidarity with the victims of some African or Asian independence struggle. While he couldn't be described as keen, he accepted the self-sacrifice without complaint. For the parents, there were also CND activities, the struggles against capital punishment and for legalised abortion, plus a growing interest in conservation and environmental protection. The latter – a particular concern of the father as his disenchantment with the human race intensified – came to a head in the early spring of 1967, when thousands of seabirds became victims of an ugly and lethal oil slick off the Cornish coast. A tanker, the *Torre Canyon*, had run aground and discharged its deadly cargo right across the English Channel. It was by far the most widely publicised wildlife disaster the country had witnessed. The Moore family sprang into action. Every Sunday they drove off on a two-hour journey to the nearest emergency rescue centre, where the sight of hundreds of helpless birds affected them deeply. As he struggled – often in vain – to wash away the foul-smelling, sticky black oil from entangled feathers, John Moore railed angrily against the polluting greed and irresponsibility of his own species. Young Tom's reaction was more sober and reflective. It might only have been birds that were dying in front of him, but it was the first time he had witnessed suffering and death at first hand. It touched him at a level that neither words nor photographs of human misery had ever managed. He had nightmares about it.

By this time Rob was approaching the end of his schooldays. Late teenage rebellion might have been anything from joining a gang of mods or rockers to going to work in a bank or an accountant's office. Yet the urge to kick against his comfortable dissenting background was never really there. Neither was there much chance of getting into mindless scrapes with rival adolescent groups when there were passionate demonstrations against apartheid and the Vietnam War as outlets for his rising testosterone levels. If, like him, it was protest you were after, then going to university the following autumn was a journey to the perfect place at the perfect time. The Americans had civil rights and Vietnam and he and his contemporaries could give full vent to their anti-war and anti-racist sentiments without any danger of army conscription or vicious Klu Klux clan gangs. They were also free to express their opposition to South African apartheid without facing the bullying regime that upheld it. So popular were these causes amongst many of his fellow students that support for them could almost be described as a fashion, distinguished by a uniform of flowing locks, beards, beads and flowery shirts.

In opting for this colourful sixties counterculture, Rob found himself part of a movement of boundless confidence and expectation. The inequalities and violence of their parents' generation were to be swept aside, replaced by a new world of peace, love and freedom. Moreover, the creation of this Utopia was to be a vibrant and joyful affair, requiring little self-sacrifice. The hedonistic tendencies natural to every healthy young life could be given full licence, with the crucial advantage that they could also be ascribed to the highest of motives and a quest for spiritual enlightenment. Music – central to Rob and his friend's social life – invariably presented itself as integral to a struggle for justice and liberation. Cannabis would induce feelings of peace and love for all human kind. Psychedelic drugs would expand creativity and help individuals to discover their true inner self. Sex, too, was a revolutionary act. You could sleep with as many 'chicks' as possible and rationalise it as an act of feminist generosity, assisting the oppressed in their pill-inspired emancipation. Your pleasure was instrumental in their conquest of centuries of servitude and sexual repression.

Rob settled easily into this life, balancing a full social calendar with a promising academic career. While he dabbled in most of the heady experiences that the period had to offer, he was far too sensible to indulge to dangerous excess. All was going well. It was such an exciting change from the stuffy snobbery of his grammar school days. Rather than dismissing popular culture – as his schoolteachers had done – his personal tutor in the second term – Professor Bob Edwards – even shared a love of Bob Dylan, considering him one of the great poets of the age. Rob was particularly thrilled when the professor was to offer an open evening lecture on the literary importance of his favourite singer – an event that drew a huge audience of admiring students from every conceivable discipline. The professor began his exploration by playing the official recording of Dylan's *It's All Over Now, Baby Blue*, followed by two further versions of the same song, each taken from poor-quality bootleg albums recorded at live concerts. Even the most hardened fans were beginning to get a bit restless by the time these scratchy, out-of-tune offerings were over. What on earth next, they wondered? Fortunately, the professor was at last ready to begin his analysis. The question he wanted to examine over the next half an hour or so – and he used the word 'examine' loosely – was the significance of the changing lyric. Why had the poet altered 'the carpet, too, is moving under you' in the official version, to 'the red carpet, too, is moving under you' on one of the bootlegs, and 'the carpet, now, is moving under you' in the other live performance? What was Dylan trying to tell us here? Professor Edwards had already advanced several interesting theories when he was interrupted by a bold voice speaking out from the audience. It was Rob's friend Steve Burrows – a no-nonsense history student, several years older than his contemporaries and widely known as Sensible Steve.

'Excuse me Professor Edwards, but do you think that Dylan might have been stoned out of his mind when he was singing live and couldn't remember the words?' Sensible Steve suggested.

The rest of the students laughed loudly. Professor Edwards couldn't see the joke.

'A very good point. Quite possibly', he responded enthusiastically. 'I've never actually been stoned myself, so I can't say what it would feel like and how it might influence the poet's thinking. Perhaps we need to look at this further.'

The audience giggled again, only less generously. In a moment the professor had lost his street credibility. He was one of the old guard after all.

One March morning during his first year at Birmingham University, Rob Moore set off by coach to London for the first large-scale demonstration he had attended without his parents. He'd been looking forward to the protest for weeks – partly because he was full of genuine youthful outrage against the Vietnam War, but also because it promised to be fun. Several of his friends were travelling on the student union organised trip and he felt sure they'd be sharing a couple of secret cannabis joints on the journey home. He was also hoping he might get closer to Miriam Levine, a young woman who had been in his seminar group during the previous term. Her long black curly hair and dark Jewish features fascinated him and he had already passed several hours glancing surreptitiously at her across the lecture room, agonising over whether the attraction was mutual.

Was he imagining that she had caught his eye a couple of times?

The journey got off to a disappointing start. Miriam turned up with a third-year drama student named James Hayes and it was clear that they were close. Everybody in the arts faculty knew James, who, though quiet and unassuming, was admired for acting skills that had seen him play one of the leading roles in the previous term's hit production of *Waiting for Godot*. He was a bit of a catch for a first year, even one as attractive as Miriam. Envy prompted Rob's hostility towards the older man. What was a third-year doing with a woman so much younger and less experienced in the ways of the world? Surely he must only be using her? More depressingly, what chance did he have of competing for Miriam's affection against somebody so widely admired?

Despite this defeat in matters of the heart, Rob felt exhilarated when he and his colleagues eventually reached the capital and viewed the sheer mass of humanity that had already gathered in Trafalgar Square. The scene filled him with optimism. This was the brave new world that would sweep away the old order of conflict and injustice. The times really were changing.

The massive turnout had only one downside. Rob had provisionally arranged to meet up with his favourite Aunt Helen. He looked out for the Winchester Communist Party banner under which she would be marching, but the crowds were so dense and the banners from communist, union and student groups around the country so numerous that it was impossible to spot her. Having tried without success to negotiate his way across the jammed Square, he eventually gave up the search and instead settled along with tens of thousands of others to listen to the speeches. Enthusiastic applause greeted each speaker, rising to feverish adoration when Vanessa Redgrave – the main celebrity of the day and a heroine of the anti-war movement – made her way to the plinth below Nelson's Column to deliver her rallying cry. Rob, who was not very tall, couldn't see her clearly, so pushed his way nearer to the front to gain a better view. How fantastic he thought she looked, dressed in a striking orange-red cloak and white hippy headband. His taste in actresses normally leaned more towards the conventionally cool, blonde and French – Bardot and more recently Catherine Deneuve – yet how wonderful he felt it would be to find a partner as powerful, committed and beautiful as this brave and enlightened English woman!

By the time the speeches were over and the protestors were led slowly out of the Square in the direction of Piccadilly Circus, Rob's attempts to get a closer look at the actress had caused him to lose touch with his colleagues. Only strangers surrounded him. Yet what did this matter? They were all brothers and sisters of the revolution, united in their mission to create world peace. Although he was well aware of some angry anti-American chants and a few potential troublemakers, the mood on the walk out towards the American Embassy, in affluent Mayfair, seemed generally calm and peaceful. Marchers were chatting away to police officers, most of whom were cheerful and friendly. It wasn't until they were almost upon the embassy building in Grosvenor Square that Rob really became aware of a change in atmosphere. While he was some distance from the front of the protest, he could hear angry jeering ahead. A sudden surge pushed the main body of the march backwards. Minutes later, several policemen on horseback charged back down the line from the conflict area, one shouting aggressively from a loud hailer that the Americans were likely to shoot any intruders who tried to break in to the embassy grounds. As a measure to calm an excitable crowd, this wasn't the brightest move in the history of policing. What do you do if a crowd is angry? Tell them that the people with whom they are enraged are even bigger bastards than they originally thought! No sooner had the officer issued this warning than he and his colleagues were pelted with missiles by groups of previously uninvolved demonstrators.

Meanwhile, at the front violence was escalating. A militant group – some later said that they were Revolutionary Marxists, others described them as anarchists – pulled up part of the embassy security fence and hurled chunks in the direction of the building. Police struggled to repel a faction trying to break into the grounds and on towards the embassy itself. The crowd behind was pushed backwards and forward in waves. More fights broke out as the whole event began to disintegrate into chaos.

The police appeared to be in a mess, scattered haphazardly across the demonstration without riot gear for protection or any apparent strategy. As they found themselves under increasing attack, some panicked and swung their truncheons rashly. More horses were ridden dangerously into the crowd. Rob felt scared. He saw a young woman accidentally trapped beneath a nervous police horse and heard her screams above the shouting and chanting. Two young men bravely went to her aid, bending down underneath the terrified animal to pull her away. As they did so, the rider leaned towards them, swung his baton and caught one of the rescuers on the back of the head. Blood gushed out as he staggered away. The demonstrators grew angrier still. Two policemen roughly dragged away a protestor, who was pleading his innocence. Chants of 'kill the pigs, kill the pigs!' broke out from one section. Some of the crowd were enjoying the battle now. Rob watched a blood-soaked demonstrator fall to the ground under a rain of truncheon blows and felt the urge to join in. His adrenalin was rising. The police were the enemy, defenders of the reactionary forces of the state. It was time to teach the oppressors a lesson: time to prove that youth and progress could not be denied. A beating was the least they deserved.

What happened next was all over so quickly that he could hardly remember the exact chain of events. Before he could act on his impulse to attack, there was a half-tug on his shoulder from behind. His heart leapt as he wheeled round. Standing there was his student colleague, Steve Burrows.

'Quick, I want to show you something!' Steve yelled. And with that, he grabbed his friend's jacket and guided him with difficulty out of the main trouble towards an area of relative quiet on the fringes of the protest. Rob slowly began to come to his senses.

'So what were you going to show me?' he shouted, accusingly.

'Nothing. I just spotted you in the crowd, saw the look on your face when you swung round and wanted to get you out of there as quickly as I could.'

'What the fuck for? Didn't you see what those bastards were doing up there? They could have killed us.'

'For Christ's sake calm down, Rob. What the hell did you expect? Do you really think you're going to achieve anything by joining in a punch-up with the police? Believe me, you're never going to win and I didn't want to see a friend of mine in jail or hospital. Besides, I thought you were supposed to be a pacifist!!'

This last remark hit exactly the right note. Rob hesitated before emitting a strange laugh cum shriek. His anger was substantially dissipated. Steve had a point. Hadn't he always been taught that violence was wrong? Did he really want to join a riot when he had come to London to march for peace? He and his friend beat a further swift retreat.

'I still wish I'd clocked one of those bastards though!' exclaimed Rob after – despite police attempts to keep everybody hemmed into the Square – they had somehow negotiated their way out of the riot and back towards the coach park. 'It was fucking disgraceful the way they let fly at innocent people.'

'You should know the score, Rob. Most coppers are fine on their own, but once you start threatening their authority they take no prisoners. That's just the way it is – whatever you're protesting about.'

They were amongst the first to arrive back at the coach and

had to wait some time for the others to return. Eventually they drifted back in dribs and drabs, some excited by events and talkative, others quiet and shell-shocked. None had been hurt, though several had a tale to tell of near-misses, fights observed or unfair arrests. Almost everybody blamed police brutality for the trouble.

The appointed departure time passed by with three students still absent – Miriam Levine, James Hayes and a friend of theirs named Al, who Rob hadn't met before but had dismissed as a bit of a hippy poser after overhearing him on the journey to London. As far as he could tell, Al found it impossible to emit any statement without either beginning or ending it with the phrase 'far out, man'.

The missing persons roll was soon reduced to two when Al appeared, making peace signs with both hands, but unable to throw much light on the whereabouts of the other two.

'It was a really heavy scene out there, man. Those cats must have split to do their own thing. It was fucking far out, man,' was the best he could offer.

'Thanks for that Al. Very enlightening' said Sensible Steve, with obvious irritation. 'You've really no idea where they could have "split" to?'

'Don't get heavy with me, man. Stay chilled. Just blame the fucking pigs, man.'

When a further period elapsed without any sign of Miriam and James, another student was despatched to telephone the nearest hospital. She was told that there was still a good deal of chaos (which they already knew from the frequent emergency ambulance and police sirens) and that not all the injured had been registered. Somebody else suggested ringing the police for news of arrests, but this was dismissed as a waste of time. It was clearly ridiculous to imagine that this gentle pair would have been involved in a fracas, however chaotic things might have become. A decision was made to head home without them. It was known that Miriam's parents lived in North London, so there was little danger of them being left on the streets with nowhere to go. Perhaps they had telephoned her family to let them know that they were unharmed and had been encouraged to stay the night? Nothing more could be done.

The mood on the return trip was rather more sombre and considerably less romantic than Rob had imagined. He couldn't escape the image of that young woman trapped underneath the police horse and the brutal blows struck at her rescuers. It wasn't until the cannabis was passed around later in the evening that the atmosphere began to mellow a little. The day's volatile events began to seem like a distant dream.

It was late by the time they arrived back at the university halls of residence. He went straight to his room and turned on the radio for further news of the protest. 'Three hundred police have been injured in the worst riots ever seen at a British demonstration', the reader announced. 'Hundreds were arrested as an estimated 80,000 marched on the American embassy in Grosvenor Square to voice their opposition to the Vietnam War'.

Despite his own experience of events, the scale of the trouble shocked him. Exhausted, he dragged himself out to the nearest telephone to let his parents know that he was safe. Then, regardless of the emotion of the day and the mystery of Miriam's disappearance, he lay on his bed, still fully clothed, and fell fast asleep.

Over the next couple of days, the story of what had happened to James and Miriam began to emerge. A bit of a scrap had broken out between a group of militant Marxists and the police, one of whom was knocked to the ground. As the attackers ran away, an irate officer rushed up and roughly grabbed hold of a bemused James, shouting 'you'll do!' Miriam protested and the crowd jeered angrily. A few tried to pull him away, but to no avail. More police turned up and James was dragged off, bundled into a police van, driven with others to a station and, after his details were taken, locked away. 'You could be looking at three years, mate,' the stern duty officer said coldly as he turned the key on the young student. Left alone, the quiet and sensitive James was filled with terror. He had led a relatively sheltered life and would probably have considered waiting in the wings to make his entrance in the lead role of the first-year production of Hamlet as his most frightening experience to date. Yet here he was imprisoned and treated without a trace of sympathy. If the police hadn't got the real troublemakers, others would have to do. They were all the same, these young left-wing hippy types. They had no respect for authority. An example must be made of somebody.

Brooding on his fate, James felt physically sick. His imagination ran riot. He pictured scenes from violent prison movies – brutal guards, pathologically violent convicts and chain gangs. As time passed slowly by, he also began to worry that he might be forgotten and left to rot in his cell. He knew that such an idea was preposterous, but he couldn't help himself.

It was late into the evening when he was taken out to the interview room and he would have said or done almost anything to get out. All that stuff he had learnt from the movies about refusing to speak until he had seen his solicitor went straight out of the window. Two officers appeared. One informed him brusquely that he was being charged with assaulting a police officer and would attend the adjacent Magistrates' Court the following morning.

'Assaulting a police officer is a very serious offence', said the other. 'I'll be perfectly frank with you, son. Given the evidence against you you're likely to end up in jail if you plead "not guilty". On the other hand, seeing as you've no previous convictions, you'll almost certainly get away with a fine or a suspended sentence if you admit to the charge. It's more than you deserve, but there you are. It's up to you, isn't it?'

'But I didn't do anything,' pleaded James, trying to sound indignant and to hide his fear. 'Find my girlfriend, Miriam Levine. She's a student at Birmingham Uni. She'll tell you. We were just trying to keep out of trouble.'

'That's not what our officers say, James. And I know who I'd sooner believe. Maybe you should have a think about it and tell the duty solicitor what you decide. Then we can take your statement and it'll all be over.'

Partly the student wanted to cry out against injustice and to question what evidence could possibly be brought against him. Yet he felt intimidated and could not bring himself to do so. The idea of admitting to a crime he hadn't committed and going back home to Miriam in the morning sounded like an invitation to paradise. He knew that a criminal record might affect his future career prospects, but what did that matter? All he wanted was to be free again – as free as he had been when the day had dawned.

By the time he made his statement, the officers were tired. It was just their luck to end up working on a night like this, processing a load of anarchists and political extremists! They weren't going to waste time going through any more details than they had to. As far as they were concerned a guilty plea with a few mitigating circumstances would do very nicely. Only three more cases to go and they could get home to bed. James agreed to some cock-and-bull story that he had punched the officer because he thought he was going to be hit first. He didn't take too much notice of the fine print. It was simply a deal to get him out of a fix.

Having made the decision to plead guilty, the student felt a little bit more at ease. He even managed to sleep for a few hours. Yet when he awoke early the next morning, the pain in the pit of his stomach had returned. His chest felt tight and hot. Partly he couldn't wait to get to court, judging that however great the ordeal, it would provide his ticket to eventual freedom. But he was still full of apprehension. The thought of abusive guards and violent inmates would not go away until he heard the judge confirm a fine or suspended sentence. The cell that had seemed so repugnant the previous evening offered comparative security. At least there were fellow protestors nearby. The couple of hours before they took him to court passed almost as torturously slowly as the previous evening.

A special sitting of the court had been set up to deal with some of those arrested. James was amongst the first cases to be heard. After the guilty plea, the judge asked to hear the evidence. The arresting officer read out his statement. The defendant, he claimed, had emerged from a group who were throwing objects at the police and shouting abuse. He had punched a colleague in the face and kicked him. At that moment, several officers had apprehended the assailant, who had resisted arrest violently. A second policeman was called to back up the story, while the alleged injured officer was absent on the grounds that he had needed hospital treatment.

The accused listened to these lies in bemused silence. It was a lot worse than the version of events he had admitted to and it just made him look more of a liar than if he had denied the charges completely. What a fool he had been to panic and admit to the assault. The duty solicitor assigned to represent him half-heartedly disputed the evidence, but even the version that he had agreed to was bad enough. When the magistrate asked him if he had anything further to say in his defence, the normally eloquent James was in such a state of shock that he could find few words. Before the implications could sink in, the whole shoddy episode was over. The judge announced that 'this sort of behaviour towards our police officers could not be tolerated' and sentenced him to six months' imprisonment. Soon James Hayes was on his way by prison van to Wormwood Scrubs.

Miriam, meanwhile, had spent a long night trying to find out where he had been taken. She had toured police stations and made endless phone calls. In the confusion – or perhaps it was deliberate – nobody had given her any firm information. It was mid-morning by the time she finally managed to track down the details of his case, by which time he had already appeared in court. She was frantic with worry. It was the next afternoon before she was allowed to visit him in prison, finding him in despair. His long blonde hair had been cut off and one warder had warned that that his life would be made a misery.

The sentence led to James missing his finals that year, the authorities refusing him special dispensation to sit his exams. It was the following autumn before Rob saw him again, walking around the university campus during a visit to Miriam. The word was that he had found the three months spent in jail particularly soul-sapping, despite being transferred to a less harsh regime within days of conviction. The experience had left him chastened and embittered. He had learnt his lesson – it wasn't worth trying to beat the authorities because there was no way you were going to win. In future he would keep his head down and avoid trouble. No more protests for him. He had his own life to lead and would get on with it as quietly as he could.

For a while, the Grosvenor Square experience had its impact upon Rob Moore, too. He had not realised that campaigning could be so fraught with danger – at least not in the UK. But he was young and the memory soon faded. Within a year the main focus of dissent around campus had switched from war to apartheid and he wasted no time in getting involved. At first his contribution to the protest against the planned South African rugby tour was fairly low-key. He turned up at meetings, collected petition signatures and gave out leaflets in local shopping centres. But he was inspired to do more by the weightier efforts of others.

Under the leadership of Peter Hain – whose parents had brought him to the UK from South Africa at the age of sixteen after they had been imprisoned and harassed for their liberal views – anti-apartheid protestors set about turning every game the Springboks played into a mini-siege. Pitches were invaded, vivid orange flour bombs were thrown during matches and tacks scattered over the playing area. Locks on the players' hotel rooms were glued, and most daringly of all, a group chained themselves to the South African team coach in an attempt to stop it reaching the stadium. Full of admiration, Rob travelled by coach to join demonstrators when the Springboks played a game in Wales and discovered an atmosphere full of brooding menace. Barbed wire fences had been erected and police prowled in large numbers, many accompanied by snarling dogs. Some of the activists were overtly confrontational, aggressively insulting spectators for supporting a pernicious racist system. In return, the rugby fans gave as good as they got, taunting the 'lefties' who dared to turn their beloved sport into a political hot potato. There were scuffles and several arrests.

Despite finding his afternoon in Wales uncomfortable, Rob was among the first to put his name forward when volunteers were sought to disrupt the England versus South Africa international at Twickenham. It seemed like a good idea at the time and it wasn't until the date grew near that his enthusiasm began to wane. What on earth had he let himself in for?

It was a grey and cold December Saturday morning at the end of the university term when he set off by train from Birmingham for the match at Twickenham, very nervous. Though shielded in part by the blind confidence of youth, he couldn't quite suppress the memory of James Hayes at Grosvenor Square. But he pulled himself together. Surely there would be little danger of similar consequences? This was to be an act of individual defiance carried out in front of tens of thousands of spectators – not to mention a massive live television audience. The possibility of serious or trumped-up charges – even if he were arrested – was negligible. He should be more worried about whether he was brave enough to strike when the moment for action arrived. That was the thing to concentrate upon.

When he reached the stadium, it soon became clear that the activists' plan was not exactly a tightly guarded secret. Every previous match on the Springboks tour had been targeted in one way or another, so it would not have taken Sherlock Holmes to assume that something similar was about to be attempted again. There were police everywhere. Moreover, unbeknown to the anti-apartheid campaigners, their organisation had been infiltrated extensively. Disturbed by the previous year's anti-Vietnam event, the government had implemented secret measures to prevent a repeat, including the creation of a police Special Demonstration Squad. The role of these undercover officers was to infiltrate left-wing pressure groups, growing their hair and beards in order to blend in. Colleagues nicknamed them 'the hairies'.

After entering the Twickenham arena, Rob surveyed the scene in order to finalise his strategy. He felt important. He likened himself to an assassin he had seen in a French film, staking out the best vantage point from which he could perform his dastardly task. Not that his role was anything like as momentous, of course, since all he was required to do was to run onto the pitch and avoid capture for as long as possible, thereby interrupting the match and gaining maximum publicity for the anti-apartheid cause in front of the television audience. It sounded so easy! Like others on the same mission, it was left entirely up to him when and how he struck, with repeated disruption the overall aim.

The more he looked around, however, the more it appeared to be mission impossible. Leaving aside the heavy police presence congregated in the area around the players' tunnel, there were three lines of burly and menacing security officers surrounding all areas of the pitch, seated astride long benches and facing the crowd. Every one of them appeared to have been recruited from the front row of the country's most intimidating rugby teams. Neither was his task made any easier by the fact that he stood out like a sore thumb. After some hesitation he had that morning reluctantly sacrificed his turquoise flared crushed velvet loon pants and embroidered Afghan coat for more conventional attire, yet still his rugby fan disguise was unconvincing. Police 'hairies' may have changed their appearance in order to fit in with the hippy set, but there was no way that protestors such as Rob were going to take comparably radical steps in the opposite direction. Dedicated to dissent though he was, no cause could be worth cutting off his hair and beard for.

As the match progressed, several fellow campaigners tried to get onto the pitch from different areas of the stadium, though as far as Rob could see the security men repelled the invasions and swiftly handed the protestors on to the police. The obvious course would have been to abandon his seemingly hopeless task, but he had a stubborn, determined streak that would not allow him to do so. He detested the idea of failure. So, with the game now well into the second half, he hatched a fresh plan. In the corner of the terrace was a section reserved for the St John's Ambulance volunteers. If he made his way onto the ground from this point, he might just surprise the security crew for long enough to get past them and onto the playing area. He would pretend that his arm was injured and plead with the crowd to let him gain access to an ambulance crew.

The tactic worked perfectly, spectators immediately making way to allow him a path into the sectioned-off first aid area. This was the moment to embark on his run for glory. Rob took a deep breath, ran past the medics, vaulted up over the wall that divided the front of the terrace from the pitch and raced forward as quickly as he could. His heart was beating as fast as he could ever remember. In that split second, the thought that flashed into his mind was of that time sat in the classroom of form 3A, waiting for the detested deputy headmaster, Old Dish Wragg, to discover his crude doctoring of the drag racing article. A similar sensation of dread overcame him. But it was already too late to turn back. Rushing the short distance towards the rugby vigilantes, he found himself greeted by a great bank of them rising from their benches to confront him, wholly unfazed by his master plan. As he approached the first group he attempted his favourite football feint – a move to the right followed by a drop of the left shoulder and a break in the opposite direction. His opponents simply stood their ground. At 5ft 6ins tall and weighing less than ten stone, he had no chance, for all his speed and determination. He didn't even have the satisfaction of making it past the front row. Four burly figures brought him crashing roughly to the ground, while another pulled back his right arm, clenching the fist as if to aim a powerful punch. The student closed his eyes in anticipation of a painful blow that never arrived. Instead, he was held fast until a group of equally hefty policemen reached the scene and expertly and painfully pinioned his arms behind his back before two of them grabbed him under the armpits. Another pair took his legs, lifting his struggling frame from the ground and carting him away past jeering spectators towards the players' tunnel. It was an undignified exit.

As soon as they were out of public view, a further ordeal awaited. Two rows of uniformed police were lined up on either side of the route to the dressing room area, ready to administer their self-appointed brand of justice. A good kicking was the order of the day. Fortunately, as it turned out, this involved releasing his legs and holding him dangling upright with his lower limbs off the ground. As the first boots were swung in his direction, Rob thrashed about as fast as he could, lifting his targeted legs far enough in the air to ensure that every kick missed by a distance.

Sore arms apart, he reached the stadium exit unscathed and unusually grateful for his short stature.

Once out of the ground, three officers led him more sedately to a police portacabin, specially erected in the far corner of the car park. It was at this point that the adrenalin rush evaporated and he began to focus upon what might happen next. Was he going to be locked up? What if there was, after all, some fabricated charge made against him? The police might claim that he had broken free and assaulted them in the tunnel. James Hayes came into his mind again. What if he ended up in prison over Christmas? What would his parents think? It wasn't too long before the duty sergeant appeared – a tall, slim young male with short blonde hair and tired, pale blue eyes. He had the air of a man who was fed up with the monotony of his afternoon's work. He wanted to show how bored he was with it all, even stopping a couple of times to yawn loudly while he took down Rob's personal details. Only when he had filled in the form and put down his pen did he look the student straight in the eye.

'Now look here, Robert. I dare say you realise that I could charge you with breach of the peace and get you taken down to the cells for the night. Maybe we could even find something a little more serious to put on the sheet. But you're in luck, mate. Christmas is coming and I'm feeling charitable. This time I'm going to let you off with a warning. OK?'

Rob nodded gratefully.

'Well, what I suggest is that you get off home as quickly as you can, before I change my mind. And just remember, we've got all your details and if we see you again we might not be quite so friendly. Do I make myself clear?'

The protestor nodded again, even more emphatically His joy was so great that it felt like Christmas Day already.

'Right then, get yourself out of here.'

And home he went to Somerset, as swiftly as he could.

Although his parents had not known in advance about his escapade, he chose to tell them the whole story almost as soon as he arrived. He received a mixed reaction. John and Margaret were proud of his courage and conviction. At the same time they couldn't help feeling angry that he had put himself at risk. There was a bit of a scene. A spot of tension had started to develop between Rob and John and the youngster ended up accusing his father of hypocrisy. He stormed off.

Watching this family mini-drama unfold, Tom's response contained none of the ambiguity of his parents'. He marvelled at his brother's bravery and longed for the time when he would be old enough to take part in similar adventures. All he wanted from life was to be like Rob, though in truth his temperament was quite different. He had little of his brother's athleticism and daring. He was a much more introspective and questioning soul, too uncertain to be a focal point for his contemporaries.

His main problem however was that he was simply too young. As much as Tom would have liked to be at his brother's side, he would have to make do with supporting his mother's rather less dramatic schemes to help the child victims of the Nigeria-Biafra war, by now entering its third year. For the first time, television reports of starving children had etched themselves into the public consciousness and images of children with wasted limbs, bloated bellies and bulging, fly-infested eyes had prompted unprecedented generosity towards those of a different colour in a far-off continent. Margaret organised fundraising events with her young pupils, plus a stream of street collections and jumble sales in local town centres. The suffering touched a nerve. Half of the nation seemed gripped by a collective sense of guilt. How could such misery occur in a world of comparative plenty?

Nonetheless, the brutal African civil war did offer one grain of compensation for parents and teachers alike, providing a potent new weapon in their enduring battle to make young children clean up their dinner plates. In school canteens, vast quantities of overcooked sprouts, sloppy cabbage, lumpy mashed potato and unappetising semolina pudding were persuaded down the gullets of guilt-ridden youngsters under the solemn instruction to 'think of all those starving children in Biafra.' In families across the land, the same tactic was employed to aid consumption of similarly child-unfriendly foods. So harrowing were the images of hungry and desperate infants that it seemed a comparatively minor hardship.

2

In the Easter holidays before Tom was to sit his 'A' levels, his father complained of severe chest pains. Despite his wife's repeated entreaties, he refused to visit the doctor. Little more than three months later he suffered a massive coronary attack and died. For the youngster, this huge shock came at a strange time. It was summer and he was in the middle of those heady days of freedom between leaving school and going off to university. He considered himself ready to flee the parental nest. So that in the weeks following the funeral, he sometimes felt guilty that day-to-day life could often still seem so pleasurable. When grief impinged, it did so only spasmodically. Sometimes he would wake in the early morning with an aching sadness after dreaming vividly that his father was alive and recovered from illness. He was left with a physical sense of emptiness. Yet for the most part life went on relatively smoothly.

After much family deliberation, it was decided that he would delay going to university to help his mother through her bereavement. Rob was rising up the ladder of a London-based publishing firm and couldn't be home as much as he would wish. In spite of Margaret's pleas that she would be fine on her own, the boys insisted that she should not have to face losing both husband and youngest son in such rapid succession. They would not be swayed.

The gap year proved not such a bad time. Many of Tom's school friends were still around and his mother was not the kind to wallow in her sadness. Indeed, it was during this period that Tom began to realise how little he had really known about his parents and their relationship. As much as he liked to think of himself as mature and sophisticated, he hadn't actually grown up to the point where he could look at them as individuals with independent lives. Their role in life was just to be his Mum and Dad and he had no critical perspective of them outside parenthood. They had married, brought up children and stayed together. Therefore, he took it for granted that everything must be fairly happy and harmonious. He was conscious of more disagreements in recent years, yet these had never seemed to run very deep. Tom was oblivious to underlying tensions.

What had been obvious was that his Dad had become increasingly irritable as he got older. John Moore had become reluctant to socialise with anybody outside his chosen few friends. He became fussy about who was and was not welcome in the house, demonstrating his disapproval of some of his wife's friends so fiercely that it became too much trouble for her to invite them. He invariably claimed the moral high ground for such intolerance, blaming materialism, shallowness, unsympathetic political beliefs or some other grave deficiency in those he wished to banish.

Tom's instinct had always been to trust his father's judgement, so it took his brother's more critical perspective to encourage a greater balance.

'It was all very convenient for Dad to blame his grumpiness on corrupt and inept politicians or other people's weaknesses', argued Rob. 'But I reckon that more often than not it was just his own discontent that was eating him.'

'Oh, that's rubbish, Rob. How can you possibly say that Dad

didn't care about the world and the way things were going?'

'I didn't say that, did I? I'm just saying that he rationalised some of his own misery, that's all.'

Rob was equally critical of his father's general role in the family.

'There's this joke, right? A couple with what seems like a perfect marriage are asked the secret of their success. "It's simple", replies the wife. "I deal with all the trivial issues, such as getting the children to school, doing the shopping, planning the food, organising holidays, paying bills, cooking and washing. Meanwhile my husband gets on with all the important issues – literature, art, politics and solving world hunger". Well, that's what it was like with Mum and Dad.'

'I don't think that's altogether fair either, Rob,' Tom defended his father again. 'I really don't. Look at all the time Dad spent taking us out and helping with our school work.'

Yet as much as he wanted to resist his brother's analysis, Tom recognised a seed of truth in it. As in the majority of families, it had been the woman who had sacrificed her own interests to the nitty-gritty of daily family existence – even if, in his mother's case, her boundless energy had meant that she still found time to get involved in lots of outside activities.

A little more than a year after his father's death, Tom was off to the north of England to take a degree course in literature at York University. He was looking forward to it, expecting to find a world of cutting-edge student protest, just like his big brother had been involved in only a few years previously. Signs were promising when he attended the Freshers' Fair and found the hall filled with groups dedicated to the 'usual suspect' causes of the day, plus the inevitable band of archetypal left-wing student politicos dedicated to union power, the workers' revolution and the ultimate overthrow of the capitalist system. It soon became clear, however, that there wasn't a lot of support for such political fervour. For the majority of students, apathy ruled and even the hardcore protesters seemed more concerned with matters nearer to home than the Vietnam war or racist South Africa – both of which were still going strong. The particular object of their wrath was their own university authorities, blamed for the heinous crimes of the high cost of campus accommodation and the government's failure to award this privileged bunch a sufficiently generous maintenance grant. The price of coffee in the cafeterias was a further source of righteous indignation. Every few months a hardcore group opposed to these momentous injustices would burst into the university administration block and occupy the premises to demand change. A clear pattern emerged. Friday afternoon saw the activists storm the building, burdened with ample provisions – notably copious quantities of alcohol – to secure their survival through the long days and nights ahead. On the following Monday morning they would call off the occupation, departing with headaches and a far lighter load than they had taken in. Despite failing to achieve an overhaul of government or university policy, the perpetrators – destined eventually to become the generation of New Labour's political class and already skilful proponents of the art of spin – invariably acclaimed their protest as an enormous success. The following week's student union campus newspaper would insist that they had sent a strong warning to the neo-fascist, bourgeois authorities, who could be left in no doubt of the dire future consequences if demands were not addressed.

The lack of revolutionary zeal amongst most students was reflected further in the music that blared out from campus bedsits. While Tom was still fixated on his old Dylan and Neil Young albums – plus, on principle, the live recording of George Harrison's groundbreaking charity event, *The Concert for Bangladesh* – it was by now Roxy Music and David Bowie who were dominating the stereo systems of his contemporaries.

Politics and protest were hardly on the agenda at all. Even the folky singer/songwriters of the day – of whom Joan Armatrading seemed the most popular – were singing mostly about the pain of love, love, love rather than civil rights and social justice. Tom felt annoyed and superior and reported these falling standards to his brother.

'I mean, David Bowie!' he exclaimed. 'What can you say about some arsehole who adopted the persona of a rock guitarist from outer space and "would like to come and meet us but he thinks he'd blow our minds"? How dumb can you get?'

'He writes some catchy tunes though. Besides, he stopped all that Ziggy Stardust and the Spiders from Mars stuff some time ago – as well you know.'

'Not for anything any more important.'

As his career began to blossom, big brother was already distancing himself from his radical hippy past and becoming increasingly measured and conventional in his views. His response surprised and disappointed Tom, who'd expected wholehearted support on the anti-Bowie front.

'Look, it's all very well going on about Dylan or Joan Baez,' Rob continued, 'but it wasn't all like that, was it? There was loads of pretentious bullshit in the sixties, too. Look at some of the stuff we used to listen to. You only have to look at the titles – *In the Court of the Crimson King, Piper at the Gates of Dawn, Days of Future Passed, Threshold of A Dream, Dedicated to Our Children's Children's Children.*'

Tom laughed.

'That's true enough, I suppose,' he was forced to admit. 'When it comes to pretentious titles, you can't beat the Moody Blues.'

'No, but they've got plenty of close rivals when you start listening to the lyrics.'

And they were off on one of their favourite rock music trivia dialogues.

'Yeah, The Incredible String Band's magical-sprites-in-the-enchanted-wood bollocks for a start. I could never see what you saw in all that. Incredibly shite band more like!' ventured Tom.

'That's a bit harsh – I still can't help liking some of it! And anyway, they wrote nothing in the class of 'the weeks passed through my brain, in their Dadaistic chain'. That takes some beating.'

'Who was that then?'

'Al Stewart, silly – fancy not remembering that!'

"You forget that I'm not as ancient as you are, Rob.'

'Nor as wise!' the older responded to this hint of sarcasm. 'The thing is, I still enjoy all that sixties 'progressive' nonsense as much as the next man, but I can't quite honestly see that most of it was any less banal than Bowie's efforts. You're just stuck in a time warp, old before your time, Tom.'

'Yes, but at least none of that sixties lot were fucking fascists.'

'Ay, there's the rub!' answered his brother, turning swiftly from progressive rock to Shakespeare in order to stress his superiority.

He had, nevertheless, hit the nail on the head. The reason Tom couldn't stand David Bowie had little to do with music. It was that interview in which he had asserted that 'Britain could benefit from a fascist leader' that was the real cause of his hostility – a sin the singer had compounded by turning up at Waterloo Station and offering what waiting journalists and photographers all took to be a Nazi salute.

Even for this unforgivable act, his wishy-washy liberal brother was ready to offer mitigating circumstances!

'I agree he must be pretty stupid. But you've got to remember the silly bastard was apparently up to his eyeballs on drugs. He probably doesn't know what he's talking about. So much for the idea that mind-altering drugs have the potential to expand the human consciousness, eh!'

The younger Moore was neither impressed nor amused by this change of emphasis.

'He certainly doesn't know what he's talking about – I'll grant you that – but I'm sorry, I don't think drugs can be used as much of an excuse. Try telling that to my Chilean friend Miguel.'

What had given Bowie's ill-chosen remarks particular resonance was the presence in York of several refugees from a real-life fascist dictator. Tom had first met two of them – Miguel and Marcos – at meetings of the university Amnesty International group. Both had been sponsored by the Chilean Solidarity Group and had been helped by trade unions, church groups and university societies to come to the UK under a scheme by which Pinochet's military government had eventually allowed some prisoners into exile. Miguel and his sister had originally been housed in South Yorkshire, where the local left-wing council – led by David Blunkett and widely known at the time as the Socialist Republic of Sheffield – had provided homes and jobs for many refugees. As a language student with impeccable English, Miguel was almost immediately found a place to study at York.

Such liberal hospitality and compassion towards the oppressed and persecuted filled Tom with an unusual sense of patriotic pride. Offering sanctuary for the victims of the Pinochets and Idi Amins of this world – that was the best thing about being British. Whatever else might be wrong, you were never likely to be faced with anything as brutal as a military coup over here! The nearest he had ever come to state-sponsored brutality had been hearing his brother's description of a few over-zealous police officers at a demonstration that had got a bit out of hand. It was a million miles from his Chilean friends' experience of imprisonment, systematic torture and the disappearance and murder of family and friends.

As the rest of the worthy Amnesty supporters gathered to compose polite letters in support of their adopted prisoners of conscience – one of whom was actually from Chile – it was obvious that Miguel and Marcos were dedicated to action more decisive. They made no secret of their bitterness or of their near-obsession with a return home to seek retribution against General Pinochet and his followers. Tom found their intensity disturbing. On one visit to Miguel's flat, the refugee showed him a vicious looking knife with a long, deathly sharp blade, hidden in the record sleeve of an album of Chilean political songs of protest. He claimed to be keeping it at hand until the time he was able to go home. Peace-loving Tom Moore couldn't quite understand. Surely it was better to forgive your enemies and to seek reconciliation – that was what he had always been taught.

Whenever Tom tried to find out exactly what had happened to create such a thirst for revenge, Miguel refused to discuss it. He learned to avoid the subject. Until, that is, late one evening when the pair were celebrating the end of term and sharing a bottle of wine. After a couple of large glasses, Tom plucked up the courage to suggest that whatever might have happened in the past, it might now be time to 'move on'. The response began as angrily as he feared it might. Miguel sobered up almost instantly.

'So you think we should forgive and forget, eh? Is that what you're saying? You just don't understand at all, do you? My family and friends have been murdered, tortured and raped. Everything I love and believe in has been destroyed. Yet you and your like – with your nice secure families and your easy, privileged lives – you want us to forget it all and get on with life. Believe me Tom, forgiving is not an option. You just haven't got a clue.'

'I'm sorry.' Tom felt the weight of his inadequacy. Why had he opened his mouth?

'No, no, I suppose it's me that should apologise. I didn't mean to insult you.'

There was a short, awkward silence before Miguel went on.

'Look, how much do you know about what's happened in my

country?'

'Not a lot, I'm afraid', admitted Tom, feeling a bit guilty about his ignorance. 'All I really know is that Allende was the popular and democratically elected president and that he was overthrown and killed in Pinochet's military coup. I also know that there are thousands of Allende sympathisers like you who have been tortured and murdered. And of course, I know about Sebastion Riveros* and Victor Java.'

Riveros was their Amnesty group's prisoner of conscience, a trade union leader still detained at a camp in the north of the country. Victor Java had been a bit like a Chilean Bob Dylan, a political songwriter who had been a famous supporter of the Allende regime. A few days after the coup, he had been arrested and taken to the national football stadium. Interrogators had crushed his hands and then laughingly handed him a guitar and challenged him to play. He defied them by beginning to sing a song he had written in praise of the elected government. They beat him mercilessly before shooting him with a machine gun and burying his body in a mass grave.

'You know what they did to Java and yet you believe that such evil should be forgotten? That we should – symbolically at least – shake hands with the animals that could do such things? Well, I'm sorry, but I cannot think like that any more. I think it would be better to cut off their hands as well, because that's the only way to be sure that they will not be responsible for such acts of cruelty again. Please don't tell me that I'm wrong to hate them, because all that I really live for now is to go back home and get even.'

Miguel went on to present his version of Chile's recent history. Before the socialist revolution it had been a country where a rich and corrupt elite ruled and the poor had absolutely nothing. At

---

* Sebastion Riveros is a fictional character. Victor Java is real and was killed in the way described

least half the population went to bed hungry each night. Then, in 1970, Allende and his Popular Unity coalition were swept to power, despite blatant attempts to fix the election against them. They had succeeded in politicising and giving hope to the underprivileged. Allende's government nationalised the main industries and many of the banks. Land reforms were introduced to address the great gap between rich and poor. Wages for poorer workers in the new state industries were increased. Education reforms allowed many children to go to school for the first time. But, of course, the powerful forces that had lost some of their wealth and influence soon hatched plans to bring them down, supported by their American investors and a US government that hated Chile simply because of its socialist agenda. 'I don't see why we need to stand by and watch a country go communist because of the irresponsibility of its own people', Secretary of State Henry Kissinger had said. The US stopped all aid reaching the country, its ambassador stating that not a nut or a bolt would be allowed to reach Chile under Allende. World market prices in copper – one of Chile's most important industries – were manipulated so that the export trade was destroyed and the economy crushed. Military takeovers were plotted. Two army leaders were assassinated because they refused to sanction a coup to overthrow the government. Everybody knew that the CIA was involved.

Tom listened to all this with a degree of scepticism. Because of Vietnam he was always happy to listen to any political treatise that contained an attack on US foreign policy – particularly when it involved condemnation of Henry Kissinger. It was he who was assumed to have authorised the blanket bombing and Napalm attacks on the civilians of Vietnam and Cambodia and he had long been a particular figure of hate for his family and other anti-war campaigners. The fact that he had since been awarded the Nobel Peace Prize added insult to injury. Yet partly because of his father's influence, Tom was already sufficiently cynical about politics to wonder whether Miguel's glowing portrait of President Allende's government was a bit too good to be true. Surely the collapse of the Chilean economy couldn't have been caused solely by US intervention? 'There's bound to have been a degree of corruption, dogma and incompetence somewhere along the line', he thought. But he decided to keep his doubts to himself. He didn't want to interrupt Miguel now that he was opening up a little.

'The Americans believed that by helping to bring the Chilean economy to its knees, they would make sure that the right-wing parties they supported would gain power at the elections in March 1973. Their plan was then to impeach Allende and get rid of him once and for all. But they had no idea of the mood of our people. Although times were very difficult, the government actually increased its share of the vote.

'So, after the failure to prevent the President being elected through the ballot box, everybody knew that things were likely to turn nasty. Life became increasingly tense. Rumours were everywhere that the Americans would help the right-wingers to seize power. Yet even though many army leaders were deeply hostile to Allende, we somehow believed that they would stay loyal to the elected government. It was strange really. Nobody should have been surprised when the coup came, but at the same time none of us – at least none of my family or friends – actually believed it would ever happen.'

With his friend more communicative than ever before, Tom tentatively risked a personal enquiry again.

'Can you really not tell me what happened to you and your family, Miguel?'

The refugee hesitated before answering.

'No, no, I'm afraid I can't. I know that maybe I should be able to talk about it by now, but I still can't. I'm sorry.'

'For Christ's sake, you don't need to apologise. It was insensitive of me to ask.'

Another silence. Again it was Miguel who broke it. His tone was quiet and considered.

'What you have got to realise is that what they did to Victor Java was not unique. Many of our families have a similar tale to tell. Once they were let loose, those bastards were capable of anything. I've heard stories of fanatics who burst into apartments, screaming while they shot parents in front of children – and sometimes even the other way around. And I've learnt too that brutality can come in many forms – psychopaths who clearly get a thrill out of torture and hearing you scream with pain; fanatical savages who kick and punch and yell 'communist scum' while they do so; ice-cool sadists who consider themselves above all the physical violence. In many ways those are the worst. They get their thrills from mock executions or describing the terrible things they have done to your family or girlfriend. Oh, they particularly enjoy the girlfriend bit – you should have heard the relish with which they described the detail. And all you can do while you seethe inside with rage and disgust is to wait for them to hand you back to the straightforward psychopaths. The only thing to keep you going is the thought that if you ever get through this, then one day you might just have the chance for revenge.'

Tom listened with a mixture of horror and bewilderment. He knew only too well that such things happened, of course, but somehow hearing it from an actual victim was different, much more shocking. Nonetheless, it occurred to him that it was still his duty to fight back from a pacifist perspective. He should point out the difference between justice and retribution and introduce his favourite Gandhi quote. 'An eye for an eye makes the whole world blind': that's what he should tell Miguel. Human history has been littered with repeated examples of similar barbarity and only by breaking the cycle of hatred and vengeance can peace ever be achieved – that should be his line. But what would be the point? No way would his friend be convinced and Miguel would almost certainly dismiss him as a comfortable middle-class do-gooder. And perhaps that was all that he was. Besides, after listening to the refugee's story, he wasn't sure how far he still believed in all this peace and love stuff, after all.

Apart from the handful of Chileans and the vociferous student Marxists, Tom Moore's university life was hardly conducted in a cauldron of political activism. There was, however, one other group that was bucking the apathetic trend. The women's rights society was full of passionate energy and zeal. Regular *Reclaim the Night* marches and vigils took place across the city, proclaiming freedom to walk the streets at any time, safe from the threat of male violence or intimidation. Great effort was also invested in renovating and expanding the city's relatively new centre for the protection of battered women and promotion of feminist values.

Despite the insurmountable disadvantage of having being born into the wrong sex, Tom liked to think of himself as an enlightened supporter of these initiatives. He even occasionally helped out with another of the group's pet projects, providing crèche facilities for students with young children. It was here that he got to know Carol Dawson, a bubbly and attractive young woman with long dark hair and owl-like, greenish-brown eyes. Carol was also in the Amnesty group and her good looks and combination of passionate commitment to good causes and love of music and books quickly captivated him.

He joined a fairly long list of Carol's admirers and began to visit her for weekend walks. She lived in an all-female household, shared by eight current and former students in a very large, rambling Victorian house on the outskirts of the city. Amongst them were leading figures from the industrious feminist community he so admired. Tom expected to fit easily into this enlightened environment of fellow radicals, anticipating that his spiritual sisters would be motivated solely by their determined struggle for sexual emancipation and equality: instead he found them fuelled by a profound distrust of all things male and soon discovered that through their eyes he would always be part of the enemy. Several of Carol's housemates were firmly at the militant end of the movement and wore the uniform of their cause with pride – short, harsh-fringed haircuts and baggy, second-hand men's clothes. Checked lumberjack shirts, dungarees and working overalls were particularly fashionable.

The house itself left the visitor in no doubt as to the politics of its occupants. On entering, you passed through a narrow hallway dominated by a huge colourful poster that proclaimed a stark message in bold print – 'A woman needs a man like a fish needs a bicycle'. The large communal kitchen at the end of the corridor was decorated with an equally imposing image, depicting a youthful and handsome Jesus Christ, arms outstretched. Underneath was the slogan, 'A man who thinks he is the Son of God is not such a rare event'.

Apart from the residents themselves, there always seemed to be other hard-edged feminists about, some of whom held every individual member of the male sex personally responsible for all of the world's evil. The most fundamental went so far as to openly declare themselves separatists, committed to avoiding all unnecessary contact with the hated enemy. 'All penetration is rape' suggested one strident voice – a sentiment that caused Tom an uncomfortable sensation around his scrotum. When a more liberal member of the group raised the difficult question of how it might be possible to eliminate men completely and still perpetuate the species, it was argued that the urge to procreate was only suffered by women who remained 'trapped within the confines of biological experience'. This was a state to be pitied and conquered if the revolution was ever to achieve its goals.

This fierce female crowd soon made it perfectly clear that they weren't going to be taken in by Tom's apparent sympathy. Although superficially polite, they imbued every utterance with underlying enmity. He felt threatened. He considered himself such a shining example of a liberated man and a true believer in their mission. Hadn't he even helped out at the university crèche? So who were these strange creatures dressed in their deliberately unflattering attire to tolerate him with such suspicion and disdain?

The more often Tom visited Carol – one of three of the tenants who were less intense in their views – the more uncomfortable he began to feel around the sexual politics. And the more intimidated he felt, the more he went on the counter-attack. He mocked and dismissed them – though not to their faces or in front of Carol. This came to a head on the night of the benefit gig for the city's women's refuge. He was excited because Carol had invited him to go with her and he had spent some time wondering whether this might be a significant breakthrough in what had seemed a long and torturous pursuit. Tom knew that she enjoyed his company: the trouble was that she had shown no real sign of wanting anything more than friendship. Could this be the night he'd been waiting for?

The evening got off to a good start. The ironically named *Prickteasers* – an energetic five-piece, all-woman band with two soaring, edgy saxophonists weaving intricate patterns above a tight rhythm section of electric guitar, bass and drums – soon had most of their audience dancing. True, he felt a bit peeved when the group changed the lyrics from *And Then He Kissed Me* into the anti-male rant *And Then He Bit Me,* and he found the bastardisation of *Great Balls of Fire* into *No Balls and Liars* equally galling. He also had to cope with the awkwardness of wanting to dance with Carol while feeling too self-conscious about his incompetence to be able to ask. Nonetheless, he was mostly enjoying himself and had to admit that the band was good. Then, quite suddenly, it all went wrong. He and his partner for the night were approached by one of the militant women's libbers he recognised from the gang of separatists in Carol's kitchen. Walking straight past Tom as if he had little right to exist, she stepped up close to his friend.

'Would you like to dance?' she asked.

'No thanks, not at the moment.'

'Why not?' insisted the libber. 'Don't you believe in being spontaneous?'

'Yes, I do believe in being spontaneous. That is exactly why I don't want to dance now.'

This incident was the final straw for Tom. It was one thing to dislike him solely on the grounds of his gender – much as he resented it – but such a blatant attempt to undermine his sexuality with overt lesbian overtures to his hoped-for girlfriend – this was going too far. The night was spoiled, despite Carol's spirited rejection of her female pursuer. As much as the moment enhanced his admiration for her, he seethed inside. 'Fools', he muttered to himself. He was deeply absorbed in his D.H. Lawrence phase (a period of initiation that seemed almost compulsory for many adolescent male literature students) and had just re-read *Lady Chatterley's Lover*. He considered the book full of wisdom. 'Don't these people realise that men and women need one another?' he thought. Yet he said nothing, partly because he was too much of a coward and also because he was afraid that Carol might disapprove. Instead, he saved his wrath for his mother, whom he was going home to visit the following weekend.

'They're so blind and limited', asserted Tom with great superiority. 'They seem incapable of seeing anything outside their own bigoted views. A couple of the girls in Carol's house have gone touring in the States and keep sending back postcards.

And you know what? The only information is whether the 'sisters' wear their hair short or long in whatever city they are writing from. Or whether there are more trousers on view than dresses or skirts. It's pathetic. There's never anything about art galleries or culture. Not even the weather gets a look in.'

He fully expected his mother to agree with him, so her response came as a bit of a jolt.

'Don't you think you protest a bit too much, Tom?'

'What do you mean, "protest too much?"' he snapped back. Why did everybody in his family always want to disagree these days: couldn't they see how right he was about everything?

'Well, usually you are so supportive of those who campaign for change. Yet you seem so worked up and angry about these women. It's as if they've got under your skin and you feel threatened by them.'

'Threatened by them! Why on earth should I feel threatened by them? They're idiots. I'm just annoyed because they pretend to be so progressive, when in reality their ideas are completely destructive to life.' (In the literary criticism jargon Tom had imbibed, any concept that you didn't like was 'destructive to life', as opposed to 'life-enhancing' or 'life-affirming' if you agreed with it).

'It doesn't sound to me as if all their ideas are destructive', replied Margaret Moore. 'Far from it, in fact. Supporting homes for battered women, upholding the right of women to have control over their own bodies and to be free from violence, campaigning for equal opportunities – I think these are incredibly important things to fight for. Perhaps if you were a woman, you'd appreciate how much we owe to the feminist movement.'

'Nobody's disputing that', responded Tom impatiently. 'But that doesn't mean they have to be so anti-men. It's not a war.'

'Well, maybe not. But look Tom, as a woman I find it very hard to be as critical as you seem to be. You forget that my mother wasn't allowed to vote and that if I'd been born a few years earlier my chances of going to university would have been practically non-existent. As it was, there were very few of us at Cambridge in the thirties. Women have had to struggle for every right we've ever gained, and who have we had to fight against? I'm afraid it has always been men. And there's still an enormous amount of discrimination and violence against women and it's still men trying to keep us down. So is it any wonder that some of these young people feel militant about it?'

His mother was really starting to get on his nerves.

'Do you mean to say', he began slowly, 'that you agree with women excluding men completely from their lives and preventing other women from having children?' (By now, he was prepared unashamedly to exaggerate and distort the views of his opponents in order to prove his point). 'Because if you do, it seems to me that, as a mother yourself, you're a bit of a hypocrite.'

She responded with exaggerated reasonableness.

'No Tom, I don't agree with that and well you know it. Some of the things you've told me about do sound a bit wild and over the top, I agree. But then you know what William Blake said, don't you? "The road of excess leads to the palace of wisdom". Sometimes you have to become a bit extreme when you are challenging established irrational customs and preconceptions – particularly when they are as ingrained as the exploitation of women.'

'Oh please, not the "palace of wisdom" again', replied Tom rudely. 'People always resort to bloody William Blake when they want to excuse some extremist rubbish.' (Indeed, he had done so on more than one occasion himself). 'I can't see that the road of excess led to much wisdom for Jimi Hendrix or Janis Joplin. They're dead. And that's what should happen to these fanatical "we should all be lesbians" feminist ideas. I can't see much wisdom coming out of that lot!'

'Really, Tom. I don't like to say it, but if you take that tone and attitude, it's no wonder these women don't like you very much.'

This really hit the mark.

'Oh, I'm not discussing this with you any longer. I'm going out for a walk!'

He slammed the door behind him as he left. The atmosphere remained frosty throughout the weekend.

While Tom was quick to voice his disapproval of her housemates to his other friends, he was keen to hide from Carol the full force of his displeasure. This proved difficult. Like most men, he could demonstrate disapproval with just a gesture, a facial expression, a quiet sigh or a meaningful silence. His opinion seeped through. It was fortunate that the object of his affection – who could often be quite sharp and feisty – seemed more amused than annoyed. While she considered herself a committed feminist and was broadly in sympathy with her housemates, she didn't share their full fervour and was capable of seeing the funny side of their unflinching devotion to the cause. Her own passionate interest lay elsewhere. In particular, it was cruelty to animals that outraged Carol Dawson. Vivisection made her angry and sick to the pit of her stomach. She was a vegetarian and felt equally strongly about the treatment of farm animals. She loathed hunting. These concerns, relatively uncommon at the time, came as a complete revelation to Tom, who had always taken it for granted that every cause worth fighting for had already been embraced by his own family. Yet despite a love of wildlife and the relatively pampered cats and dogs who had always been part of the household, their sympathy had been of a wholly different nature to Carol's. His parents believed that humans, as the most powerful species on earth, had a duty to care for domestic animals and to protect wildlife habitat. They supported the emerging efforts to save whales and seals and disliked hunting. But they had never thought about giving up meat. The only vegetarian he had really known before his university days had been Aunt Helen, whose refusal to eat animals he had always put down to her loveable but faintly cranky extremism on just about every conceivable issue. It was a complete eye-opener for him to be faced with Carol's belief that 'non-humans' – as she called them – were every bit as deserving of protection from exploitation as people.

'They value their lives just as much as we do and they feel pain like we do. For me it is as intolerable to kill and inflict deliberate suffering upon them as it would be to harm a human being,' she declared unequivocally.

As he came to know her better, Tom came to understand that Carol's sympathy for animals was actually far more instinctive and deep-rooted than the philosophical arguments she relied upon in discussion. It seemed to have been part of her almost from birth, though nobody could quite work out why. On trips to the seaside, the toddler howled in protest when her father tried to entertain her by catching crabs and shrimps in a fishing net. Fascinated though she was by the anemones, shrimps and other darting little creatures that lived out their lives amongst the warm water and seaweeds, some natural impulse dictated that she wanted to watch and never to trap. At the age of seven this feeling was reinforced when she witnessed a fisherman removing line and hook from the torn and bloody mouth of his catch. She looked at the bloodstained rock beneath with horror. The wider implications of the victim's grotesque bulging eyes were not lost on her. In spite of parental disapproval she soon afterwards resisted attempts to feed her meat and fish with such dogged intensity that they eventually had no choice but to accede to her wish to become a vegetarian. And it was no fad. As her teenage years advanced, the strong-willed Carol became even more determined. She began to dedicate increasing amounts of her spare time to a whole range of worthy causes, but particularly to those against animal cruelty. She would write letters, organise petitions at school and raise money from sponsored events. She threatened to go out sabotaging hunts. Her parents simply couldn't understand and worried that her behaviour was abnormal. It wasn't that they were cruel or callous: on the contrary, they were kindly folk who would help anybody close to them and in need. But their compassion was limited to those in their immediate circle – family, neighbours, or even their pets. They were far too busy looking after their own to find much time to worry about the wider world. For them, the abiding objective in life was to ensure that their two daughters gained opportunities that they themselves had been denied, having had to leave school at fourteen to earn a living. Their sense of mission was so strong that education had almost become a religion in the Dawson household. From an academically undistinguished comprehensive school serving their rough and sprawling housing estate, Carol and her sister had worked assiduously to fulfil their parents' ambition, so that when the younger began to spend time that could have been devoted to study on writing to the Prime Minister about seal culling, they objected on principle rather than out of hostility to the issue itself. They soon came to realise, however, that there was no stopping their daughter.

Had Tom understood the depth of Carol's feeling for her fellow creatures, his pursuit of her might well have been a little less tortuous. In his awkward and inexperienced way, he had tried everything he could imagine to win her affection. A few clumsy compliments about her physical attractiveness and passionate character had apparently fallen on stony ground. Attempts to engage her in conversations on issues close to their hearts – nuclear disarmament and power, environmental degradation, prisoners of conscience and shared contempt for David Bowie – had led to nothing more than lots of intense late night conversations. They always ended with him facing a cycle ride home in the middle of the night, partly exhilarated by their apparent spiritual bond but also frustrated that it had led no further. Then, inadvertently, he hit the jackpot. As he sat on the end of her bed talking one night, he came up with what proved to be the sixty-four million dollar question. 'So tell me, how exactly do they slaughter cows?'

As a seduction line, most experts would have dismissed this as unpromising, but in Carol's case it proved little short of irresistible. The moment seemed subtly to change her attitude towards him and she began to treat him more as a potential ally. What he had actually done to deserve such promotion was not easy to fathom, since he found the smell of sizzling bacon and the taste of juicy steak far too attractive to make the decisive sacrifice of giving up meat and following her cause. But obviously she saw something there to work on. Eventually, their emerging intimacy grew to the point where the photographs she thrust before him of veal calves solitarily confined in narrow cages and hens packed ruthlessly into battery cages had the sought-after effect. Whether Tom's conversion to a meat-free diet should be ascribed to empathy with other species or an overwhelming desire to win favour with a member of his own was not altogether clear, but whatever his motives, he felt unable to continue his carnivorous habits any longer.

Carol Dawson held her controversial views on animal rights with such strident conviction that they seemed to provoke regular heated discussion amongst fellow students. She had total confidence in her beliefs and never seemed to tire of defending her position. One evening during an Amnesty group meeting, things became particularly tense after Carol refused an end-of-term glass of sherry on the grounds that it might include gelatine, a substance derived from animal bones. Penny Painter, the society's secretary, was irritated. Later, in the student bar, she went on the attack. 'Isn't that gelatine business going a bit far? I don't see why you spend so much of your time bothering about animals when there are so many more important problems to worry about.'

'In what way do you think caring about animals prevents me from campaigning against what you call "more important problems"?' replied Carol, calmly. She had read a spate of recently published books on the subject of animal rights and was familiar with almost all the arguments likely to be put forward. Her answers were well rehearsed. 'It's a matter of priorities', continued Penny. 'Look at what happened to Miguel and Marcos – not to mention thousands of other torture victims around the world. Look at apartheid, Idi Amin in Uganda or the Indonesian invasion of East Timor. Yet you want us to worry about pigs, chickens and mice.'
'I find that really offensive, Penny. How can you possibly accuse me of caring about animals instead of Chile or South Africa? What do you think I'm in the Amnesty group for? When have I ever compared the way a pig suffers to what Miguel and his family and friends have been through? That's not the point at all. I've told you, I just want to go through life causing as little suffering as possible and I don't see why that shouldn't include animals as well as people. I'm really not the least bit interested in whether they are capable of suffering more or less than we are: the point is that I know they suffer enough. And I'm sorry, but I don't see why it's any less important to fight against one injustice than any other. As far as I'm concerned the important thing is to do what you can to prevent them all.'
'Oh, come on', responded Penny, further annoyed by what she considered Carol's sanctimonious tone. 'How can you even begin to compare the suffering of animals with people? You can't possibly think that they have feelings that are anything like ours? That's preposterous!'
'Not only do I think that animals have feelings: I know they do. Just look how pleased my dog is to see me when I go home. Don't tell me that it isn't an emotion similar to my Mum and Dad's. Watch a group of lambs in a field – they play together, they're

full of energy one moment and fast asleep the next – just like young children. They need their mums, just like kids do. If you use your eyes and ears, I think you can watch animals and realise that they experience joy, sorrow, loneliness, excitement – nearly all the same emotions as we do.'

'That's rubbish. What you're talking about is instincts. Animals live in the moment. They have no awareness of what's going to happen to them in the future, so how can they suffer in the same way?' Sally Wilson, a conventionally glamorous postgraduate student from the Department of Medieval Literature, interrupted. There was always an unspoken hostility between her and the rebellious Carol.

'I'm sorry, Penny, but I've got to go. For what it's worth though, I think the difference between animals and us is that they are incapable of those great achievements of the human soul. Our spirit is capable of so much more. Animals can't produce great art or literature. They can't appreciate a Bach symphony or a Giotto mural.' 'I'll grant you that', Carol acknowledged in a tone that showed she wasn't actually conceding anything. 'Neither can they launch a military coup or build a concentration camp. What was it Mark Twain said? "Man is the only animal that blushes – or needs to".' It was a cheap jibe, but she wasn't going to let the medievalist get away with sounding more cultured than she was. Sally's reaction was simply to ignore. She stood up and rather ostentatiously put on the fox fur jacket that had turned Carol against her from the first moment she had spotted it. Already stirred by the discussion and feeling less composed than her polished answers betrayed, Carol stared coldly at her adversary. If looks could kill! Penny Painter and one or two others also looked slightly disapproving. Medical research was one thing; wearing fur was another.

'Oh. I'm not the least bit sentimental about animals', said Sally, aware of Carol's anger and smiling condescendingly as she spoke. 'I'm not sentimental about animals either. And neither am I

the least bit sentimental about stupid women who are so vain that they think that wearing the skin of dead animals makes them look good. One woman, one skin – that's enough for me.'
'You must feel very superior then', replied Sally, keeping her calm while inwardly flustered by the intensity of the attack.
  'I *am* superior.'

Both the personal attack and the last comment were a bit much for the rest to take. There was an embarrassed silence. Some drank nervously and others looked down into their beer or wine glasses, carefully avoiding the two protagonists. Sally left, trying to hold back tears. The group split up slowly into twos and threes and left the table where they had been sitting together. Tom hugged and reassured Carol, who was also upset and crying. She knew she had blown it. For him, however, she could do no wrong. Sally had got what she deserved. As he had watched the whole discussion unfold, he had felt increasingly proud of his loved one's performance. He adored her feisty nature and the certainty of her beliefs. He marvelled at her grasp of the subject and her ability to bring relevant information quickly to mind. He loved her bravery in defending her position against all comers. He envied her powerful debating skills. He was awe-struck at the way somebody from her poor background could achieve so much, dispelling the idea that protest movements were exclusively the realm of the privileged and middle-class (even though he knew that the vast majority were, like him, exactly that). He was consumed with youthful, romantic love, robbing him of the ability to judge the object of his affection with any degree of disinterest.

By the beginning of their third year at university, Carol and Tom were living together in a terraced house close to the river on the north side of town. They shared with four other students and were revelling in their domestic tranquillity. Tom, in particular, felt blissfully happy. All he really wanted to do was to stay at home and spend every minute of every day in the company of his beloved. But she was made of sterner stuff. They – or rather Carol with Tom in tow – formed a group to oppose factory farming. One Saturday each month they gathered at one of the city centre pedestrian areas, a tree-sheltered square at the end of a fashionable cobbled street known as *The Shambles*.

'Intriguing, isn't it', he pondered, 'the way that abattoirs used to be known as shambles and that now that word has come to mean chaos and disorder?'

'You may find it intriguing but the only thing of interest to me is closing the fucking places down!' Carol replied impatiently. 'As far as I'm concerned, hell would be a better word for them.' Sometimes Tom's pontificating got on her nerves.

They handed out leaflets and collected petition signatures. Given that animal issues were not yet much on the political agenda, it was surprising quite how much sympathy and support they attracted. Soon their group had a number of members. They felt they were getting somewhere. But they also learnt that trying to convert even the more sympathetic members of the Great British Public could prove a frustrating task. On one occasion, Carol managed to get hold of a real-life battery cage in an attempt to highlight the plight of factory farmed hens. Soon after they had set up their stall for the day, two elderly women approached.

'What's that?' asked the first.

'It's a battery cage for laying hens', replied Tom, ready to launch into his prepared monologue on the subject. 'On most poultry farms they pack five birds into one of these. It's only twenty inches wide, so each hen has only four inches of cage space. They can't spread their wings or even turn around.'

'Five hens in there?' came the incredulous reply. 'That's disgusting!'

'It certainly is', responded Tom, pleased with the positive

response he had stimulated.

The woman turned to her friend, who was clearly a little hard of hearing and straining to follow the conversation.

'They keep five hens in there, Alice,' she shouted. 'Isn't that disgusting?'

Alice nodded her agreement.

The questioner turned back to Tom.

'You ought to be ashamed of yourself!' she exclaimed indignantly.

'Sorry?'

'I said you ought to be ashamed of yourself, keeping five hens in a cage that small.'

Tom tried to suppress a giggle.

'No, no,' he explained. 'You've got it wrong. It's not us that keep hens in cages. It's the farmers. We're trying to stop it.'

'Farmers as well, eh? Well, you all ought to be ashamed of yourselves.'

And with this the women walked away, his critic continuing loudly to expound her version of events to the deaf Alice.

'Five hens in a cage like that. They ought to be ashamed of themselves,' she went on, looking back disapprovingly.

Then there was the type that Carol chastised as 'the self-satisfied petition signers'. More often than not they were women in their thirties or forties, who would rush up to the stall and declare their 100 per cent support.

'Anything for animals, me!'

Tom would offer a leaflet.

'No thanks, love. I can't stand to read about it, or see the pictures. It upsets me too much. Have you got a petition I can sign?'

And so they would sign the petition and hurriedly depart, their pained expression at the thought of being handed literature giving way to a smile that indicated total allegiance to the cause.

It was clear that this swift and simple gesture offered the best and cheapest therapy in town, allowing the signatory to go home safe in the knowledge that they had done their bit of caring for the day and were now absolved from any further responsibility.

Every Monday he cycled along the river towards the university for his morning lecture, singing joyfully as he rode along. How could life be this good? Locals out walking their dogs would smile indulgently as they heard him rolling out the lyrics of his favourite songs of the moment. Almost always there was the Bill Withers' hit *Lovely Day* ('Then I look at you, and the world's alright with me/Just one look at you, and I know it's gonna be/ A lovely day'). And sometimes he would switch to a lusty chorus of the most successful protest song of the time, *Glad to be Gay*, the street credibility of Tom Robinson's composition endorsed enormously by a broadcast ban from the BBC. ('Sing if you're glad to be gay/ Sing if you're happy that way'). The latter tended to provoke a less sympathetic reaction amongst some of the dog walkers, one or two glancing in his direction as if he was suffering from a deadly infectious disease. It was 1978 – towards the end of a decade which had started with the formation of the UK Gay Liberation Front and its initiative to allow homosexuals 'to express their feelings openly and without shame'. The campaign had made great progress, moving away from an almost apologetic plea for tolerance towards an assertion of Gay Pride – celebrating difference and cultural identity. Yet remarkably, it was also little more than a decade since the first legislation to decriminalise homosexual acts between consenting adults and still five years before a Labour parliamentary candidate, Peter Tatchell, would be defeated at a by-election after a vicious homophobic witch-hunt. As the words of *Glad to be Gay* made only too clear, prejudice and bigotry were still widespread. Indeed, much as he would have denied it, Tom was not entirely free from unease himself.

Although he liked to imagine that not a drop of prejudice infected his politically correct blood, he wouldn't have wanted his singing to be interpreted as anything more than a gesture of solidarity with the underdog. In plenty of circles, even that was still enough to earn a severe beating.

On leaving the river to cut across town towards campus, he would stop at the cheap and cheerful wholefood co-operative called *Seeds* to stock up with provisions for the week ahead. It was one of several co-operative ventures started up by hippy ex-students who had decided to make their futures in the city of their exciting university days. Elsewhere there was a bicycle repair and renovation shop, the refuge for abused women and a community newspaper that gave voice to the alternative culture that flourished around the town – mostly music, complementary therapies and spiritual regimes based upon Eastern influences. Tom wondered with regret why his brother and some of his university friends had not taken a similarly unconventional path rather than opting for lucrative careers in conventional business – or else teaching or social work. Even though the latter occupations were relatively more acceptable, he thought that everybody with radical tendencies should really be devoting themselves to small-is-beautiful alternatives to the capitalist economic agenda.

Seeds was a successful if chaotic venture, run from cramped and slightly shabby premises about a mile from the university. The shop floor was packed with hessian sacks filled with beans, grains and cereals. It had a permanent window display, consisting of a wide range of dried herbs and spices kept in old sweet jars, each identified by colourful and flowery hand-written labels stuck on the outside with selotape. Looking in from the street, some of these were obscured by rows of classified advertisement cards, mostly promoting yoga, eccentric spiritual and healing groups, self-awareness meetings, alternative medicine practitioners and rooms to let in community households.

'Sixth woman sought for holistic vegetarian, feminist household. Ideal home for young sister committed to self-discovery and seeking to reconnect to the strength, intuition and power of the feminine spirit. Must also possess a sense of humour.'

Apart from the many students who bought up the beans and hand-mixed muesli, the store also attracted a significant number of local residents, particularly older folk seeking out porridge oats and bowel-clearing prunes and bran at bargain prices. By the time Tom reached the shop – soon after the official 9am Monday opening – two or three of these characters had already assembled outside, vainly awaiting signs of life from within. A further delay invariably ensued before a bleary-eyed member of the co-op eventually emerged from the living quarters above the premises. Unlocking the door, the unshaven figure known as Alf stared, mole-like, into the morning light, running his hands wearily through his dishevelled mop of greasy hair. As the relieved customers filed in from the cold, Alf scratched his head, coughed, yawned and generally offered no attempt to disguise a severe hangover from the weekend's revelries.

'What can I get you, love?' he at last enquired.

'A pound of bran, please', ordered the patient female pensioner at the front of the queue.

More time was then lost while the appropriate sack was located and prised open. Alf plunged his metal scoop into the grain, only to discover yet another impediment to progress in the shape of a small moth, who immediately flew out from the grain and up onto the ceiling. The best bet might have been to apologise or pretend that the insect had not been spotted, but feigning ignorance was apparently not an option. The previously sleepy staff member sprang brightly to life, pursuing the despised and rejected creature doggedly around the premises. With customers looking on with a combination of embarrassment and alarm, Alf leapt over sacks, jumped up towards the ceiling and swatted thin air with his scoop in an ultimately futile attempt to exterminate the fugitive.

Reluctantly abandoning the chase, at last he returned to the waiting pensioner and restored his weapon to its rightful purpose. Shovelling the bran into a recycled paper bag, he attempted to reassure the watching crowd.

'Mice and rats are not such a problem in this game,' he began in a friendly and confidential tone. 'But we do get a lot of moths. Weevils, too. They love this stuff.'

The old lady nodded in anxious agreement, handed over her coppers and left as quickly as possible – no doubt weighing up whether it was worth enduring the environmental health hazards and the eccentric service in order to save a few pennies. Probably it was.

After he completed his degree, Tom decided to hang around for a year while Carol completed a teaching qualification. Despite volunteering for this and that and doing some seasonal work helping with the potato and sugar beet harvest on a local farm, he was at a bit of a loose end. He became increasingly dependent upon his girlfriend for stimulation. She began to feel stifled by him. When an opportunity came up for a voluntary service post in Tanzania, Carol decided to take it. Not only was it a job she wanted to do, it would also get her away from Tom without having to make a clean and painful break. The possibility of them being together on her return would still be there.

Tom's hurt – considerable though it was – proved less of a problem than her parents' opposition. They were horrified. They had expected their daughter to become a lawyer or university academic – a journalist or teacher they could just about put up with. But a volunteer in a far-off country, working for a pittance of a wage! What sort of a job was that? Had the sacrifices they had made for her education all been wasted?

The prospect of his girlfriend's absence at least spurred Tom into some sort of action. He decided that he needed to make a fresh start, nearer to his childhood home. Without any great conviction, he successfully applied for a teaching course in Bristol. Soon after Carol's summer departure, he headed back down to the south-west.

3

The first months of Tom Moore's homecoming were not the easiest of times. He wasn't particularly interested in his teaching course and though he corresponded regularly with Carol, as time went by it was obvious that the more involved she became with her work, the less time she had for him. Love was on the rocks. Soon after Christmas came the letter he had been dreading. She had met someone else, a fellow volunteer. She hoped nonetheless that they could carry on being friends. He was devastated.

He sought solace mostly by throwing himself into the pressing campaign issues around the city. These turned out to be nuclear disarmament, followed soon afterwards by animal rights. CND was in the very early days of a dramatic revival, fuelled by Mrs Thatcher agreeing to site American cruise missiles in the UK and intensified by publication of the government's 'home defence' information booklet, *Protect and Survive*. This was meant to offer reassurance that the effects of nuclear war would not be as devastating as all that. All you apparently had to do to save your family from bombs with the power to destroy whole cities – followed by the catastrophic effects of radiation fallout – was to hide under the dining room table and stock up with a few extra tins of food and bottled water. It proved an even greater gift to the anti-nuclear cause than the occasion back in 1961 when Home Secretary Sir Alec Douglas Home declared that the British people were 'prepared to be blown to atomic dust if necessary'. Speak for yourself, Sir Alec! What really got up everyone's nose –

apart from the fear of annihilation itself – was the certainty that while they were waiting to be blown to smithereens, politicians such as Hume and Thatcher would be installed in their luxurious underground bunkers.

When Mrs Thatcher came to power in 1979, CND had just over 4,000 members and 150 local groups. The next year both figures had doubled. Two years further on there were 50,000 members and 1,000 groups. This spectacular rise reflected widening divisions within the country. Those who supported the PM's assertion that the USSR would waste no opportunity to invade and conquer the West were full of praise for the decision to allow US nuclear weapons on our soil. The large minority who hated everything she stood for opposed it vehemently – a minority that grew stronger still after the official Labour Party briefly returned to its traditional anti-nuclear stance. It felt to Tom as if almost everybody he knew was joining CND. Every week there were large demonstrations and meetings to attend or coaches organised to cross the Severn Bridge in support of the initiative to declare Wales the first nuclear-free country in the world.

Animal rights on the other hand, was not nearly so mainstream and when Tom first made contact the local group was very small. But it was growing fast and the fact that everybody knew one another was part of its attraction. He needed to meet new people, so it fitted the bill perfectly. There was some crossover with the CND people as well, notably with the Reverend Tony Swallow, a tireless and inspirational vicar from a comfortably wealthy parish in North Somerset. The Reverend was a little eccentric and something of a local celebrity, well known for his anti-nuclear activities and weekly missives in the local newspaper against greed and excessive wealth. His particular passion was fighting world poverty, highlighted through his association with Christian Aid and regular visits to local schools. He was also a vegetarian, and tried to find time to help local campaigns by turning out at the occasional demonstration.

After completing his course, Tom decided to hang around and delay taking a teaching job, funding himself by working part-time in a bar. He became increasing involved with the animal rights group, which, as the new decade kicked in, seemed full of passion and boundless energy. Fifteen or so industrious characters – a couple of teachers and middle-aged women alongside a core of committed youngsters – religiously held information stalls in the city centre and travelled around the country to attend demonstrations or sabotage hunts.

As with most successful voluntary groups, this vibrancy was inspired predominantly by one individual. Marie Westwood was an unusual and charismatic young woman in her very early twenties with bright, almond-shaped brown eyes that lent a vaguely oriental touch to her appearance. She had developed an intense empathy with animals from parents who had spent a lifetime giving refuge to stray dogs, cats and rabbits – so much so that the word seemed to spread inexplicably around the homeless four-legged community that they had only to turn up at the back door to claim entry. At eighteen, Marie made what she saw as a serious career decision: rather than join her school friends in going off to university, she would instead devote her life to the alleviation of animal suffering. Activities would be funded by a combination of part-time work and state benefits. She felt no qualms whatsoever about taking taxpayers' money, reasoning that the fight to end factory farming and vivisection was far more valuable to society than studying science or becoming a doctor or lawyer. It was a more important and ethical use of government money, even if the public were yet to appreciate it.

In many ways Marie possessed the unmistakable qualities of a true zealot. She had no doubts about the justice of her mission and was dedicated and fearless in its pursuit. Such certainty and devotion inspired confidence and loyalty amongst her colleagues.

They looked up to her. Yet uncommonly for one so young and with such uncompromising beliefs, she could also show surprising tolerance towards those with different views. She possessed a precious ability to laugh at herself and laugh with others. When it suited, she could even charm opponents whose attitudes she despised.

Alongside Marie, the majority of the group would have passed any 'appeared normal' analysis with flying colours, but, as with most minority causes, there were also a few strange characters who added credence to the popular theory that it is predominantly misfits and the insane who stand out against the received wisdom of the age. Particularly striking was a young man in his mid twenties who, as a result of an incongruous fascination for Roman history, had renamed himself Septimus the Severe. It had been the ancient Septimus's doctrine of retribution that had attracted him to this identity, though in practice his bark was far worse than his bite. Despite his somewhat dour character, always dressing in black and rarely smiling, he wasn't one for a fight or even an argument with his enemies. In fact, the title Septimus the Separatist might have been more appropriate. He was a vegan (as was Marie) and didn't believe in mixing with anybody who wasn't of the same persuasion, though he just about tolerated the presence of lacto-vegetarians such as Tom. When challenged on this policy, he was uncompromising.

'I wouldn't want to mix with child killers or torturers, so why should I have anything to do with people who feed off the dead bodies of murdered young animals?'

This fundamentalist stance had alienated him from his family and almost all of his old friends to the point where he lived a relatively solitary existence in a small cottage situated on the southern edge of the Cotswolds. For company, he had a growing community of rescued animals and three likeminded souls and fellow hunt saboteurs from across the country who got together as regularly as they could to play what might loosely be described as music. *The Liberators* – as the quartet had named their hardcore punk band – made a lot of aggressive noise and wrote songs whose titles confirmed a single-minded approach to lyrical content. Their titles included *People Are Shit, Fuck You Vivisectors, Meat Eating Bastards* and a more reflective piece, *Hunt Scum, Your Time Has Come.* Away from this contribution to the Arts, Septimus's main passion was wandering the countryside in search of snares and traps, regarding himself as on a personal mission to defend helpless wildlife against rural savagery.

Equally unusual was Denise Oakley, a short, buxom, blonde-rinsed woman in her early forties who, on first acquaintance, would have been taken for an unexceptional – if a little loud and brash – wife and mother. Her most notable feature was a pair of breasts that appeared too large for the rest of her body, so that she waddled a bit like a duck when she walked. It came as a shock to find that inside this slightly comical frame lurked a self-appointed medium for almost everything that exists outside our earthly realm. Denise considered herself an expert on all matters pertaining to horoscopes, healing, angels, communication with spirits or any form of alternative medicine. As a vehicle for her gifts, she had formed her own organisation, Spiritualist and Pagan Animal Welfare Network (SPAWN).

It seems to be a feature of almost all protest movements that odd little Jesuses emerge from the main pack to cater for even smaller minorities with incongruous spiritual, religious or political beliefs – Marxist Stockbrokers for Womens' Rights, Alliance of Religious Fundamentalists for Gay Pride, One-Armed Osteopaths Against Nuclear Power and so on – and it is therefore not altogether surprising that Denise chose to pursue her own area of special interest, independently from the rest of Marie's group. Neither was she the only member to do so. Right-Wing Roger, as his colleagues knew him, was prominent in another recently formed organisation, the Conservative Animal Alliance. Roger had risen dramatically to a position of prominence within this society, admittedly without encountering the stiffest of competition. Although the UK's first female prime minister was only in her first term, the vast majority of protestors – whether their cause was animals, the environment, poverty or peace – were already demonising her as the personification of reactionary evil. Roger, on the other hand, remained adamant that she and her government would prove themselves radical reformers and firm friends of the furry creatures. He also stood out from his fellow campaigners by his dress code, turning up on anti-hunting demonstrations as if he were about to take a lead role in an amateur dramatic society production of a Noel Coward play. No older than Marie, he would often wear tweed jacket and bow tie or cravat and was never to be spotted in anything more casual than a plain collar and tie.

As Tom struggled to recover from the loss of Carol, he found himself increasingly drawn towards the company of Marie. When he was away from her, he would talk about her virtues at great length. At Easter, there was a family gathering at which he waxed lyrical about her dynamism and her unusual brown eyes.

'Good God, Tom', commented his mother, 'you do seem to pick 'em! Carol was fanatical enough – and don't get me wrong, I thought Carol was a lovely girl – but this Marie sounds frightening. I don't know why you go for these strong-willed, headstrong types.'

Rob – who was bouncing his baby daughter up and down on his knee while his wife collected the dropped bits of food and discarded toys from the kitchen floor – looked up to the heavens.

'Oh no, mother, I don't know where he gets it from!' he exclaimed, casting a mockingly stern stare in her direction.

'What **do** you mean Rob? I'm not a bit like that.'

'Mother, when it comes to campaigning you're indomitable... and you know it.'

Margaret Moore looked offended. Far from the overprotective type, she nonetheless didn't want to believe that her son could possibly be attracted to somebody in any way similar, let alone entertain the thought that such a young woman might become equally influential in his life. Besides, the focus of Marie's and Carol's social consciences didn't quite measure up. Margaret accepted this animal rights business to a point and was quite willing to cook and eat vegetarian food when Tom was at home, but she couldn't help feeling that it wasn't quite as important as the issues on which she had fought.

Tom's fascination with Marie continued to blossom. Often, they would travel considerable distances together in her battered old banger to take part in some demonstration or other. These were almost always fairly friendly affairs, even after they began to include an inevitable minor outbreak of civil disobedience. After a couple of years of marching politely and optimistically around various city centres, the more impatient young activists had concluded that this tactic alone was not going to bring about an immediate end to factory farming or vivisection. A rallying cry went out for more strident action, a call to which the passionately committed responded with enthusiasm. Soon, no protest could pass by without some gesture of unauthorised defiance. Mostly it was of a harmlessly mild and predictable nature – a brief sit-down protest in the middle of a town shopping precinct, a rooftop occupation of a factory farm or slaughterhouse, trespassing onto the site of a laboratory and so on. Sometimes a few arrests and minor charges would follow, but there was no hint of violence and more often than not the offenders would be sent home after a couple of hours in the cells. The police remained largely tolerant.

One Saturday afternoon in late autumn, it was the turn of

Marie's group to organise their own regional protest. The target was a poultry slaughterhouse – or processing plant as it was officially known – for the local company, Sunny Chicken. To the organisers' delight, about three hundred people turned up, making quite a show for the modest size of the market town. Apart from Septimus the Severe and his mates – dressed in grim reaper black as usual – plus the unfashionably smart Right-Wing Roger, it was a predominantly fresh-faced crowd, unexceptionally attired in casual sweaters, jackets or anoraks. It might have been the post-punk era, but hardly a bright dyed haircut or a pierced ear was to be seen, let alone a lip or eyebrow stud. Indeed, the only thing that really distinguished the marchers from the Saturday afternoon shoppers were their placards. Slogans carrying the anti factory farming message were everywhere to be seen, though Septimus once again distinguished himself by creating a homemade poster with a more puritan agenda. *Are you a Vegan or a Nazi?* was the simple question it posed, a choice that left both the public and the majority of his colleagues firmly in the fascist camp.

After a long delay, the demonstrators set off through the two streets that constituted the entire shopping centre. While the less vociferous chatted away amicably to the small number of police assigned to keep them in order, the more robust yelled out their greatest hits from the uninspiring world of protest chants, endlessly repeating *What Do We Want and When Do We Want It, Meat Means Murder,* and *Factory Farming – Out, Out, Out!* for the benefit of local shoppers. Their performance was co-ordinated by an acknowledged champion in the key role of megaphone man, known to regulars only by the nickname of Ho Ho. He took his position seriously, carrying his personal loudhailer from venue to venue like a virtuoso musician with a favourite instrument.

'Ladies and gentlemen, I have a different chant for you today', he had announced one day in his finest BBC voice. 'It goes like this:

He,he,he,
ho,ho,ho,
factory farming has to go!'

This wasn't exactly the tone or sentiment that the young and angry wished to convey. It was like asking Septimus's punk band to sing *Chirpy Chirpy Cheep Cheep* or *Granddad We Love You*. From that moment the name of Ho Ho had stuck firm.

On this dull and breezy October afternoon, Ho Ho was in full swing, urging on the chanting until the protest left the busier area and wound its way through quieter countryside in the direction of the isolated industrial estate where Sunny Chicken's headquarters was situated. Most of the marchers settled down to chatter peacefully among themselves, only reverting to demonstration mode when they reached their ultimate destination. Despite finding the buildings apparently deserted and with nothing to indicate the bloody nature of the enterprise, the laid-back afternoon stroll immediately gave way to a more excitable atmosphere. The obligatory act of civil disobedience had been pre-arranged and so, to the cheers of the rest of the crowd, about fifteen of the fittest and most committed activists climbed over the locked gates, clambered athletically up the drainpipe and made their way onto the low flat roof of Sunny Chicken's administrative building. An impressively designed banner was unfurled and Marie shouted down a message of defiant explanation for the benefit of the four or five gathered members of the local press.

'One million poultry are slaughtered every day in this country and we're here to show Sunny Chicken that this can no longer be tolerated in a civilised society!'

More enthusiastic cheers rang out from below.

After this initial flurry of activity, things became a little dull. The police request to end the rooftop protest having been refused, there was a period of quiet stand-off. The media had got their photos and quotes, the direct action group couldn't think of anything else to do, and watching a few people sit on a roof soon lost its entertainment value for everyone else. An hour or so passed and everybody was feeling uncomfortably chilly. The police officer in charge – a burly, round-faced West Country man named Sergeant Goss – made a second attempt to urge the roof-invaders to come down. Borrowing Ho Ho's megaphone, he implored them to go home.

'You's made yer point, the press 'as got 'ems photos, so please come down and we's can all go 'ome peacefully', the Sergeant politely reasoned.

Marie bluntly rejected this request. Goss looked a bit frustrated. After discussion with a colleague, he retired to a quiet corner and picked up his police radio. Tom noticed this development from his position alongside the rest of the legal demonstrators, outside the gates. He began to fret. Were things about to turn nasty? He decided it was time to intervene.

'What are you going to do to end all this?' he asked, feigning to share the officer's belief that it was time to call a halt to the afternoon's proceedings.

'I think yurll find id'll soon be over', the policeman responded ominously, looking up towards the sky as he did so. Tom felt even more apprehensive. Had the sergeant sent for reinforcements to storm the roof? Were the demonstrators about to experience decisive and violent police action?

Sergeant Goss revealed his master plan.

'We's gunna leave 'um up there a while. Look at they dark clouds. I's been on ter weather office and they say there's a good chance of rain sweepin' in from the west in the next 'arf 'our or so, dun 'um. Thad'll do the trick.'

This cunning strategy was presented with all the gravity of a man who had decided to call for the riot squad and water canons.

Regrettably for Sergeant Goss, the meteorological office let him down. The predicted rainstorm never arrived. The crowd stood around for a further period, until the reporters concluded that nothing more thrilling was going to happen and that they would make do with the copy and photographs they had already acquired. Soon afterwards, the rooftop crowd also decided to call it a day. Sergeant Goss made a half-hearted attempt to take names and addresses before giving up and allowing everybody go home quietly. Nobody had been hurt; no damage had been done. The activists felt satisfied with the limited success of a probable front-page story and exclusive photographs in the next edition of the free local weekly newspaper, plus news headlines and a very brief interview with Marie on both *BBC Radio Somerset* and *Voice of Bristol Radio*. Given that the limited Saturday afternoon audience for both stations consisted almost entirely of sports fanatics in search of up-to-the-minute news of their local football and rugby teams, it is questionable how much influence her words of wisdom might have had upon their listeners.

Months later, Sergeant Goss's weekend duties brought him into further contact with Marie, after she and ten others were arrested for staging a sit-down protest outside a vivisection laboratory on the outskirts of London. Police arrived swiftly from all directions, long before the media could be summoned for the planned photo opportunity. The campaigners were carted away and dispersed to several police stations across the capital. Most were locked up for the night, where they met with contrasting treatment. Some were left to stew in their cells and ignored. Requests for vegan food were treated with contempt: 'Eat what you're given or go hungry'. Others were shown more sympathy. Marie, at her most charming, was soon offered fruit and nuts and given magazines and newspapers to read. When she pleaded that her parents wouldn't know where she was and would worry, an understanding duty sergeant immediately agreed to contact the local force. He was a parent too and knew how he would feel if his young daughter had gone to London and disappeared for the weekend. Sergeant Goss was contacted and decided he would go in person to deliver the news of her arrest.

'No need to worry yerself too much', he immediately reassured a shocked Marie's mum when she opened the door and found a uniformed policeman on the step. 'It's just that yer Marie 'as got 'erself into a bit o' bother up there in Lurndon and they's keepin' 'er in overnight. It weren't much as far as I can see – just lying down in front of a building or summat like that. I'm sure she'll be 'ome soon. To tell you the truth, we wouldn't 'u bothered too much with that sort of thing down 'ere, but they Met boys – they's a bit different.'

The next day, all the protestors were released.

Even Tom started to get a bit more adventurous. One Saturday afternoon he joined a hard core of the nation's anti-nuclear campaigners in London as they poured into Downing Street and sat down in the middle of the road outside Number Ten. Despite the IRA terrorist threat and the left-wing rhetoric constantly accusing the Thatcher government of turning the country into a police state, the street still remained open for visitors to enter and peer at the Prime Minister's house. Security was understandably tight however and the protest didn't last long. He was scared when they roughly bundled him into the police van and locked him away, but after a couple of hours in the cells, he and his colleagues were all surprisingly released without charge.

Next – and against his better judgement – Tom was persuaded to join the transit van load of hardy individuals who, each Wednesday and Saturday, set out across the countryside to protest against local hunts. His involvement was reluctant and partly to impress Marie, who had been a regular saboteur since the age of sixteen and was well known to many of the region's hunting fraternity. She could be charming to the upper classes, too: so much so that one or two of the traditional old redcoats rather liked her. They maintained that she was different from the rest of the despised 'antis', simply a bit misguided rather than a member of what they dismissed as a Kremlin funded rent-a-mob. In the face of the rougher hunting elements she was fearless, on one occasion even attempting to throw herself across the underground entrance to a lair in which a fox had gone to ground in order to prevent the terrier men calling in their dogs. In what proved ultimately to be a futile gesture, she yelled her defiance at the men, women and pursuing hounds who gathered around as two men hacked at the earth with spades and iron bars. The youngster screamed hysterically, loudly drawing attention to the sexual inadequacy of anybody who could take pleasure in such activity. Her language was coarse. As the soil crumbled around the underground tunnel, the two dogs that had been loosed below ground were exposed, almost at the climax of their deadly attack. One snarling terrier seized the dying fox by the shoulder, shaking and pulling his exhausted prey. His owner reached into the pit and grabbed the blood and mud covered dog by the scruff of the neck, releasing his teeth from the fox's flesh. With the other arm, he grabbed the dying vixen by her tail. One eyeball had burst. The second terrier man reached for his spade and brought a final blow crashing down with full force upon the victim's head.

Tom's career as a hunt saboteur got off to a bad start when violence erupted on only his second outing. It happened after they had successfully distracted the hounds and prevented the hunters from achieving a kill. The saboteurs had returned triumphantly to their van and were about to drive home when three or four vehicles roared up and hemmed them in. A group of seven or eight men jumped out and started to destroy the van's tyres. Tom sat rigidly in his seat, scared stiff. Marie leapt from the vehicle and attempted to strike a tone that lay somewhere between reason and remonstration. She was immediately surrounded. One of the gang, in an uncontrollable rage, began to threaten her. All this occurred so quickly that only when the blows began to rain down did the rest of the saboteurs – Septimus and Tom at the rear – pile out of the vehicle to defend their comrade. Almost before they could reach her, the incident was over. Such had been the viciousness of the assault that the rest of the hunt supporters had come rapidly to their senses and restrained the attacker. They hurried back to their vehicles and roared off. Marie looked a real mess, blood streaming from her face. Her ribs were giving her great pain and she couldn't lift one of her arms. Police were called and she was rushed off to hospital.

In the pub that evening, Tom discussed the day's activity with a few of his fellow activists. He knew Septimus the Severe and Greg, a student from the university, but the rest were new to him. Colin, in his mid-thirties, turned out to be a graphic designer from Dorset, who had been a hunt saboteur for fifteen years – since the early days of the organisation. As the evening progressed and the beer flowed, he entertained the others with nostalgic anecdotes from his protesting past.

'It was different in those early days, back in the late sixties. We were a bunch of softies really. Most of us were long-haired "peace and love, man" hippies wearing CND badges and the hunters largely put up with us. It's true that there were always one or two rural thugs who would turn nasty, but we soon got to know who they were and to run like fuck when we saw them coming! Nowadays, it's different. There always seems to be a whole bunch of psychopaths out there, like that bloke today, and if I'm honest, there's often a couple of sabs up for a good scrap as well.'

'What's wrong with standing up for yourself?' Septimus responded, indignant at what he took to be criticism of the more militant elements. 'Those Neanderthals deserve everything they get as far as I'm concerned. I wouldn't shed any tears if somebody gave that cunt that attacked Marie a good kicking. Violence is the only language these bastards know.'

'That's fighting talk for someone who was almost as reluctant to get out of the van as me', Tom thought, but kept it to himself.

The discussion went on. Dave Dryden, a tall, angular figure with a bald head and rather doleful blue eyes, was eventually brought into the discussion. Previously he had sat silently in the corner, too shy to join in.

'How did you get involved in all this, Dave?' asked Colin.

'Through Denise from the Spiritualist and Pagan Animals Welfare Network', he muttered nervously.

'Oh, I know Denise,' Tom intervened. 'She's part of our local group. How come you know her?'

'She's High Priestess of our pagan community and Ron, her husband, is the High Priest.'

A few suspicious glances were exchanged around the table, and Colin tried his best to defuse any awkwardness by steering the conversation in a less bizarre direction.

'And what do you do for a living, Dave?'

'I work as a chemist, though actually I'm an Elfin King.'

Tom caught Colin's eye and took a deep breath to stop from bursting into laughter. Even though he knew of Denise's standing as the brain behind SPAWN, he hadn't been aware of her status as High Priestess. He found the whole business a bit off the wall. When he had first been introduced, he had expected to find a tall, thin witch-like creature with long dark hair and fingernails rather than a middle-aged, buxom blonde. Similar prejudice had informed his first visit to her home, which he had visited with Marie to pick up some rescued chickens. He had imagined some damp, detached residence hidden deep in darkest countryside, strewn with cobwebs and strange artefacts. Instead, he discovered a newly built semi-detached on a comfortable modern housing estate that reminded him of a children's television toy town.

Denise had greeted them warmly.

'Hello Marie. Hello love. Would you mind taking your shoes

off?'

Tom thought that this request might be a prelude to some dark initiation ritual. He was certainly hoping for something a little more unusual than the hygiene measure it turned out to be. The briefest glance inside revealed greater attention to cleaning fluids than potions or totems. The house was immaculately tidy from top to bottom and the furniture was disappointingly plain, modern and functional. The whole set-up was more MFI than ESP. A strong smell of synthetic pine filled the air. Denise led her guests into the living room, where High Priest Ron and teenage son Robin were eating a light tea consisting of toasted white sliced bread, Marmite and blackberry jam. Neither of the Oakley males was very communicative, so there was an awkward silence while he waited for Denise and Marie to collect the birds from a shed at the bottom of a small, neat back garden. It wasn't until the five chickens were safely packed into Marie's car that Tom experienced what he took to be his first piece of hocus pocus.

'Would you like a nice hot cup of Slippery Elm before you go, love?' enquired their hostess.

'At last, something a bit weird', Tom thought, accepting the offer a little apprehensively. It was a decision he soon regretted, finding the taste bitter and unpalatable. Out of politeness he managed to drink half. Denise looked suspiciously at his unfinished mug and was prompted to an astrological enquiry.

'You must be a Capricorn, Tom?'

'No'

'Aries then?'

'No, I'm Sagittarius actually.'

'Aah yes, that figures. Of course, the centaur. Yes, a typical Sagittarius, ambitious and optimistic.'

Tom was astounded. How could such things be deduced from his failure to enjoy a beverage derived from tree bark? Had Denise secretly been setting him a test? Was there some mystical connection between how a person responded to this unappetising substance and astrological charts? On the way home he asked Marie about the spiritual significance of the slippery elm.

'Oh, I don't think there's anything particularly spiritual about it. Everybody who's into alternative medicine is drinking it these days. It cleans out the digestive system or something like that.'

'So Denise is into alternative medicine as well?'

'Oh yes, she does consultations and healing in her spare time.'

The rescued poultry collected from Denise were not, as had been expected, rescued battery hens. They had come from a farm that reared poultry for eating rather than for their eggs. They were feeble creatures, cheeping away like baby birds and yet hugely fat and immobile. Tom knew that such chickens were killed when they were only about seven weeks old and concluded that these juvenile giants must have already lived slightly beyond their normal slaughter weight. They took them to Septimus, where they joined a group of twenty or more ex-battery hens who enjoyed a contented retirement, spending the daylight hours wandering around a large and untamed back garden. When new birds arrived, they simply stood around, dazed and confused. They had never felt earth or grass beneath their feet or had the opportunity to roam around and breathe fresh air. Yet within days they rediscovered the instincts they had been born with. They bathed in the dust and pecked in the ground for worms and other insects. They searched out secret places to make nests and lay eggs.

Unlike their egg-laying sisters, the latest arrivals from Denise did not so easily recover. If they left their shed at all, it was only to huddle in the corner of the porch. They seemed unwilling or unable to move. They had grown so fat, so quickly, that their legs were unable to support them. It seemed as if straying very far was too painful and difficult. They were black-humouredly nicknamed 'the zombies'. Within weeks they had all died, keeling over one by one.

One Saturday evening soon after these events, several members of the local group were gathered in the local pub. Septimus was telling them about the zombies' unhappy fate and explaining what he thought might have happened.

'I reckon they all had heart attacks – their limbs and organs just couldn't keep up with the weight of their bodies, poor things.'

Before any of his colleagues had a chance to react, they were interrupted. A short, squat figure waddled busily across the pub floor.

'Hello Marie, hello everybody', began Denise the High Priestess. 'So sorry to hear about the chickens, Sep. Believe me though: they've gone to a better place now. I should know because I've been there and I've seen it. You needn't worry about them.'

And with this reassuring testament to her extraordinary powers, the founder of SPAWN disappeared off into the night.

Although he had played only a peripheral role in the incident in which Marie Westwood had been attacked, the violence he had witnessed was enough to cure Tom's ambitions as a saboteur. But it would have taken far more than that to deter the young woman herself. After only a few weeks, the cuts and bruises had healed and she was back in the van, ready to face the enemy again.

This was also the time in which the Animal Liberation Army or ALA had begun to gain more widespread support amongst campaigners, and, as in many other areas of the country, some of Marie's colleagues became involved in more daring adventures. These nocturnal raids were almost exclusively confined to taking away pet animals that had been reported to them as ill treated, or else stealing poultry from factory farms. Often the victims of these minor crimes chose to put up with it, preferring to keep secret their location and fearing a hostile reaction to the nature of their occupation. Both media and public tended to react to such activities with more admiration than condemnation.

Despite these illegal operations, Marie and her friends seemed essentially an innocent bunch. It was true that they sometimes sat around late into the evening, pontificating upon such weighty issues as whether it was ever justifiable to perpetrate violence against individual animal abusers if it would put an end to animal suffering. And admittedly some concluded that they could envisage 'certain circumstances' in which such a deed could be defended. Septimus the Severe went further, believing that the death of vivisectors would clearly be legitimate when you considered the pain they inflicted upon innocent animals. He personally would not be sorry. It was equally true that in a more severe and paranoid political climate, such talk might easily have been interpreted as conspiracy or incitement to serious crime and have resulted in grave charges and media outcry. But it was essentially very hypothetical stuff. Listening to Septimus reminded Tom of the Christian Union meetings he had overheard in his university days. One night he had suddenly been woken by a voice from the next room shouting to his fellow believers, 'Jesus did say that! As Christians we do have to give away all our possessions'. He didn't imagine than many of them ever did so. Similarly, he was convinced that Septimus was all talk. This was little more than passionate young people enjoying the drama of debate.

While Tom Moore lacked the temperament to be at ease with these illegal raids, he did find something in the secrecy and illicit nature of the enterprise partly irresistible. Whispering in the dark and creeping through the night sent the adrenalin levels soaring, particularly when Marie was close by. A network of similar undercover groups across the country began spreading news of each other's efforts through voluntary regional press officers. Contact for Marie's group was invested in an eccentric pensioner named Norma, who entered into the intrigue with gusto. She basked in the importance of her role and was rarely off the telephone, keeping everybody up to date with a series of snappy, coded messages.

'Norma here', she would declare in her most conspiratorial, "I will say this only once" sort of tone. 'I thought you'd like to know that five naked ladies have arrived from Peterborough.'

'Just to let you know that the lentils have been in soak since yesterday evening.'

The only problem was that she made up the code as she went along and never bothered to let anybody else into the secret. Any communication from Norma invariably had to be followed by a further round of calls in which those who had received her messages sought to decipher what on earth she had been talking about. It is impossible to imagine an exercise more likely to attract police suspicion, so it was fortunate that it didn't much matter. Although it added to the campaigners' sense of danger and importance to imagine tapped telephones and secret surveillance, the reality was that neither the authorities nor anybody else was very interested.

It was eventually agreed with some confidence that the naked ladies from Peterborough must refer to more rescued battery hens, many of whom were devoid of feathers because of aggression from cage mates. There was less certainty in the theory that the soaked lentils referred to a rather unlikely group of elderly women from a northern town, almost all of whom were in their seventies and had won a reputation as a sort of animal protection version of Hell's Grannies. They were notorious for meeting up in the middle of the night and sneaking across the town to rescue and re-home abused dogs and rabbits.

Other messages from Norma remained a complete mystery.

'The tofu has been marinated'.

'I've yet to receive any apricots for the muesli'.

While deeply scared of detection, donning his balaclava and dutifully joining in with clandestine raids briefly became a routine for Tom. Rescuing dogs neglected by their owners and tied up in barren outside yards didn't cause him too much anxiety. Such procedures were carried out quickly and efficiently and there wasn't much risk of being caught. Trespassing into battery units in the darkness he found far more of an ordeal. Fear and excitement mingled in equal measure, the former ensuring that his instinct was to grab a few birds as quickly as possible and get away. Unfortunately, some of his fellow intruders had different ideas. The female contingent were so laid-back and apparently unaffected by nerves that they would hang around the farms for what seemed like an age, methodically working through a criminal schedule that intensified as confidence grew. One of them would painstakingly daub some long-winded message on the wall. On some occasions graffiti was not enough and they would set to work on destroying property, meticulously pouring sugar into petrol tanks, puncturing tyres and putting egg-grading machinery out of action. Tom wasn't sure how far he approved, but was spurred on by the excitement and the desire to impress Marie. He didn't want to be seen as a coward either, though he was always mightily relieved when finally a few birds were taken away and the gang were safely on their way back home.

The criminal damage left Tom feeling increasingly uneasy and he plucked up the courage to challenge Marie about his misgivings.

'Something just doesn't seem right to me. We're supposed to be rescuing animals because we oppose violence, and yet we're happy to smash up equipment and vehicles.'

'That isn't violence, Tom. If we were cutting brakes, starting fires or doing something that might hurt someone, then I would agree. But nobody is going to get hurt by us stopping them from starting up the lorries and driving chickens to the slaughterhouse.'

'Yes, but it won't save any birds either, will it? They'll still get killed in the end. It's not the same as rescuing them.'

'But we can't rescue millions of chickens, can we? We have to hit these bastards in their pockets because that's all they care about. It might not save animals in the short term, but it'll make a difference when the factory farms start closing down because they're losing money and their insurance premiums go through the roof.'

'I've heard that argument before', replied Tom a little impatiently. 'I still think there's something essentially corrupting about the way we all enjoy the sabotage – that adrenalin rush when we're out there smashing things up. We're justifying our actions by claiming that we are doing it to reduce violence, yet it feels like a part of us is giving in to the very impulses we are supposed to condemn.'

Marie gave a characteristic giggle. She was always amused when Tom attempted to philosophise – as he so frequently did.

'Oh Tom, you're such a bloody intellectual. Look, have you seen the film of the Michigan monkeys yet?'

'No, I haven't.'

'Well, you should watch it. This ALA cell broke into a laboratory in the States. Although they couldn't get to the area where the primates were actually kept, they did get hold of some disgusting videos. These poor macaques had had their brains damaged and the researchers were mocking and laughing at them. Some of it was shown on television over there and it caused real outrage. People were so disgusted by the cruelty that nobody gave a shit that the activists later went back and were able to smash the laboratory equipment to bits. Do you really think that they were wrong to do that? Because I don't and I don't think that many other people would think so either. It's no different to seeing a person hitting someone with a stick and grabbing the stick and snapping it. You're not causing violence: you're actually preventing it.'

This made Tom think. That was the trouble with arguing with Marie. She was always so certain of her moral ground. Eventually he responded.

'So who is it who decides when you are morally justified in smashing stuff up and when you are not? Are you saying that it's simply a matter of public perception, rather than the nature of the act itself? If there's enough support then it's OK? If not, you shouldn't do it because then you might be labelled an extremist or worse?'

'That's not what I think, but for what it's worth, I do believe that the public are on our side when they learn what goes on in those factory farms and laboratories.'

'Yes, but I want to know what you think!'

'You know what I think, Tom. It's OK to damage property that's used to abuse animals, but not if it causes harm or threatens other animals or people. That's why I would never set fire to anything – you never know what might happen and at the very least you'd be killing all those little creatures that live in the wood or crannies.'

'I'm still not so sure, Marie. It would be different if somebody was actually caught in the act of hurting an animal – or a person for that matter. Then you'd actually be stopping an act of cruelty by destroying their weapon. Economic sabotage is different. It is just aimed at putting up the costs. As I said before, no animal is actually being saved.'

'Yes, we've already been through that, Tom. As I said, it might be true in the short term, but you just can't tell the long-term impact.'

'Even if that's true – and I'm not saying that I think it is – it still worries me that you are committing a kind of violence against someone who comes into work and finds graffiti on the walls and machinery smashed to smithereens.'

'Not if that machinery belongs to some nameless and faceless business that doesn't give a toss about its workers – let alone the animals it exploits.'

'Oh, I don't know about that. Are you now claiming that there's a moral difference between causing economic damage to an unethical big company and a similarly disgusting small business? …. Well, maybe there is. To tell you the truth, I'm not sure what I think about it all.'

'Believe it or not, I do understand what you're saying, Tom', Marie interrupted, switching to her most understanding manner. 'If you're not happy with it, you shouldn't do it. It's as simple as that. There are plenty of other ways to campaign.'

'I suppose I want to feel it's possible to persuade people by the force of our views and the strength of our argument, that's all. Otherwise, once the other side start to take the same line and to justify smashing up our property, then you end up with war.'

'Yes, but the difference is that we're right and they're wrong. And you know that's true, Tom. Besides, they don't need to resort to subversive tactics to get their voices heard. They already have all the power.'

Soon after this conversation, Tom Moore gave up his involvement with the shadowy side of protest. He liked to think it was down to the ethical dilemma he faced, but he was self-aware enough to wonder whether he was just rationalising his own fears. He didn't really have the temperament to take such risks and he also knew that any criminal conviction would be likely to scupper his anticipated teaching career. He decided that his role lay elsewhere, with the more mundane. Words were his chosen weapon, so he feverishly wrote slightly long-winded letters to newspapers, gave talks in schools and found himself sometimes acting as the group's spokesperson on local radio. He performed these tasks with sufficient skill to get noticed by one or two of the expanding national animal protection societies. One offered him a senior post, based at its headquarters on the southern outskirts of the capital. He thought hard about it and concluded that, tempting though it was, he didn't want to move away from Marie. He loved being around her. So he plucked up the courage to write a letter, telling her how much she meant to him and asking if there was any chance that their friendship might go further. Her reply was a model of tact and diplomacy. She was very fond of him, too, and valued their friendship enormously. But she didn't know what she wanted from a relationship and wasn't going to get involved until she was sure. Besides, she was far too consumed by her campaigning mission.

Tom was hurt and disappointed, yet surprisingly not broken-hearted. Without knowing it, Marie had helped him through the crisis of losing his first love, Carol. He was over the worst. At least her gentle rejection made his decision easier. He would take the job with Save Animals From Exploitation (SAFE). It seemed a more exciting option than teaching.

4

'And I know that change has not come as rapidly as any of us would have liked', Wendy Walters began the conclusion to her talk. 'But as I have tried to show, great progress has been and continues to be made. What we all have to do now is to put aside our differences, keep united and work even harder for the rights of animals. For we must always remember that they have no voice other than ours.'

A reasonable level of applause followed from the hundred or so in the audience, but there was little enthusiasm from a certain section and several hostile stares in her direction.

It was seven months before Tom Moore's job offer and more than three years since Wendy had begun working for SAFE, though she had only recently become one of its public speakers. It seemed rather a dubious honour this sunny Sunday afternoon in North London, where she was answering an invitation to address a gathering of GAFA (Grassroots Activists Forum for

Animals). Although she didn't want to be there, it would have been politically impossible for her organisation to refuse and Wendy had drawn the short straw. Some of the most zealous and determined supporters of the cause travelled great distances from around the country to take part in these monthly meetings and although the majority were friendly and supportive, a vociferous handful were extremely critical of SAFE and any other society that employed paid staff. It didn't take long for one of them – a tall and skinny young man with staring blue eyes – to rise from his seat and express his antipathy.

'What I'd like to know', began Geoff Turner in a broad Liverpool accent, 'is why vast amounts of money raised by national societies such as SAFE are being wasted on meaningless demonstrations, full-colour leaflets and expensive salaries, while dedicated activists like us are willing to spend every day and every night risking our freedom, without funding and without financial reward.'

While he spoke, Geoff Turner jabbed his finger accusingly in Wendy's direction.

'We've had 100 years of trying to change the world by political means and it hasn't worked', he continued. 'The only way to end the torture that animals endure daily is to bring these people to their knees through a concerted, co-ordinated campaign of economic sabotage. What we need is more and more direct action!'

He sat down to cheers and loud applause from a significant proportion of the audience. You only had to mention the term 'direct action' at a GAFA meeting and you were guaranteed an enthusiastic reception. Nobody ever needed to clarify exactly what they meant by the expression.

Before Wendy had a chance to answer, another critic was on his feet. This was Dave Howard, a small bespectacled figure who was probably about twenty years old, but looked little more than fifteen. He also wore something resembling a beard, which, as he barely needed to shave at all, consisted of little more than a few fluffy tufts of light hair strewn irregularly across his chin.

'I wonder if Miss Walters would be kind enough to tell us exactly how much she earns as a professional campaigner? Because I've heard that it is at least £15,000 a year.'

Wendy felt a mixture of fury, frustration and indignation, partly on behalf of her colleagues, but more particularly for herself. She earned less than half of that amount, though she'd be damned if she was going to defend herself to this lot.

'I don't see that what I earn is any of your business', she responded spiritedly. 'All I would say is that you don't want to believe every rumour you hear, or spread them around for that matter. Whether you agree with the campaigning we do at SAFE or not, we all work incredibly hard and believe in what we do. Believe me, none of us are growing rich out of it.'

Many of the audience responded to this a bit more generously than they had to her speech. One man – a little older than the previous contributors – even got up to chastise her critics.

'Look, we may have differences of opinion about campaigning methods, but that's no excuse for treating our speaker so badly. Wendy has been kind enough to come and talk to us and the least we can all do is to show her some common courtesy.'

All went quiet for a moment, partly out of respect for the speaker and partly out of guilt, before a further smattering of applause spread amongst the crowd.

While there was still a bit more criticism for Wendy to take, the discussion soon drifted into other areas. A dispute arose between Geoff Turner and another character called Jem. Turner considered himself a tactical genius when it came to organising direct action, having been one of the masterminds behind a couple of successful break-ins at animal laboratories. The group for which he was a spokesperson – The Merseyside League for Animal Rights – had obtained some damning film footage of animal cruelty and, to great acclaim amongst fellow activists, this had had been broadcast sympathetically on national television news.

'What we have to do now is get away from the decentralised structure and autonomy that still exists amongst many direct action groups', he was arguing. 'This promotes a highly inefficient and anarchic approach that cannot possibly attain the ultimate aim of liberation. What we need instead is a more targeted and disciplined strategy, based on the blueprint we have provided with our successful actions at the Merseyside League.'

Jem – who sounded like and actually was a politics student – responded with an equally vehement defence on behalf of the decentralist agenda.

'With all due respect to what the League has achieved, I have to disagree with Geoff. It is precisely the individualistic, non-patriarchal nature of independent, self-empowered groups that is the strength of this and every other radical liberation movement. I'm not denying that the type of actions favoured by the League have a place in the struggle, but the fundamental duty of grassroots campaigners is to promote an alternative to the kind of institutionalised hierarchy that Geoff is proposing. By encouraging a centralised elite he is doing little more than imitating the structure of the very organisations that are the main perpetrators of abuse in our so-called civilised society – namely the evil and corrupt multinational corporations. With the greatest respect to Geoff and his fellow campaigners, it seems to me that the Merseyside League is advocating a thinly disguised dictatorship. And since we are living in what is undoubtedly one of the most repressive regimes in the history of humanity, the last thing we need to do is to follow the neo-fascist policies of Thatcher's Britain.'

Before too long, this ideological dispute was in full swing, fuelled by egotism and envy. The ill feeling that already existed between the two protagonists and their supporting factions spilt over to the point where their disapproval of Wendy was quite forgotten. The silent majority grew restless and bored.

When at last the meeting was over, several of the audience did take the trouble to come up to Wendy, thank her for coming and apologise for her treatment – including the man who had stood up to defend her.

'I'd just like to say sorry again. I thought it was a good talk', he added generously. 'But you have got to remember that they're all young, idealistic and frustrated by lack of progress. They'll learn.'

'Well, so am I young and frustrated by the lack of progress', she responded, unimpressed and still uncharacteristically upset. 'That doesn't mean I go around insulting everybody I disagree with – particularly when they're supposed to be on my side'.

She let out all the sense of injustice on her boyfriend, Bill Stockland.

'Stupid bastards!'

'Oh don't be so naive, Wendy. You know the score by now. It's near impossible for a bunch of radical activists to last long without falling out and treating each other as if they're worse than the people they're fighting against. What did you expect?'

'Yes, but not everybody is like that', continued Wendy. 'What about that bloke who backed me up? He was all right. You don't know who he was by any chance?'

'You mean you really don't know? That was Cliff Preston.'

'Was it really? Bloody hell!'

Cliff had become a bit of a legend in the small world of animal protection. He'd been involved since he joined the Hunt Saboteurs in his late teens, in the early 1970s – long before there was any real momentum for campaigning. Later, he had hit the newspaper headlines for stealing three beagle dogs from a laboratory. This event had been greeted with almost universal media praise. Cliff was characterised as a brave Robin Hood type figure, rescuing helpless cuddly animals from callous scientists. A few years down the line he had become one of the first animal activists to serve a prison sentence after rescuing several rabbits from a laboratory and then smashing part of the place up. Since his release he had kept a fairly low profile, despite remaining a bit of a role model for many of the increasing number who were following his example.

'He seemed such an ordinary, nice guy', said Wendy.

'I think he probably is', Bill Stockland replied. 'What did you expect – that he would have horns growing out of the top of his head?'

'No, of course not. It's just that I expected him to be somehow – different, that's all. A bit more exceptional in some way.'

'Whether you agree with him or not, Cliff is just an ordinary bloke who felt strongly about things and had the nerve to do something about it. He's not like some of this lot nowadays, who have latched on to the issue because it's the trendy cause of the moment and a good excuse to play at being subversive.'

'Oh, don't be so cynical Bill. That's just not fair. There can't be many like that.'

'Perhaps not', the world-weary Stockland unconvincingly conceded. 'But those that are sure know how to produce a disproportionate amount of noise!'

Part Two – Corruptible seed

5

He had landed the kind of job he had always hoped for. He saw himself at the cutting edge of a vital campaign for social progress and imagined he was entering an enlightened kingdom. He was aware that his predecessor, Wendy Walters, had become disenchanted by the disagreements and rivalries amongst some local activists, but he still expected to be joining a community full of principled people living by superior moral values. Everybody would be ready to put aside their personal egos and petty differences to unite in their chosen struggle for justice and reform.

SAFE had been formed only six years previously and its progress had been rapid. But recently its impact had started to slow down just a little. In the earlier days, it had believed that constant demonstrations and giving out leaflets was all that was necessary to win the revolution. Only relatively recently had staff come to realise that victory wasn't going to be as straightforward as they had hoped and that campaigning methods would have to become more sophisticated. Negotiation and political compromise could not be ignored. As a result, various attempts were being made – with differing degrees of success – to bring together all the organisations fighting on similar issues under a coalition to present a joint manifesto for political progress. Meetings of the great and the good were held under the chairmanship of respected Liberal peer Lord Fairclough of Oldham and took place in the eighteenth-century splendour of a traditional London gentlemen's club – obsequious servants formally dressed in coat and tails, high ceilings, elegant chandeliers, heavy oak and mahogany furniture, walls adorned with stern portraits of ex-colonials. Tom was sent along to represent SAFE and, in spite of his declared disdain for such pomp and ostentation, experienced a guilty sense of awe at both the setting and the illustrious company he was keeping. In addition to his Lordship, there were many leading figures from the campaigning world to which he felt privileged to have been admitted.

Yet rather than the anticipated oasis of harmony and disinterested co-operation, he soon discovered that he had walked instead into a cauldron of petty jealousies, fragile egos and bitter rivalries. Some participants were far more interested in elevating their own status and glorifying the organisation they represented than in meaningful collaboration. One-upmanship, snide remarks and recrimination over past disputes lurked never far below the surface. It was a professional version of exactly the same problems that Wendy had encountered at grassroots level – though with a great deal more name-dropping. No sooner had one member proudly given the details of a fruitful working breakfast with Jeff Eastwood MP, than he would be trumped by another boasting about a luncheon appointment with well-known actress Rita Miller. Loaded discussions over who had managed to make an appearance on this or that recent television programme were even more commonplace. Had it not been for the skilful intervention of the ageing Lord Fairclough, it could easily have descended at times into an unseemly slanging match. But things were normally kept in order by a combination of overwhelming respect for his Lordship's status and his tactic of responding to any statement he didn't like by pretending not to have heard it.

'What?' Fairclough would bark in the direction of any errant speaker, grimacing and exaggeratedly placing his hand against his ear as he did so. Such venom was instilled into this performance that the recipient usually felt too intimidated to dare a repeat. Mysteriously, his Lordship's hearing problem disappeared completely whenever an opinion he agreed with was put forward. By utilising this selective deafness at regular intervals, he had an uncanny knack of steering everybody in roughly the direction he sought.

In addition to the bickering, meetings were lengthened inordinately by the efforts of old-fashioned socialists demanding a detailed recap on every minute point to avoid the possibility of misinterpretation and others who were decades ahead of their time in their love of management babble, endlessly invoking 'ongoing situations' and other contemporary clichés. It was almost a gift, the way that some people could use so many words to say so little.

It soon became clear that, despite the best endeavours of his Lordship and others who wanted to co-operate and get things done, the egotism and self-importance of the loud minority were going to present a formidable barrier to progress. Whatever the merits or otherwise of the cause they represented, the problem was that it was not, after all, being pursued by a race apart from the rest of humanity. To Tom's disappointment, he swiftly realised that some of his colleagues were subject to the same flaws as everybody else. It was no different from how he imagined lesser mortals such as politicians, businessmen, academics and celebrities. Within the tiny world they inhabited, these were people at the top of the ladder, and however pure their original motivation, some had come to relish their minor authority and to guard it jealously.

After what seemed like months of wrangling, one major decision was eventually taken. It was agreed that a collective national demonstration against animal experiments should be held in London. Tom swelled with pride when he was asked to be part of the organising team.

6

As a seasoned student of social protest, Tom Moore was well aware of Trafalgar Square's status as the UK's headquarters of protest. Actors had the National Theatre, footballers had Wembley Stadium and campaigners had Trafalgar Square, with its proud history of demonstrations dating back more than a century. Courageous souls had defied police bans and government crackdowns in order to assemble there and stand up for what they believed in – particularly in earlier times. First it had been political reformers such as the Chartists and the desperate unemployed who had held centre stage. Later it was suffragettes, hunger marchers and anti-fascists. In modern times, anti-nuclear and anti-war protests had drawn the largest crowds, with tens of thousands of demonstrators venting their opposition to Suez, Vietnam and, very recently, the Falklands. There had been peaceful summer afternoons of comradeship in the sunshine and occasional angry days of riots, confrontation and arrests. Sometimes, of course, it had been the bad guys' turn to voice their indignation – Oswald Mosley and his anti-Semitic British Union of Fascists two years before the Second World War began; an anti-immigration National Front rally soon after Enoch Powell's famous 'Rivers of Blood' speech in 1968, the same year as mass left-wing student protests reached their peak.

There was, of course, no place for Mosley's blackshirts, right-wing extremists and their like in Tom's vision of protest. His consciousness was filled only with noble causes and heroic sacrifices in the name of justice and freedom. He remained unflinchingly romantic about such matters, with the hundreds of thousands of committed citizens who had assembled to make their voices heard over the decades an inspiration to his own agenda. He thought of his grandmother listening to Sylvia Pankhurst's plea for women's rights at a rally that had turned violent and led to many arrests. Only a few years later she had been joined by his grandfather, the couple making the slow journey by car from their home in Hampshire to listen to Keir Hardie's passionate speech on behalf of the emerging Labour movement. Almost half a century later it had been his mother's turn to represent the family at an anti-Suez rally at which Aneurin Bevan had spoken, not long before his death. And then there had been big brother Rob, travelling to London for that anti-Vietnam protest which had eventually descended into chaos outside the US embassy in Grosvenor Square. Now, amazingly, it was to be his own turn and what's more, he was actually going to deliver a speech in the famous Square. As the date of the demonstration drew near, he grew elated and nervous in equal measure. He worried over whether he would manage to give his talk without panicking or forgetting the words. Would he remember the intonation and hand gestures he had been practising?

While there was undoubtedly some degree of self-glorification in these musings, young Tom was under no great illusion about his own standing. Speaking at an anti-vivisection rally – even if it was probably going to be the biggest ever held – was the campaign equivalent to the Amateur Cup rather than the big match itself. At best, he could hope for 10,000 to turn up. It was small fry compared to the anti-nuclear weapons march he had attended relatively recently, where there must have been in excess of 100,000 crammed into London. But then didn't all campaigns have to start somewhere? He was convinced that one day the world would judge his cause with the same sympathy that it had come to look back upon anti-fascists or the opponents of racism. Surely he and his colleagues were also pioneers, ahead of their time? If so, was it not possible that his contribution might earn a mention when history came to be written? Perhaps future students, studying the emergence of animal protection as a significant social development, might come to view the book he was writing as a key text? This prospect of some limited degree of immortality was exciting. With the confidence of youth, it simply did not occur to him that the movement he represented might never capture wider public acceptance or could fade into relative obscurity, just as many others had done before. Such an idea was inconceivable. Human kindness would continue to evolve. In time, the circle of compassion would be extended to protect animals from persecution, just as it had been to black people and women.

A few days before the big day of the demonstration, the office receptionist rang through to his extension number.

'The Reverend Peter Wignall is on the phone for you.'

'Who? Never heard of him.'

'I'm sure he said the Reverend Peter Wignall. He sounded as if he thought you should know him.'

'Better put him through, I suppose.'

The Reverend greeted him in the sort of gentle, slow and melodious tone customarily associated with a man of the cloth.

'Oh hello', he began, slightly hesitatingly. 'I don't know if you remember me. A few weeks ago I sent you a copy of a book of prayers I had written on animal themes. I was just telephoning to see whether you had received it and to check whether you might consider doing a little review in your members' magazine?'

As soon as the Reverend mentioned it, Tom vaguely remembered who he was and knew that he'd seen the booklet somewhere. While Peter Wignall was still speaking, he sorted through the untidy piles of papers and documents that littered his desk, vainly hoping to find it and make some pertinent comment. He was always being sent these little literary efforts that some supporter or other had proudly put together and thought vital to changing the world. Most were cheap, slim little typed volumes with indistinct print and unattractively designed covers.

'Yes, we have received it', Tom reassured the Reverend Wignall as he continued the search, 'and I'm sure we could give it a mention'. He chose the word 'mention' carefully, trying hard to strike a tone that was polite and encouraging, without raising expectations too high.

Clearly he failed.

'And I was also wondering', the Reverend responded, 'whether it would be possible for you to stock copies and sell them to the public through your organisation?'

Tom tried to be tactful.

'I wish we could', he said disingenuously, 'but I'm afraid we can only sell a limited number of books because of lack of space and staff time. We really can't take on any more right now. I'm very sorry.'

Undeterred, Wignall returned with a further proposal.

'I also thought you might like me to speak at your rally on Saturday. I'm sure that many people might be pleased to hear something from a Christian perspective. Perhaps I could read one or two of my prayers?'

This was starting to get a bit troublesome.

'I'm sorry to disappoint you again, but I'm afraid that won't be possible either. We're already having trouble fitting all our speakers in to the timetable and it's impossible to get anybody else in.'

'Well, you can sod off then!' shouted the Reverend Wignall angrily, slamming down the phone.

Once Tom had recovered from the shock, the incident reminded him that, in addition to rejecting unwelcome volunteers, it was also his job to check that there were no problems with the celebrity speakers who had agreed to give talks. Out of a hundred or so invitations, two MPs and one well-known actress had offered to speak. One of the politicians was a popular Labour left-winger and the darling of many a protest movement. The only problem was that his time was precious. His secretary had warned that he could only speak between 4pm and 4.15pm because he had a meeting of the San Salvador Solidarity Group beforehand and was booked to address a conference on the potential environmental impact of acid rain immediately afterwards. The other parliamentarian had a less busy schedule, but created a different kind of difficulty. He was an elderly right-wing Tory who had always spoken out unflinchingly on animal issues. He hated vivisection. The trouble was that he believed that part of the solution was to experiment upon criminals instead.

The third celebrity speaker was well-known actress Rita Miller. By now in her mid forties, she was well respected for her commitment to humanitarian issues. Although no longer quite on the celebrity A-list, she was well enough remembered as the glamorous young star of several popular British 'angry young man' social comment films of the 1960s to be considered a decent catch, quite likely to attract some media attention. Tom was rather pleased with himself for having Rita's home telephone number and for being on first name terms with her. Sometimes he found himself casually dropping her name into conversations and it still had the power to impress. While her theatrical voice and manner left no doubt that she was 'in the business', Rita worked hard to play down her fame, trying desperately to convince Tom that her life was completely unaffected by stardom. On a previous occasion when he had reason to telephone, she had told him he'd caught her cleaning the toilet and asked if he would mind waiting a moment while she removed her rubber gloves. This time the Spanish au pair answered and once again he was asked to wait. Minutes elapsed before the actress reached the phone, dramatically breathless.

'So sorry to keep you waiting, darling. I was just at the bottom of the garden clearing up the dog poo.'

Rita assured Tom that she 'would have to be on her death bed' before she would miss Saturday's event, yet despite the prospect of appearances from both her and the politicians, advance press interest in the demonstration had been disappointing. A few pieces on local radio, a short piece in *The Guardian* and a planned feature on North-West Television's late Friday night discussion programme, *Northern Weekend*, were the highlights. The TV booking demanded a flurry of complicated travel arrangements for Tom, ensuring that he raced up and down the country for a couple of days in a warm glow of self-importance. He would catch the train up to Manchester on Friday, stay overnight after appearing on the programme and then travel down to the march and rally with local supporters on their hired coach.

Other than a train delay, the first part of the schedule went relatively smoothly. After taking a taxi to his hotel, Tom spent the hour or so before he had to leave for the television studio playing around with the free gadgets. He fiddled with the remote control television, soaked luxuriously in the bath and even utilised the trouser press. These limited opportunities for entertainment exhausted, he practised the next day's speech in front of the large bathroom mirror.

This isn't the first time he has appeared on *Northern Weekend* – a depressing, tabloid-formula chat show that goes on air just as the pubs are about to shut and broadcasts through until midnight. During that one-and-a-half hour period three issues are debated, with 'experts' from both sides and contributions from an invited studio audience. Some of the latter are selected specially for their partisan interest in the subject, while a supposedly impartial group make up the numbers, brought in from local clubs and institutes to represent the views of 'the man in the street'. Heated argument is what the programme seeks and animal issues are popular because they usually provoke strong reaction. Tom knows at heart that the whole thing is probably a waste of time, but gaining publicity on television is one of the most tangible ways in which a pressure group measures its success. No invitation can be refused.

It turns out that his thirty-minute section of the programme – entitled *Is it right to experiment on animals?* – is to be the second item on this evening's show. It follows an opening session that raises the question of whether we can transform our lives for the better simply by adopting a more positive attitude. This is to feature as main guest Mary-Jane Nicks, a tall, glamorous, blonde Californian of roughly Tom's age, author of several self-help books and currently touring the UK to promote her latest effort, *Twenty Easy Steps to a Happy Life*. After Tom's part in the night's entertainment, the finale will be given over to discussion on a sexual theme. Sex – the programme's producers are well aware – is the issue most likely to increase the viewing figures, so they are always pleased when they manage to come up with something juicy. This particular evening the production team believe that they have achieved a bit of a coup in securing an appearance from Madame Whipcrack, a hugely well-endowed young woman in her mid twenties. Only a few days earlier she has been the subject of a lurid front-page story in one of the Sunday tabloids, exposing the unusual sexual fantasies of a married government cabinet minister who numbers amongst several celebrity clients at her North London massage parlour. Further revelations are promised for the upcoming weekend.

Before the programme goes on air, the audience is to be entertained by Wally, the resident warm-up artist. His task is to get them in the right mood for the main debate. Tom has seen Wally three or four times before and always found his stand-up comic routine unconvincing. It invariably began by engaging the crowd in a bit of lively banter. 'Hands up everyone from Oldham Rotary Club!' 'Give us a wave if you've come down from Bury Women's Institute!' 'Anyone here from Stockport?' The local flavour continued with a standard routine that consistently centred upon the range and quality of Marks & Spencer underwear and featured some predictable and slightly smutty jokes about its impact upon the sex lives of spouses and mothers-in-law.

The studio reaction to Wally on this particular Friday night can best be described as lukewarm. The evening's guest community – the Rochdale Christian Fellowship – has been chosen in the hope that it might take offence at the unorthodox sexual goings-on at Madame Whipcrack's establishment and be prompted to some fiercely disgusted response. They are not quite the right audience for Wally's underwear humour. Fortunately, it matters little in the great scheme of things, because Mary-Jane Nicks needs no warm-up.

'OK', she begins confidently in response to an invitation to outline just a few of the life-transforming measures she advocates.

'A few simple things. Firstly, each evening before you go to bed, try to recall something that you have achieved that day. Tell yourself that any negative experiences are now a thing of the past and that tomorrow offers great opportunities for a new beginning.

'Secondly, always smile. By smiling you send out a message that accentuates the positive and releases your negative energies.

'And thirdly, make sure that you say something nice to those around you at least once a day. It can be someone close to you, or just a work colleague. Either way, the energies we give out to others are reflected back to our own inner selves and allow us to grow into the new person that we want to become.'

Tom listens for a few minutes before being whisked away to the make-up room. Mary-Jane's supposed expert opponent, Edward Evans, is finding it hard to get in a word edgeways. He's been introduced as a 'commentator and cultural historian' and Tom is unsure what this means. What he does know is that Evans is always turning up on second-rate radio and television shows to express a not very original opinion on whatever subject is required. His main talent is to give an air of intellectualism to a range of clichéd opinions, gesticulating impressively and usually prefacing his remarks with phrases such as 'in a sense' or 'as it were'.

When Mary-Jane eventually lets up for long enough to allow Evans a say, he takes – to the producer's disappointment – a largely conciliatory line. He acknowledges that, in a sense, her ideas have grown out of the Californian hippy tradition of the 1960s and obviously have some merit, in, as it were, encouraging us to consider the possibilities of personal growth. Nonetheless, he is concerned that we are now dealing with a much more difficult world, requiring what we might call much more complex avenues of enquiry.

The Californian is soon back in control, dismissing this criticism rather aggressively as typical of the kind of negativity she is always encountering to her books and 'so destructive in our journey towards self-awareness and fullness of being'. She continues with a shameless self-promotion, interrupted only when the female presenter manages to intervene and ask whether scepticism about her programmes makes her angry. She replies without hesitation.

'OK – good question. The answer is that I don't get angry and neither will anybody else who follows my programme in *Twenty Easy Steps to a Happy Life*. Anger is such a negative emotion. When we are angry, it impacts upon our creativity. What we have to do is defend ourselves from those harmful emotions. One exercise I recommend in my book is what I call "finding moments to sing and be free". All you need to do is find a favourite location and literally sing your favourite song as loudly as you can. I've had great results with this technique.'

By now watching on a screen from the studio reception room, Tom can't see any reason why you should want to stop being angry with much that went on in the world. Mrs Thatcher for a start. Besides, Mary-Jane has already annoyed him in a brief introduction before the transmission. 'I have some sympathy with your goals,' she had told him after finding out the subject of his portion of the show. 'But I think the really important thing is for us to learn how to listen to our own inner voice.'

He feels himself becoming increasingly impatient with all this navel gazing.

The TV discussion ends with Mary-Jane inevitably grabbing the final word. A member of Rochdale Christian Fellowship censures her for promulgating 'an unchristian agenda that ignored the fact that our Lord Jesus Christ offers the only true path to happiness and salvation'. The irrepressible author disagrees.

'OK, so what are we actually saying here? Jesus told us that we should always turn the other cheek, right? So my "finding a place to sing and be free" exercise actually helps us to live a Christian lifestyle by controlling our anger. In fact, I like to believe that if Jesus were alive today, he'd most likely make use of my techniques to help spread his message of love and peace. I'm proud to tell you guys that I fail to see any conflict between what I'm trying to say in *Twenty Easy Steps to a Happy Life* and any conventional religious teaching.'

Time is up and the presenter hastily brings things to a close, thanking her guests for offering plenty to think about. The floor manager gives the audience a pre-arranged signal to applaud loudly, the adverts begin, and Mary-Jane Nicks and Edward Evans are ushered speedily out of the studio, to be replaced by the next set of experts.

The discussion on animal experiments is to be presented by Gary Lucas, a smooth-talking and well-manicured man in his late thirties, who generally enjoys a reputation as a bit of a heartthrob. Certainly, he himself has no doubts about his attractiveness to the opposite sex. He treats his celebrity status with the utmost seriousness, keeping a pile of signed photographs to hand out – whether solicited or not – to any female studio guests who take his eye. Lucas also enjoys a well-earned reputation for media professionalism, always carrying out his research thoroughly and possessing a rare ability to display a wide range of emotions. Concern, sympathy, disdain, righteous indignation, anger and cynicism – all come easily to him, as does the talent to switch from one to another with seamless ease.

The debate itself is to centre on three main speakers. Professor Brian Dalton, a leading animal researcher, is pitted against Tom, with Dave Howard from the Animal Liberation Army (ALA) also given a prominent role. Tom hasn't been told beforehand that Dave is to be his sidekick and his heart sinks at the news. Howard has recently completed a degree in philosophy at the University of East Anglia and has become increasingly popular with the media over the past couple of years because he can be guaranteed to offer extreme views. Moreover, he's prone to speak with a rather unattractive scowl upon his bespectacled features. On the positive side though, his beard is now considerably fuller than in earlier days.

The discussion opens with the usual salvoes. Professor Dalton – an old adversary of Tom's – argues that scientists would much prefer not to use animals, but, regrettably, it is necessary if we are to find cures for cancer, heart disease, Alzheimer's and Parkinson's. It is his customary 'necessary evil' line. Tom responds- rather impressively he thinks – with a well-rehearsed statement of intent.

'Vivisection can never be justified. It is the extraction of information by violent means from prisoners held against their will. If it was carried out on people it would be defined as torture.

'What is more', he adds hurriedly, 'there are also important differences between other animals and humans that make it impossible to treat the results of tests on dogs and mice with any degree of confidence. Where are these cures that Professor Dalton promises? Forever just around the corner?'

With a rather self-satisfied expression, he then leans back in his chair, picks up his glass of water and sips smugly, prompting – as hoped – a smattering of applause from those of his persuasion in the studio audience. A rather good start, he thinks.

He is expecting Gary Lucas to go back to Professor Dalton for answers to the points he has raised and then plans to get personal and focus upon Dalton's own experiments. Instead, however, the presenter switches straightaway from 'let's get to the facts' investigator mode to his most sympathetic and caring tone.

'Professor Dalton', he begins. 'Now you've been targeted by extremists because of your use of animals, haven't you? Would you like to tell us about some of the terrible things that you and your family have had to contend with?'

Dalton gravely lists the incidents he has endured – poison pen letters, hoax calls and death threats to himself and his family. Tom has heard it too many times before to feel much sympathy. He wants the Professor to defend the research that has earned his notoriety – experiments in the field of pain that involve inflicting varying degrees of trauma on dogs and rabbits and are always defended as somehow vital to future treatment of cancer and arthritis sufferers. Dalton's main ploy, however, is to play the role of helpless victim – the man whose quest to help humanity has led to persecution of him and his family.

When the Professor has finished, Gary Lucas doesn't return to Tom again, but marches determinedly to confront the bloke from the ALA. This time he adopts the tone of a man who represents the moral indignation of the nation.

'Dave Howard of the Animal Liberation Army, you've heard what Professor Dalton and his family have had to deal with – incendiary devices and death threats that even involved an innocent young child. What have you got to say about these acts?'

'Live by the sword, you've got to expect to die by the sword', responds Howard unequivocally.

Jeers from a section of the audience; outraged indignation from the presenter. 'Oh shit!' thinks Tom.

'Now hang on a minute', exclaims Lucas, holding his hand up to quieten the noisy element. 'Let me get this absolutely clear. You're saying before a live television audience that Professor Dalton and those like him, who carry out what they say is vital medical research to find cures for cancer and other killer diseases – you're saying that they deserve to be subjected to intimidation, violence and worse?'

'That's exactly what I'm saying', confirms Dave Howard, shouting above a rising crescendo of hostility that half drowns out the rest of his reply. 'What the likes of Professor Dalton endure is nothing compared to the pain and misery they inflict upon defenceless animals.'

Uproar from those hostile to Howard, particularly from one large man in his fifties with receding, greyish hair, who stands up and starts to yell abuse, both at the ALA man and at a section of the crowd in the studio who have already identified themselves as supporters of the anti-vivisection viewpoint. Things are starting to get out of hand. Even the super-professional Gary Lucas is struggling to keep control.

'Please calm down, sir. I promise you'll have a chance to have your say later.'

This measure proves ineffective. The troublemaker continues to shout and bawl, though Tom can't make out exactly what he is saying amid the rising din. So great is the hostility between the various factions that even a mega-dose of the formidable Mary-Jane Nicks' anger management would have been hard pressed to cool tempers. Dave Howard manages to make himself heard again.

'What you've got to remember is that if non-human animals could stand up for their own rights they would be at war with their abusers. Whatever action we liberationists take is merely self-defence on behalf of those who can't fight for themselves.'

This is the final straw for Mr Angry in the audience. He is beside himself now, red-faced and shouting even louder.

Gary Lucas issues a final warning:

'Sir, I promise I'll come back to you later, but if you don't keep quiet now, I'm afraid I'll have to ask you to leave the studio.'

This seems to inflame 'sir' even further. He rises from his seat and rushes towards the ALA man. Dave Howard stands up to meet his challenger, applauding him mockingly.

'On your bike', he shouts contemptuously, pointing towards the exit.

Within seconds, Howard is sent flying over the back of his chair and onto the floor. His adversary leaps on top of him and, as the wrestling match gets into full swing, the camera crew rushes on to break up the fight. An extended commercial break is hastily convened. It's pandemonium out there. All the main participants are ushered out of the studio and a swift decision is taken to abandon the item and bring forward the Madame Whipcrack feature.

It subsequently turned out that the intruder actually had nothing to do with animal experiments. He was a fur trader whose shop windows had been broken several times and slogans painted on his walls and windows. Fur had lost its public appeal to the extent that sympathy for those like him was limited, even when their premises were vandalised. His business had closed down, leading to financial problems. He was angry with the Animal Liberation Army and had been invited onto the programme to attack their methods, though it was assumed that his role would be performed with words rather than fists. As for Dave Howard, he suffered nothing worse than a cut lip and a few bruises.

Far from proving a disaster for *Northern Weekend*, this chaotic scene proved to be its defining moment. The next day the scrap even made it onto the national news.

'And finally', the smiling presenter had begun – indicating clearly that this was the moment to lighten up from the daily dose of hard current affairs – 'it wasn't only fur that was flying during a television debate on animal rights last night.'

Viewing figures soared over the next few weeks. Tom even received letters from acquaintances on the other side of the world who had seen the clip on their news programmes. It turned out to be his most enduring moment of television stardom, catching his expression of open-mouthed bewilderment as Dave Howard was sent tumbling backwards towards the curtain at the back of the studio.

From this moment, there was no stopping the programme's researchers. Every few weeks they invited Tom to take part in some debate or another – bullfighting, puppy farming, hunting or circuses – even though he often knew very little about the subjects he was required to discuss. He clung doggedly to the view that they were after his skilful debating skills and camera-friendly features, when the true motive was the hope that he might contribute towards another punch-up. From a 'good television' perspective, his cause had gained the dubious honour of being the next best thing to sex.

Back in his hotel room later in the evening, Tom found it impossible to sleep. Being a guest of the television company might help to inflate his ego, but faceless hotels can feel lonely and sterile as the dark hours pass by. His mind was racing. He kept playing back the evening's chaotic entertainment – partly amused by it all and mostly frustrated by the brevity of his contribution and the damage he believed that Dave Howard had done to his cause and beliefs. He was also increasingly preoccupied with the next day's demonstration. How many people would be there? Would the television crews turn up? He rehearsed his speech again, several times. Finally, his thoughts turned to Madame Whipcrack, who he knew was staying in the room next door. Whips, straps and sticks – how strange to imagine those instruments of pain transformed into objects of sexual pleasure! He began to fantasise a little. All that leather and the like wasn't really his scene of course. Nevertheless, he couldn't help wondering what would happen if the notorious dominatrix were suddenly overcome by the voracious sexual appetite attributed to her by the Sunday newspaper revelations. What would he do if an uncontrollable urge led her to open the door and attempt to ravish him? How would he react? With such unlikely thoughts, the campaigner eventually drifted off to sleep.

The next day's journey got off to an eventful start. Len, the appointed coach driver on the demonstration special from Manchester to London, belonged strictly to the awkward and bad-tempered school of officials. He was a short, elderly man, whose pale and unhealthy appearance suggested that he should have retired several years ago – one of those part-time workers that bus companies drag in at the weekend when short-staffed. He soon made it clear that he'd rather not be there. The last thing on earth he wanted was to spend his day driving what he considered a load of unemployed wasters to some mass gathering of the loony left. His opinions were formed predominantly from tabloid newspapers and therefore he believed that all such protesters were likely to be fanatics and extremists. Money was scarce, however, and the opportunity for a decent day's pay on double time was too good to miss.

Not that the initial delay for their departure could be laid at the driver's door. Three or four people were late arriving, notably a young woman named Yvette and her boyfriend. As the minutes ticked by after the scheduled leaving time, Len became more and more agitated, prowling around the side of the coach, looking pointedly at his watch and complaining to the organisers.

Eventually Yvette and her friend arrived and completed the party. She had been held up, she yelled from the front of the coach, by a severe bladder infection that had forced her twice to seek out public conveniences.

The twenty-odd minute postponement might not have been too troublesome if Len hadn't then compounded the problem by setting off in the wrong direction. Even though his slightly erratic handling of the vehicle had immediately betrayed a degree of rustiness, the passengers assumed that he had at least taken a trip out of Manchester some time over the many years since the opening of the motorway network. Unfortunately, this presumption was thrown into grave doubt when they found themselves headed east in the direction of Leeds rather than south towards the Midlands. By the time the error had been pointed out, a suitable turning point found and the correct road located, the schedule was starting to look a little tight.

The crisis then deepened considerably when Len ruled that the coach toilet was out of order, thereby forcing Yvette to plead for a couple of unscheduled service station stops to relieve her problem. After some resistance, the morose driver reluctantly gave way, insisting that he would not accept any responsibility if they arrived late at their destination.

'Why do these coach journeys to demonstrations always seem fraught with difficulties?' Tom pondered as the coach sped down the motorway. He'd been on a few in his time and there often seemed to be something going wrong – vehicle breakdowns, campaigners lost, arrested or left behind after coffee breaks. The passengers, too, seemed typically idiosyncratic. While the majority chatted away jovially (on this occasion there was a good deal of heated debate about events on the previous evening's *Northern Weekend,* plus the inevitable comparison of vegetarian lunchbox contents), the back seat was, as usual, occupied by a group of scruffy youngsters who mostly kept to themselves. A young woman called Toyah was the most striking in appearance, her inch-thick mascara and black lipstick contrasting sharply with bright green hair lacquered into the shape of a cockerel's comb. Equally original was the juxtaposition of red training shoe on left foot and black, lace-free plimsoll on right. Her four colleagues sported similarly unorthodox combinations of brightly dyed hair and unusual adornments, ranging from safety pins through the ear to eyebrow studs and campaign badge-covered jackets.

And there was Yvette, of course. She was another zealous convert to the cause who believed that, since vegetarianism was responsible for everything that was good in her own life, it must therefore also provide all the answers to everybody else's problems. One minute a meat-free diet was the complete answer to world hunger, the next it was the source of unrivalled pleasures in her bedroom.

'Me and Tony are vegans and we do it five times a night', she proudly informed as many of her fellow coach passengers as would listen. She was clearly of the opinion that no carnivorous couple could possibly be capable of such a feat. Tony – sat beside her – wasn't sure whether to look embarrassed or triumphant.

The consequence of a whole series of mini-crises was that they were a little late arriving at the assembly point in Hyde Park. They had to hurry off the coach and tag along at the back of the procession as it began to wind its way slowly out towards Pall Mall. This was the bit that Tom enjoyed most, for he could now relax for the first time in the knowledge that the demonstration was well attended. Ignoring the indefatigable attempts of megaphone man Ho Ho to stir the masses into chanting mood, he marched along with a contented swagger, stopping now and then for a quick word with a few of the supporters he recognised.

By the time they reached Trafalgar Square he was feeling high on a heady excitement that protected him from his nerves. But as soon as he began to move slowly through the assembled crowd towards the speakers' plinth beneath Nelson's Column, apprehension belatedly crept in. He checked several times whether the notes for his talk were still tucked safely into his back pocket. Good, they were. His anxiety was eased again. He pushed on and reached one of the ornamental fountains, around which he spotted the odd-shoed Toyah and her friends, sat at the water's edge and swinging their legs against the concrete walls. The area had evidently become rebel's corner, occupied by a row of equally rough-and-ready youngsters, some of whom were swigging lazily from lager cans. Tom was close enough to hear one youth turn to another:

'What's happening next?' he asked.

'Not really sure. I expect that wanker Tom Moore is going to speak though.'

Tom halted in his tracks, ego instantly bruised to the point where – rather than taking a sensible moment to reflect and ignore – he unwisely turned to demand an explanation.

'Why is he a wanker?' he enquired, trying to sound calm and disinterested.

The two teenagers looked up at him.

'Why? Are you him?' asked the individual who had identified his masturbatory tendencies.

Tom had no choice but to acknowledge that he was indeed the aforementioned Sherman Tanker – a confession that failed to induce even the slightest trace of remorse or apology. His accuser's only response was to take another swig of alcohol, while his friend simply nodded repeatedly. As far as they were concerned, his intervention had confirmed beyond doubt the accuracy of their original diagnosis.

While this damning indictment was a temporary blight upon Tom Moore's big day, its impact was relatively minor. Standing on the plinth next to one of the sculptured lions at the side of Nelson's Column was too momentous an experience for him to feel any more than a slight pang. There were MPs to greet, an actress to embrace, fellow campaigners to acknowledge and notes for his short speech to sift through one last time. Tom looked down with pride as the cheering thousands responded excitedly to a forceful rallying speech from the ubiquitous Labour MP. Such a large gathering and display of fellow feeling thrilled him. All these people who shared his hopes and beliefs! It was almost overwhelming. He was far too full of the justice of his cause to reflect on darker instincts that can always be unleashed by mass chants, adulatory cheers and whipping up of emotions with slogans and clichés. It didn't occur to him that almost any mass gathering of partisan human beings stands on the verge of bigotry, regardless of how fine the motives might be for their shared conviction. The dividing line between passionate solidarity and hate-filled prejudice is inevitably wafer thin.

On this, as in the majority of occasions, however, that line was not crossed and the mood remained peaceful and upbeat. His own talk went well enough, though rousing demonstration speeches were not really his strength and he forgot one or two of the hand gestures he had fastidiously practised. Compared to Rita Miller's dramatic and emotional outpouring, it seemed a bit amateurish. The audience, in generous mood, applauded encouragingly as he marched off, yet he failed to rouse them as much as others.

When all the speeches had been delivered and the fond farewells to Rita and the rest of his colleagues concluded, Tom's spirits began to flag a little. He felt tired, and despite some relief that it was all over, a gnawing sense of discontent that, after so much time and effort, his big project was now at an end. Rather than rush off home, he decided to drift back into the dispersing crowd and drag the last dregs out of the day. If the truth were told, his main motive was to seek compliments on the smooth organisation and reassurance on the quality of his performance. He carefully avoided the area where some of the punky gang were still congregated by the edge of the fountain, feeding the pigeons who had returned to occupy the area vacated by the demonstrators.

7

As the years passed and Tom became better known as a spokesman for his movement, he had come to depend increasingly upon others' approval. At first this had all come as a bit of a surprise to him. He travelled across the country giving talks at public meetings and, as the issue still attracted widespread interest, many of them were remarkably well attended. Once the beginner's nerves had calmed, however, he came to consider himself rather a powerful orator and to feed on the spotlight. Imagining himself a bit of an intellectual force, he also wanted to show off his culture and learning, offering his audience something a little more sophisticated than the run-of-the-mill exposé of harrowing cruelty they might have been expecting. Literary and philosophical references were scattered among his speeches to impress. Since the D.H. Lawrence phase was still going strong, he searched painstakingly through novels and essays in search of any quotation that might be relevant to his subject. At last he found something:

'And as the white cock calls in the doorway, who calls? Merely a barnyard rooster worth a dollar-and-a-half? But listen! Under the old dawns of creation, the Holy Ghost, the Mediator, shouts aloud in the twilight. And every time I hear him, a fountain of vitality gushes up in my body. It is life.'

Tom was too engrossed in his sense of mission and importance to notice the minority who sniggered and considered him a pretentious fool, choosing instead to focus upon the more generous members of his audience who praised his lofty utterances and nourished his blossoming ego. Although he was not as good a speaker as he imagined, the applause was normally enthusiastic enough to reinforce his sense of importance. It soon became clear that, just as he desired to be recognised as a bit of a celebrity, there were those out there among the SAFE followers who were only too happy to transform him into one – albeit of a very minor variety. Royal, rich, famous or powerful he was not, but even a medium-sized fish in a miniscule pond could enjoy a moment of comparative fame, standing out proudly from the crowd. While it was far from film or pop star stuff, the same basic human instincts were at work as if he had been singing to an adoring crowd on *Top of the Pops*. Lift your head above the parapet and some will be impressed – that seemed to be the way of the world. He and his listeners complemented each other's needs perfectly.

What came as even more of a pleasant surprise was the discovery that his small impact upon the campaigning world also had a mildly seductive element. This should not be exaggerated. When the detested (and frankly deeply unattractive) US Secretary of State Henry Kissinger had declared that 'power is an aphrodisiac', he must certainly have based his assertion on a more substantial female following than Tom Moore was enjoying. Nonetheless, there were one or two advances that even this fairly innocent and inexperienced young soul couldn't fail to notice – the inviting touch on the arm, the oh-so-welcoming offer of a place to stay should he ever be speaking in the Manchester or Newcastle regions again. As much as he welcomed this attention, the possibility of such liaisons held little temptation. He was almost priggish in his disapproval. When a fellow campaigner boastfully declared 'I've had more nookie since I've been in this protest lark than ever before in my life', he felt only disgust. Tom wanted attention for his fine intellect and brilliant campaigning skills. He wished to be recognised as a moral crusader on a powerful mission to achieve vital social progress. Anybody could be a philanderer and he didn't want to be just anybody. When his thirties kicked in, however, he was no longer quite so sure. He started to perceive middle age around the corner. The prospect of dwindling sexual potency raised its scary head and he started to look back with regret upon one or two of those missed opportunities. Sometimes he even wondered whether the time he turned down the possibility of a night of passion with that attractive redhead with the long pre-Raphaelite curls was not a bigger source of disappointment than his failure to create a world of universal peace and harmony.

While female interest was especially flattering, Tom also grew far from indifferent to the attention of a handful of male admirers who also latched onto him as a source of enlightenment. Andy Knowles was a particular fan – a tall, blonde, fresh-faced and eager young man who worked as a builder and whose life was changed after he was reluctantly taken to a public meeting by his girlfriend. Much to his surprise, he found Tom's presentation compelling. At the end of the talk, Andy went to congratulate the speaker and asked him to suggest further reading. Tom, enjoying the role of mentor, was happy to oblige. Just as his father had been a kind of guru to some of his students, he rather fancied himself in a similar role. He and Andy corresponded regularly. His pupil read avidly, became a vegetarian and soon afterwards a vegan. Before too long he was devoting all his spare time to campaigning for animals and frequently seemed to be in the audience when Tom was speaking.

'I've been thinking about what you said about trying to reach out to people rather than expecting them to come to us', Andy began after approaching Tom on one such occasion. 'I think you're so right about that and I've had this really good idea. I've organised a quiz night at a pub in town. It's a really popular venue and they allow different charities to hold an event every month to raise money. Loads of people go. It'll be a great way of educating ordinary people as well as raising funds. I was wondering whether you might come along as guest and present the prizes?' Travelling fifty miles to make a special appearance at a pub quiz night was not a role that particularly appealed to Tom, but he was flattered by his position as Andy's inspiration and didn't want to dampen his pupil's enthusiasm. Consequently, one frosty Sunday night a couple of weeks before Christmas he found himself listening to an embarrassingly lengthy and complimentary introduction in the smoky *Three Horseshoes*, in front of an audience of local quiz enthusiasts who didn't know him from Adam and didn't really care who he was. All they wanted was to get on with the questions and take home the prizes.

Andy at last finished heaping praise on his star guest and was ready to begin.

'The first round is on general knowledge', he declared, 'and the first question is -

'Worldwide – to the nearest figure – how many animals are killed for meat every year? Is it:

a) 20 billion b) 30 billion or c) 40 billion.'

A collective look of puzzlement filled the room. 'I'm bound to be winning', thought Tom, who, apart from Andy's animal rights mates, was probably the only person who knew that the answer was 40 billion.

'Question two,' continued the quizmaster after allowing suitable pondering time, 'what is the LD50 test? Is it:

a) Slang for a half-marathon – 50% of the longer distance.
b) The estimated accuracy for lie detector tests.
c) An animal experiment in which 50% of the creatures experimented upon are poisoned to death with a lethal dose of the test substance.'

This was about as subtle as it got. Andy's idea of general knowledge didn't venture much beyond the number of turkeys killed for Christmas or the methods employed to slaughter Arctic foxes for fur. All might have been well had animal torture been an area of expertise among the quiz participants at *The Three Horseshoes*, but unfortunately they were more geared up to answer questions on the length of African rivers, the names and order of Henry the Eighth's wives and the history of the Eurovision Song Contest. By the end of the round there were loud murmurings of discontent and Tom was beginning to worry that the natives might turn nasty. He was relieved when Andy announced that the next session was to be on sport.

'Thank goodness for that', he thought. 'Not much room for propaganda there.'

How wrong he could be! Andy's grasp of sporting matters had little to do with football grounds or cricket scores.

'Question one. How many horses were fatally injured at this year's Grand National meeting?'

Tom groaned inwardly. People were starting to get angry.

'Question two. The season for which so-called sport begins on August 12?'

Admittedly the quizmaster did manage to throw in a couple of questions about football and rugby, but Tom reckoned that was only because he ran out of bloodsports to ask about. The evening descended into chaos. People walked out in their droves, moaning about 'bloody fanatics'. Some demanded the return of their entrance fee. Round three on celebrities was the final straw. Question one – how many of the Beatles were vegetarian?

Question two – which member of *The Goons* was a strong supporter of the campaign against hunting? And so it went on.

At the post-mortem, Andy was unrepentant. The fault lay wholly with the audience and their uncaring ignorance. Even if they found the questions difficult, they should have been delighted by the educational opportunity to learn about slaughterhouses and laboratories in such an entertaining format.

'I just thought it was a perfect chance to teach people about the suffering that goes on out there every day', he declared defiantly.

'It's clear that people don't know about it and what really annoys me is that it looks as if most of them aren't interested in finding out. Somehow or other we've got to make them listen.'

Tom said nothing.

Events such as the quiz evening apart, Tom enjoyed socialising with his organisation's supporters. By nature he was a little awkward and self-conscious, so he revelled in situations where his status ensured that he did not have to promote himself. It gave him confidence. People knew who he was and what he did. And they respected it. As he travelled around, one of the members would invariably put him up for the night and, though they came from vastly different backgrounds, they were almost always generous in their hospitality. Some became firm friends. In particular, there was a big friendly giant of a humanitarian called James Quick, who had been involved in animal protection throughout his life and seemed to be around at every major demonstration, whether it was for human rights, the environment or animals. His lofty frame ensured that he always stood out from the crowd. Tom had first met him giving out leaflets to homeward-bound commuters on the concourse of Waterloo station. Most people had been sympathetic, but one smartly dressed young man insulted the protesters as he raced past.

'Why don't you get a job, you wasters?' he sneered.

James followed him, his legs so long and strides so full that he quickly caught up.

'Come here, chum', he commanded in his deep booming voice, beckoning his critic with his forefinger as he spoke. The commuter immediately stopped in his tracks and peered up anxiously, like a frightened animal cornered in headlights.

'Thirty-two years in the City, ten years in the RAF before that, including active service in the war. So don't start telling me to get a job, Sonny Jim. I think you'd better think twice before you speak next time.'

The young man looked up, nodded sheepishly and then slunk away. Only when he was well clear did he break into a brisk, relieved trot.

Then there were Simon and Diane Potter, a middle-aged couple who worked tirelessly to treat and rehabilitate wild animals and birds – most of whom arrived at their door as victims of human viciousness or ignorance. Diane was one of those women who had a gift for anything maternal, never happier than when she had a young creature to nourish and nurture. With her five children grown up and no longer needing her constant attention, these healing skills and protective instincts were focused increasingly upon birds, badgers and hedgehogs. Whatever the species, she had an uncanny ability to nurse back to health wild animals who seemed to have no possibility of survival. Soon the Potters had built a reputation across the local region. If a suffering animal was discovered and the finder cared enough to do something about it, the victim was likely to end up in their sanctuary. The work was exhausting and unrelenting. Often, despite their best endeavours, they had to cope with failure and death. Yet despite the disappointments and exhaustion, their dedication to these bruised and battered creatures never waned. A fox or hedgehog successfully treated and re-introduced to the wild made all the effort and heartache worthwhile. Watching a bird they had miraculously restored to health never failed to revive sinking spirits. What a joy it was to watch a recovered swift soar high into the sky out of Diane's hands, pausing to find its bearings before decisively heading off on the long journey south!

Yet it was inevitable that, as well as the Quicks and the Potters of this world, Tom also came across one or two strange set-ups on his travels where a desire to stand outside the status quo seemed to be on display rather too overtly for his taste. Human nature being the way it is, these bizarrer encounters tended to make a more lasting impression than the ordinary and uneventful. How, for instance, could he ever forget his visit to the Green Alternatives Festival in West Wales, where he stayed in an anarchistic, hippy household containing a posse of wild youngsters offering their republican alternative to the traditional game of cowboys and Indians? 'Fuck the bourgeoisie!' yelled one young cherub as he chased his sister cheerily across the battered sofa. 'Down with the monarchy!' cried his older brother, filled with similar revolutionary zeal.

Also, of course, there were the devoted animal lovers. Tom was fond of cats and dogs himself, but he sometimes found smelly households packed with rescued animals a bit much. This was particularly true when the family included some large dog, rescued from a life of abuse and understandably a little bit neurotic about strangers on the territory. Tom spent several sleepless nights holding onto a painfully full bladder, too afraid to cross to the bathroom in case the aforementioned Rover was keeping guard on the landing. Neither did he particularly enjoy those evenings when he was kept up into the early hours trawling through endless photo albums of Flopsy, Mopsy and a succession of other family pets.

'Do you know who the previous owner was?' Tom asked politely after listening to one heart-warming story of a rabbit who had been delivered from a lonely past life in a barren hutch.

'We don't use the word "owners",' came the sharp reply. 'It's people thinking that animals are ours to own that causes a lot of the problems. We prefer to think of ourselves as their self-appointed guardians.'

It wasn't until he next made one of his three or four visits a year to his brother that he came to view such dedication with a greater degree of sympathy. Rob had little time left for protest these days, maintaining some degree of political credibility only by boycotting South African apples, paying his annual subscription to several worthy causes and always finding time to read *The Guardian* on Saturdays. His career in the publishing world had continued to flourish and he was already managing director of a medium-sized company specialising in children's fiction. He worked long hours and earned good money. In the limited hours when he wasn't at work he tried hard to play the happy family man, indulging his two daughters, Natalie, then aged about five, and Lottie, who was three. A third child was on the way. Wife Mary, a history graduate who had also gone into publishing, had given up her career and thrown herself wholeheartedly into motherhood. Anyway, on the hot July Saturday in question, they all decided to get out of London and head for the beach at Brighton. It seemed like a good idea at the time. Tom started out convinced of his great affection for his nieces and full of enthusiasm for the trip. By the time they reached the coast, however, he had already had enough of the noise, demands and bickering. And that's how it continued for much of the day. Mary had a newfangled video camera and was anxious to capture every detail of the trip for posterity. Lottie was filmed messily eating an ice cream, while Natalie pulled attention-seeking faces in the background. Later there was a game in which the two girls were attempting unsuccessfully to throw a beach ball to one another, blighted by Lottie's inability to catch, throw in any pre-determined direction or understand the complicated rules of the game imposed by her older sister.

'I can hardly wait for this evening', thought Tom cynically, knowing full well that it was likely to feature a playback of the day's filming and detailed footage of the recent family holiday in Mauritius. The sooner he could get back to his world of campaigning the better! And it was only at this point that he began to compare his brother's life of apparent domestic bliss with some of those animal-friendly hosts and their devotion to cats and rabbits. Was there really that much difference? Perhaps it was true that love for our human families usually ran far deeper than any emotional kinship we could share with dogs, cats or rabbits. Surely the same level of intimacy was impossible when, for a start, you didn't even share a common language? There was something natural about caring for your own offspring or even your own species above every other, and maybe individual animals were replaceable in a way that the people who are close to us were not. But not everyone felt the same. What if you didn't share a desire for human children or were unable to conceive them? What if experience of your own kind left you sad and disillusioned? If so, was it necessarily so crazy to bestow your protective instincts upon suffering animals instead? The world might consider it a limited fulfilment, but what harm was it doing to bring some comfort to the lives of the neglected four-footed – other, that is, than keeping him up half the night pretending to share their unstinting affection for Gus the guinea pig or Hoppy the three-legged cat?

8

On a couple of occasions Tom found himself sharing a platform with Elizabeth Plant, Director of the Society for the Promotion of a Vegan Diet. In appearance, there was nothing exceptional about this homely looking woman, well into her sixties. She was soberly dressed in a plain cotton cardigan over a rather old-fashioned floral patterned dress. She wore no make-up to disguise the passing years and her comfortable mop of greying hair was unfussily styled. Her talks were infuriating. She ignored time limits, appeared to have no notes and rambled wherever her thoughts took her. By accepted public speaking standards, she talked far too fast. There were no punch lines. In comparison with his own efforts, there seemed to be no sense of performance. Yet there was something compelling about her. Partly it was the apparent absence of ego, but also there was something visionary in the content that grabbed his attention. She spoke reverentially about her pioneering predecessors, who had adopted a diet free from animal products at a time when medical orthodoxy had assumed it would lead to certain ill-health and probable early death. She talked about her own conversion, inspired by an incident in which she had watched a new-born male calf suckling from his mother and had realised for the first time that she had been drinking the milk that nature had intended for the cow's young. She spoke about her passion for the struggle against world hunger and the pivotal role that trees could play in feeding the world and protecting the land from floods and drought. She stressed the need to lead by practical example, describing her own efforts to grow as much food as possible on a council allotment. She urged her audience to purchase everything they could from local sources. What impressed Tom above all, however, was Elizabeth Plant's assertion that her main reason for embracing an animal-free diet was a belief that ego-free compassion was the most valuable and important impulse for any human endeavour.

The more Tom considered her ideas, the more he felt inspired. He, too, would aspire to a life of ego-free compassion. That would be his religion. He couldn't see any problem as far as the ego bit was concerned and becoming a vegan would be an easy step on his road to spiritual perfection.

Actually, it didn't prove quite as simple as he had imagined, despite the fact that the choice of foods available by the mid 1980s would have seemed luxurious to those hardy pioneers from Elizabeth's days and beyond. They had lived through post-war rationing, where now commonplace products such as nuts and fruit were not freely available. Even tinned fruit had been a rarity. The options available to Tom were comparatively varied, yet still he didn't find the range particularly inviting. He wasn't much of a cookery enthusiast and most of the recipes he discovered came via the journals of the rather puritan Society for the Promotion of a Vegan Diet rather than the more exciting vegetarian cookery books that were beginning to emerge. They mostly seemed to involve soaking soya beans for about three and a half days and then cooking them for a further four hours until they eventually softened. He considered life too short! So instead, he came to rely mostly upon a few convenience foods, produced by a couple of small specialist companies – the largest of which rejoiced in the name of Tofu Towers. It was hardly the sort of fare likely to convince the unconverted. Ostensibly there was a range of eight or nine products to choose from: the only problem was that they all tasted much the same as the company's most popular tinned item, the uninspiring *Soya Spam*. It was about as appetising as it sounded. Then there were a handful of dry mix foods made with the attractively named TVP – textured soya protein. These consisted of a combination of flavoured soya and pellets of hydrogenated fat, a thick layer of which stuck to the pan after water had been added and the final product fried. Compared to the gristle, sinew and rind finding their way into meat sausages, *VeggySos* may perhaps have warranted its label as a healthy alternative to animal products, but it was certainly nothing to write home about. Oh well, not to worry! Tom could live with it. After all, where was the virtue without self-sacrifice? Limited choice and absence of flavour only added to a sense of moral worth.

Accepting his role as an ambassador for his new diet, he decided to make more of a culinary effort when he had visitors. Alas, he was no creative genius and his endeavours did little to enhance the reputation of dairy-free foods. When Penny Painter, his old colleague from the university Amnesty group came for dinner with Glen, her new Australian boyfriend, he slaved away for hours preparing the obligatory soya beans and trying to convert them into an interesting casserole.

'Food all right, folks?' he asked after they had taken a few mouthfuls. He already suspected from the silence that it wasn't.

'Fine thanks, Tom,' answered Penny.

'Yes thanks, lovely', added Glen, prompted by a kick under the table from his girlfriend. 'A bit tasteless, though.'

'Tasteless!' an offended Tom exclaimed.

'No, no, sorry mate, not tasteless', responded the blunt Aussie. 'That's not what I meant at all. It's more sort of ... flavourless.'

Despite struggling to eat as much as they could, a fair amount lay untouched when Tom collected the plates. The dessert – a plain fruit salad – fared less controversially and any awkwardness over the failure of the main dish was temporarily dissipated. Then he served coffee. A warning on the soya milk tin advised that the liquid might curdle in hot drinks and that is precisely what it did – though 'curdling' hardly did justice to the mess that Tom embarrassingly handed over to his guests. It resembled frogspawn.

'Crikey. I don't know how you drink that stuff, mate,' said Glen, grimacing. 'Tastes worse than a wrestler's jockstrap.'

9

Andy Knowles couldn't really understand why Tom Moore should want to come and see him. What was the point? Moore was a paid employee of one of those despised status quo organisations that had condemned truly committed activists like him, so why waste one of his precious prison visits? Nevertheless, he had agreed to the meeting. After all, it was less than two years ago that he had admired and quite liked Tom, inviting him to come and give the prizes on that ill-fated quiz night. So although he had now rejected all those fine words and peaceful demonstrations in favour of hard-edged, illegal campaigning, something about the request had pleased and intrigued him.

Tom was also a bit puzzled by it all. What had motivated him to write to the prisoner? Was he desperate to be liked and to court favour with Andy and those like him? Or was he genuinely concerned, feeling a twinge of responsibility for the activist's initial conversion to the cause? It wasn't as if Tom had any hidden sympathies for the criminal spree that had seen the prisoner convicted of a range of offences, including setting fire to livestock lorries and a slaughterhouse and then issuing death threats to animal experimenters. On the contrary, campaigners like Andy and his small band of fellow militants had been making his life increasingly difficult, ever since that damp and dark November morning when an Animal Liberation Army press spokesperson had claimed that an undisclosed number of Neptune chocolate bars had been poisoned in response to the company's funding of research on monkeys. It was a hoax, of course, but with its characteristic capriciousness, the media had seized upon the incident to present animal rights activists as ruthless terrorists, threatening all civilised values. The 'fanatics' and 'maniacs' had to be hunted down. And worse was to follow. Next the hack columnists and 'security experts' got in on the act, disclosing the supposed dark intentions of animal terror cells. The nation was faced – they declared –with merciless terrorists second only to the IRA in fanatical intent: secret networks had been established with all the bogeyman organisations of the day, from Basque separatists to Palestinian guerrilla groups.

It was nonsense, but to some extent it had been coming. A tiny minority *had* become steadily more outrageous, resorting to bigger incendiary devices, arson, increasing vandalism and threats. Press coverage had understandably become less sympathetic. Yet still nobody could have foretold the degree of condemnation that came after the chocolate bar hoax.

Besides its adverse effect upon public opinion, this emerging status as the nation's newest sinister threat acted as a rallying cry to a certain mentality of disaffected youth. Nothing could be more exciting than to be stigmatised as an evil menace to civilisation and there were those who were only too happy to supply the frantic media circus with sensational boasts and hideous plans. Rough, home-produced newsletters urged their small audiences to adopt a policy of maximum devastation. The whole process took on an inevitable momentum. The more severely the media condemned, the more enthusiastically the extreme minority feasted upon their notoriety. The rhetoric grew increasingly inflammatory, championing the 'lethal violence of the IRA'. Violent anarchist groups got in on the act, turning up at demonstrations bent on their class war agenda and aggressively planting black flags and *Smash the System* banners at the front of marches. They goaded the police into conflict whenever they could, thus provoking further condemnation.

In the great scheme of things, it was still relatively low-key stuff and nobody was physically harmed, but nevertheless activists were suddenly treated as a police priority and dealt with severely by the courts. Those arrested faced harsh prison sentences and, as in all such instances when the State wants to flex its muscle, it was not only the guilty that fell foul of the justice system.

Tom had found himself tarred implicitly with the terrorist brush. Some top reporters – the kind of A-team news personalities who in time would come to prove their commitment to good causes by performing song and dance routines on annual television charity extravaganzas – were wheeled out to grill him.

'Have you ever witnessed the charred remains of innocent children blown to bits by terrorist bombs?' accused one self-righteous presenter, summoning every ounce of moral indignation he could muster into the interrogation. Even when criticism was less extreme, a deep-seated disapproval could be detected. 'You're not one of those people who sends letter bombs are you?' became the common response whenever he declared what he did for a living.

Nobody, however, could accuse Andy Knowles of jumping on a pseudo-terrorist bandwagon. His belief in 'the cause' and his moral certainty in the justice of his actions was absolute. He was unrepentant in the face of the heated backlash against his activities. Above all, it had been the intimidation that had particularly enraged the press. Writing to that university professor and threatening to kidnap his children and treat them like he treated the animals in his laboratory had led to one of the tabloids characterising him as an 'evil fanatic'. Furthermore, Tom thought that Andy was a bit of a fool for getting caught so easily. After all, if he was going to threaten people, it wasn't very wise to make the calls from a girlfriend's house, nor to keep a stash of incriminating evidence in his own flat. Given the current political climate, it was little wonder that the Farnham Five – as sympathisers had nicknamed Knowles and his fellow conspirators – had received stiff sentences. Andy, branded as the ringleader, had been given six years and had only recently – after six months in a higher-security jail –been moved to the more lenient regime at HM Hill House Prison.

Tom had never visited a prison before and didn't know what it would be like. Things turned out to be rather more relaxed than he had expected. True, he was searched on arrival, but this was relatively swift and unobtrusive. It might have been even more so, had not the officer become slightly suspicious of the three bars of Tofu Towers' latest confectionery product he had brought as a gift for the prisoner. In keeping with much of the company's output, not an enormous amount of attention had gone into presentation and the sickly mauve wrapper, bearing the bald message CAROB – WITH NO ADDED SUGAR, did little to conform to the world's idea of what a chocolate bar should look like. Real confectionery was described as rich, delicious, smooth and creamy: this came with the less seductive sub-heading of A COMBINATION OF UNSWEETENED CAROB, SOYA FLOUR AND STABILISERS. After carefully reading the ingredients and feeling the texture, the searching officer nodded in disbelief as he returned the bars to Tom. If it was an escape plot or an elaborate form of drug smuggling, it was way too complicated for him to comprehend!

The meeting with Andy took place in a plain and functional communal visitors' room. Initial greetings were cordial, if a little awkward and tentative. Fortunately, the Tofu Towers confectionery helped to break the ice.

'I've brought you some chocolate… well, carob actually. Would you like some? Don't worry, I've cleared it with the guards,' said Tom.

'That would be great. Thanks,' replied the prisoner, glancing at the overseeing officer for confirmation that the gift was acceptable. 'Do you mind if I eat some now – I'm really hungry?'

'Sure, you go ahead.'

Several moments of silence followed. According to tradition, eating chocolate is supposed to be sensual experience, the substance melting seductively on the tongue. By contrast, Tofu Towers' no-sugar carob stuck doggedly in thick wedges to the roof of the palate. It took a considerable chewing effort, rolling the tongue around the top of the mouth while swallowing repeatedly, to produce anything that remotely resembled a melting effect. Tom looked on with a mixture of amusement and concern as Andy struggled to digest.

The prisoner didn't seem to mind too much.

'Mmm, thanks a lot. I really enjoyed that', he said – apparently without irony – after eating half a bar. 'I'll save the rest until later if you don't mind.'

'You're welcome. It must be difficult getting much to eat in here?'

'It's the worst thing about prison. Ask any of the animal rights prisoners, they'll tell you the same thing. They don't cater too well for us vegans.'

It emerged that this was an understatement. As Andy explained his dietary difficulties, Tom felt annoyed with himself that he hadn't given much thought to the kind of responses that these vegan inmates were encountering when they asked whether their meals were suitable. 'I'll just check with Chef whether the stock in today's casserole is obtained purely from vegetable sources' was not amongst them. Breakfast requests for soya milk to be added to porridge and tea tended to be greeted with similar disdain. The least sympathetic of the kitchen duty prisoners came to regard it as something of a challenge to create the most inedible combinations. Overcooked tinned carrots covered in brown sauce were a culinary treat when compared to lumpy mashed potato topped with white sugar. And heaven knows what secret ingredients were added to Thursday's curry in order to teach the fussy new arrivals a lesson. It didn't bear thinking about.

Hunger apart, Andy Knowles had few complaints about prison life. He was soon in full flow with the activist rhetoric, dismissing any deprivation he was enduring.

'Prison is nothing', he declared defiantly. 'Whatever hardship I face behind bars is nothing compared to the suffering of animals. I've got six years; theirs is a life sentence. It's a war out there and sacrifices have to be made if we're going to win it. People have to stand up for what they believe in.'

Tom took this as veiled disapproval of his own role. Soon the criticism became more explicit.

'Not being personal or anything, but the national societies like SAFE have let the animals down. We've had over 100 years of cosying up to politicians and handing out leaflets. What has it achieved? Nothing. Animal abuse is worse now than it has ever been. Some of us are not willing to put up with it any longer.

'It really gets on my wick', he continued. 'You get all these people on fat salaries – and I don't necessarily mean you – sitting on their arses and blaming us for trying to do something about it. But things will change. The day will come when it's the animal abusers who are imprisoned for their crimes, not freedom fighters like us. Look at the civil rights leaders and the feminists. They had to break the laws, yet nobody condemns them any more.'

'Yes, but aren't we supposed to be about non-violence?' Tom felt compelled to point out.

'We are non-violent. Nobody gets hurt by threats or setting fire to slaughterhouses.'

Eventually Tom managed to divert the conversation and find out a little more about Andy's life in jail. Most of his fellow inmates, he said, looked upon him with amazement. They simply couldn't understand how anybody would risk their freedom for the sake of a campaign for animals. But he had managed to have interesting conversations and had won some sympathy and respect. Hundreds of letters of support and food parcels had also helped to maintain his spirits. A further boost had been copies of activist newsletters that the authorities had surprisingly allowed him to receive. These had hailed the Farnham Five – as well as the Newcastle Nine and Hastings Seven – as heroes and had sworn revenge for every hour their brothers and sisters spent behind bars.

It was an odd meeting. Despite Andy's hard line, there was something that Tom couldn't help liking about him. He found him naïve, impressionable and obsessed with his cause to the point that he was blind to any other perspective. But in spite of the prisoner's deeds, he found it hard to think of him as the evil monster portrayed by the press. Certainly it was impossible to doubt his conviction, even if to Tom it all seemed a bit of a waste. What good had it done, getting locked up like that? And how could Andy swallow all that fundamentalist freedom fighter rhetoric quite so uncritically? For now at least, the distance between their views was impossible to bridge. Tom was glad to get away. He watched the prisoner disappear through the visiting room door, dressed in his blue uniform and clutching the remaining carob bars.

'Thanks again for the chocolate,' he called out as he was led back through the door towards his cell.

When Tom visited Elizabeth Plant from the Society for the Promotion of a Vegan Diet to discuss the prisoners and their dietary problems, he was surprised to find her adamantly unsympathetic.

'These young people don't understand the damage they cause', she responded brusquely.

'What do you mean?'

'All this militancy – it's misguided and counter-productive,'

'Well maybe it is, Elizabeth – I'm not particularly in favour myself – but Andy is really sincere – and so are lots of others. They're just frustrated by the rate of progress, that's all. They say that a century of lawful campaigning has achieved nothing and we need to get tougher. Everything moves too slowly for them and they don't have the patience for changing public attitudes or political progress.'

'Patience! Don't give me that nonsense, Tom. I doubt if most of these people have been around for 100 weeks, let alone 100 years. If you're prepared to resort to threats and violence – and making threats is violent as far as I'm concerned – I'm afraid you simply don't understand the message. It's as simple as that.'

'"Don't understand the message"? What do you mean by that?'

'I mean that they don't really grasp how very radical this cruelty-free living idea actually is. Look at human history. To date, most of us have proved incapable of displaying consistent love and empathy towards anybody outside our immediate families – and many of us can't even manage that. It's proved impossible for us to live with our neighbours for any length of time without conflict breaking out over some petty difference or rivalry. And now some of us are calling for this same tribal species of ours – that can torture and murder its fellows at the slightest provocation – to behave with care and compassion towards cows and sheep. Do you really expect the whole human race to look at things the way that you or I do overnight?

'Look Tom', Elizabeth continued, without waiting for an answer. 'There may be some of us who look at an animal in a cage and understand that she suffers loneliness and despair – and that's even before we do something unspeakably vile like experiment upon her or take her to the slaughterhouse. But it'll take a very long time, probably far beyond even your lifetime, before it is ever likely to be accepted by the majority. So please don't talk to me about angry young people not having patience.'

'I think that's a bit harsh, Elizabeth, I really do. As I said, I agree entirely that some of this direct action has gone too far, but they're only doing what they believe to be right. Whatever you say, it does take a lot of courage to risk your freedom for your principles.'

'No, I'm sorry. Brave in their misguided way, perhaps yes, but I won't accept the principles. They are wrong. These militants are simply imitating the tactics and motives of warmongers. They're saying, "I'm better than you", "I hate anybody with opposing views and I have the right to inflict my opinions upon them through intimidation or violent means".'

'No, that's not always true. Mostly, it's trying to rescue animals from farms and laboratories – directly saving the oppressed from suffering.'

'That's different. I'm not quarrelling with that or with any other appropriate form of non-violent civil disobedience. But it isn't just that any more though, is it? What I object to is sending incendiary devices through the post, arson and that sort of thing. That has nothing to do with rescuing animals. It's warmongering, plain and simple. It's the tactic of the bully boy, just as surely as we, as a species, bully animals.

'Listen', she continued, 'the last thing I want to resort to is the "wisdom of old age" argument, like some boring old woman. But you must realise that my generation has seen things that yours has not. My father lost his brother in the Great War. My own brother was killed in the Second World War, as were several of our friends and many other young men in the Yorkshire village where I was brought up. I've lived through some of the most violent times in human history and I've seen more than enough vicious, callous treatment of both people and animals to convince me that it can only be through a message of non-violent and selfless love that the world will become a better place. I know that might sound very corny and wishy-washy to you and your contemporaries, Tom, but it's the one thing I'm really sure about. This period of relative peace – at least in our region of the world – gives us a unique opportunity to nurture the power of compassion and I hate to see it wasted by anybody who glorifies militancy.'

'"All you need is love", eh?' responded Tom. 'Well yes, I suppose I believe in that as well. It still doesn't get over the problem of what you do when the world isn't interested in compassion and won't listen to reason though, does it? What **do** you do then?'

'"Listen to reason"? Are you really suggesting that humans are uniquely rational beings who behave logically, Tom? I'm afraid that's a hopeless myth. If we were rational there is no way we'd behave the way we do – killing, stealing and destroying the planet that sustains us. We *rationalise*, that's for sure – justifying everything we do according to our personal prejudices and selfish motives, but you only have to look at the nuclear arms race or religious and racial hatred – to name just a couple of examples – to know that there's nothing rational about the way we behave.'

'God, I find that even more depressing, Elizabeth! If there's no rationality to appeal to, what hope is there for change at all? If you really believe that, how on earth do you keep going?'

'That's easy. Even if we're not rational beings, I do believe that we have a spiritual dimension that can be appealed to. I don't personally believe in an omnipotent God, but, as I always told my children, I still maintain that humans possess a capacity for selfless compassion that springs from those spiritual qualities. In the end, I think that this will somehow shine through.'

'Are you sure that's not just another of those rationalisations you've just mentioned?' half-joked Tom, smiling despite the bleakness of his question.

'Quite possibly I suppose, Tom – quite possibly. Let's hope not though, eh!

'Anyway, to get back to matters more immediate, what did you say this chap in prison is called again?'

'Andy Knowles – or Arson Andy as he's known in the trade!'

'Silly boy!'

'He's very popular with the more militant wing, I believe,' added Tom, provocatively.

'I'm sure he is. The only trouble is that every time he opens his mouth he probably alienates the other 99.9 per cent of the population!'

Despite her disapproval, Elizabeth took up the prisoner's diet with customary vigour. By lobbying her local MP, she was able to pressurise the Home Office into entering into discussions. To her surprise, the junior Tory minister responsible for prisons was not unsympathetic. After negotiations, the government agreed to accept veganism as a choice of principle. Provided that they were fully paid-up members of the Society for the Promotion of a Vegan Diet, all prisoners would be entitled to specially agreed ingredients, providing minimum nutritional requirements. Rather than inedible combinations of junk foods or worse, they were soon enjoying meals that included soya milk, fresh fruit and salad. While it certainly wasn't cordon bleu, it was luxury compared to usual prison food and other inmates looked on with envy. 'I wouldn't mind a bit of that myself', some thought. The word soon spread around the country's jails.

As a consequence, the Society was suddenly faced with a significant increase in membership. The organisation – set up to promote a message of compassion and non-violence to all living creatures – found itself welcoming a rush of criminals, including a few convicted for the most heinous of offences. Inmates – many of them barely able to read or write – saved up their fag money to raise the membership subscription for the 'vegun klub'. It was impossible to tell how many were genuinely converted by the passionate views of fellow inmates or whether they were solely motivated by a desire for more edible food. A handful of lost souls would even turn up on the doorstep of the Society's headquarters after release, hoping that membership might entitle them to a bit of financial help and a roof over their head. Poor old Elizabeth Plant found an increasing amount of her time given over to finding lodgings for ex-cons, buying them a meal out of her own pocket and trying to ensure that some cynical journalist didn't get hold of the story. She could just imagine the headlines – 'Cereal Killers', 'Mad Axeman is from Planet Vegan'.

Fortunately, her secret was safe.

10

As if the militants were not trouble enough for Tom Moore, there were plenty of other political events to feel miserable about as the years passed by. Like everybody else with left-wing sympathies, he loathed Mrs Thatcher and her government with intensity. Had it been feasible to do so, he would have implicated them in every one of the decade's disasters, but try as he might, it was difficult to lay the blame for events such as the Ethiopian famine, Chernobyl nuclear disaster, Tiananmen Square or the Bhopal chemical catastrophe at Norman Tebbit or Mrs T's door. That still left plenty of scope for righteous indignation though – the poll tax, the arrival of cruise missiles, the treatment of miners and the Falklands War just for starters.

There was more personal tragedy for Tom too, with his mother's sudden death after a short illness, soon after her seventieth birthday.

Yet in spite of this heartache and the unsympathetic political climate, it remained mostly an exciting and fulfilling period. Nothing could make him feel sad for too long. His status as a minor hero in his chosen field grew significantly when, four years into his employment with SAFE, he managed to find a publisher for *Getting Away With Murder – the true costs of animal abuse* – a book he had put together from research undertaken for his talks. What a fantastic feeling it was when the letter arrived, confirming that the manuscript had been accepted for publication! It was surpassed only by the magical morning when he opened the small brown package and found inside the first six complimentary copies of the glossy-covered paperback. There, printed across the bottom, was his own name in large, bold letters. How proud he felt! Not even the pangs of sadness that his parents were not around to share his moment of glory could detract from his sense of achievement. And this was only the beginning of the ego boost. There was a favourable review or two, followed by queues – admittedly not very long – waiting to purchase signed copies at the end of his talks. As a child he had spent hours developing what he considered an interesting signature, imagining himself a novelist, pop star or politician. Now there were real people wanting him to inscribe *his* book. He did so with an eagerness artfully disguised by a show of modest reluctance. It was still far from fame, but it was some kind of semi-celebrity status and very intoxicating. His confidence grew to the point where he even learnt to take advantage of the occasional sexual favours that came his way. These liaisons invariably struck an unusual if distinctive pattern, particularly when it came to post-coital conversation. The conventional subjects of pillow talk were of little interest to Tom and his equally committed vegan partners. Rather than reassurances on the quality of sexual performance, details of past lovers or intimate revelations about the year at which virginity had been lost, familiarity was established instead by discovering at what age the meat habit had been kicked or whether hummus and cucumber was preferred to peanut butter and lettuce in lunchtime sandwiches. The prospects for future compatibility were judged not by comparing musical, film and literary taste, but by the more burning question of whether you shared similar preferences when it came to dairy-free substitutes on pizza.

By the end of the decade, life for vegans had changed dramatically. For a start, there were a lot more of them. Informed nutritionists had dramatically changed their tune, praising the health-enhancing qualities of plant-based diets rather than warning of their deficiencies. A combination of health scares about animal foods – particularly BSE and salmonella – and growing concern over animal welfare had also made a difference. The range and quality of foods to feed the growing ranks improved massively. Interesting recipe books appeared, filled with mouth-watering dishes from around the globe. Innovative new food companies burst onto the scene, offering tasty dairy-free ice creams, yoghurts, cheeses, mayonnaises, chocolates and cream. Soya milk now tasted good enough for dairy users not to spot the difference in their tea. Even *VeggySos* and its like took on more attractive formulas, and were beginning to eliminate the hydrogenated fat content in line with the growing health scares.

A few veterans felt betrayed by these advances, hating the loss of their refugee status and bemoaning the intrusion of commercial interests upon their oasis of purity. The majority, however, were delighted that their diet no longer demanded any feats of self-denial. They could be greedy as well as virtuous. Tofu Towers looked out of touch with the times and was threatened with insolvency until it was taken over by one of the slicker new outfits on the dairy-free block. While rejecting animal products had hardly become fashionable, it was no longer considered completely freakish or beyond the understanding – let alone the tastebuds – of ordinary mortals.

By this time, Tom was living with Wendy Walters. After he took over her job at SAFE, they had come across one another regularly at meetings. Intimacy had developed slowly but surely. He had a circle of like-minded friends whom he liked and respected. A combination of personal contentment and fulfilment at work lent him boundless energy and optimism. The counter-culture to which he belonged appeared to be thriving. From his entrenched position near its centre, he believed that the world was changing and that he was playing a significant role in the revolution. So many around his social circle were turning to vegetarianism or getting involved in Green politics that he assumed that the whole world would eventually follow. Ideas that not long ago had been dismissed as extreme were becoming almost mainstream. Commercial whaling had been banned, Europe had outlawed the import of seal skins, wearing fur was considered socially unacceptable. Cruelty-free cosmetics were on the high street.

There had also been those inspiring displays of communal public protest throughout the decade that had reinforced his positive outlook. Marching against cruise missiles with a quarter of a million others for CND; surrounding the nuclear base at Greenham Common one cool Good Friday morning in support of the women camping there; the Band Aid concert to help Ethiopian famine victims that had captured the public imagination to an unprecedented degree, and for which even the despised David Bowie had partly redeemed himself. It was true that some of his protesting colleagues dismissed this event as an extravagant exercise in celebrity ego-massage, but his response was less sceptical and full of admiration for Bob Geldof's uncompromising passion.

And then, as the decade approached its end, events far more momentous stirred his optimism still further. People Power created revolutions against the Soviet empire in Hungary, Czechoslovakia and Romania, culminating in the triumphant dismantling of the Berlin Wall. Peace and liberation were breaking out everywhere. It would only be a matter of time before things would change almost as decisively here, despite Mrs Thatcher. How freely the wine flowed as he and Wendy celebrated the spectacular success of the Green Party at the 1989 EU elections, gaining fifteen per cent of the national vote. (The fact that hardly anybody bothered to turn out was conveniently ignored!). Membership of Friends of the Earth was rising astronomically. Newspapers took up the Green agenda eagerly. One morning he picked up one of the national papers and was amazed to find a whole page dedicated to an exposé of the secret world of a registered UK slaughterhouse, He read the article with a combination of horror, excitement and disbelief: *'the air is heavy with a demonic mist, a mixture of blood and foul water. It splashes and froths up from the bleeding troughs where animals are hung by a back leg after their throats are cut. And it washes in great black waves from the scalding tank as each newly slaughtered pig is dumped in.'* Three thousand words given over to graphic descriptions of deliberate cruelty, and 'medieval' barbarity: *' the noise, in some locations like a roaring mechanical tide, elsewhere the explosive sound of metallic slamming and clanking, chains and hooks coupling and uncoupling, the hiss of power hoses, the bang of the "captive bolt" as it penetrates the skulls of cattle, and, mingling throughout, the shrieks of terror from doomed beasts'.* *

When he had first become involved with these issues – less than fifteen years earlier – it would have been impossible to imagine such high-profile revelations. Not even a tinge of envy of the writer's courage and skill could diminish Tom's amazement and admiration. Surely, nobody could read much of this sort of stuff and remain unaffected?

* From 'Slaughterhouse Tales' by Andrew Tyler.
First published in *The Independent*, March 13 1989

Part Three –
This place don't make sense to me no more

11

On a warm Friday evening in late autumn, Tom Moore stands on platform 9 at Waterloo Station, awaiting the late-running service to the West Country. It is packed with long-distance commuters, similarly tired and irritated by the delay. When the train eventually pulls in, it's a fight to get to the front of the queue and guarantee a seat. As he can't face the crush tonight, the choice is either to stand in the crowded corridor or struggle through the carriages and confront one of the breed of passengers who routinely occupy the seat nearest the aisle and plonk their briefcase and jacket on the place next to the window. It's an increasingly common habit, the offender usually pretending to be deeply absorbed in the newspaper and unaware of fellow commuters left standing.

Although Tom normally considers it his civic duty to claim the spare seat, tonight he can't be bothered to push his way through the packed train. Instead, he resigns himself to standing in one of the non-smoking compartments, next to two young men in fashionably cut dark suits who sound like they almost certainly work in the City. After a bit of office gossip, their conversation moves on to weightier matters.

'I never thought I would catch myself saying this', one of them begins, 'but I'm really starting to believe that a Labour victory would be good for this country. We need some fresh, blue sky thinking, that's for sure.'

'Oh, absolutely', replies his colleague. 'Blair's completely obliterated the fear factor.'

It's sixteen long years since Mrs Thatcher came to power and somehow her shadow still looms large over everything the government does, despite concerted efforts to soften its image since ditching her. The country has had enough of perceived sleaze and greed and is at last ready for a change. It may be a full eighteen months or so before the next General Election is expected, but there is already a sense that the Conservative reign is coming to an end. The get-rich-quick times of the 1980s have long passed and even its staunchest allies in the City are deserting the Tory ship.

'We're still downsizing, despite the signs of economic recovery,' one of the two businessmen reveals to his colleague. 'In fact, almost all the firms I know are engaged in some form of workforce imbalance correction.'

'Oh, quite. I hear that Phillips and Bradley are planning another half dozen negotiated departures within the next couple of months. Everywhere you look there's ongoing restructuring.'

'Yes, you never know what's round the corner these days. I know that our MD has been working on some pretty robust contingency plans.'

Despite the discomfort of standing in a crowded railway carriage, there's a part of Tom that enjoys straining to pick up snippets of conversation from the hordes of homeward-bound commuters. He likes to feel a bit superior and contemptuous of their vulgar world of business and trade, considering them almost from another, lesser planet. He has always dismissed as nonsense any suggestion that this heartless world of capitalism has any connection with his own higher calling.

'Business creates affluence, and affluence enables people like me to help fund organisations like yours', brother Rob had once defended himself when Tom had criticised his purchase of utility company shares, sold off cheaply by Mrs T's government. 'More than that, it seems to me that without economic stability you're unlikely to get a great deal of understanding and tolerance of minority views. Thatcher may have taken it all far too far, but I don't see that there's fundamentally a better alternative.'

Tom didn't buy his brother's argument at all. Didn't capitalism inevitably create greed? Wasn't Thatcher's Britain the logical outcome of the philosophy – yuppies with obscene and ostentatious wealth alongside the homeless, destitute and discarded sheltering in doorways? And what about animals? Wasn't greed and capitalism also responsible for those drug companies and their vile vivisection laboratories?

'Are animals really that much better off in Soviet Russia or China?' had been Rob's response to this – a question to which he had no convincing answer. Yet nothing his older brother could say was going to make him feel part of the same human family as the get-rich-quick city slickers.

Nevertheless, like it or lump it, he couldn't deny that for the moment he appeared to share the same political aspirations as many of them. He, too, felt optimistic about a change of government. Tony Blair's New Labour had talked about an ethical foreign policy, a ban on hunting with hounds and the need to tackle environmental problems such as global warming with vigour. Whatever they did, they were bound to be better than the hateful Tories!

It may have been five plus years since her departure, but Mrs Thatcher had lost none of her power to inspire his intense loathing. Her seminal sins still loomed large in his mind – the Falklands War, confrontation with the print unions and miners, home repossessions, poverty and unemployment, the riots at Brixton, Broadwater Farm and against the poll tax. As for the issues that particularly mattered to Tom, she had simply dismissed them as irrelevant or worse. After summarising her brief period as shadow minister of the environment as 'boring and humdrum', she had gone on as PM to consider environmentalists as part of the condemned 'enemy within'. She had even shunted hostile and unsympathetic Nicholas Ridley to the Ministry of the Environment in order to confront the vociferous Green lobby – a role to which he had brought a potent combination of ignorance and aggression. Organic farming he rubbished 'as a way to rip off customers'; sea pollution could be ignored because the oceans would 'destroy all viruses that have ever been invented'; the campaign to ban CFC aerosols was rejected on the grounds that 'this would not be a scientifically valid thing to do'. Green Party polices in general were ridiculed as 'a wish-list of unscientific rubbish based on myths, prejudices and ignorance'. 'They are poets, perhaps, but not realists', the irascible Old Nick had said of Green politicians.

What a time they had been, those Thatcher years! How could he and his colleagues ever have imagined that they were changing the world, when those in power had shown such disdain for their beliefs? How young and naïve he had been.

Not that things had improved much after Maggie had gone. John Major's administration had brought Tom a new object of loathing in the shape of Minister of Agriculture and Church of England Synod member John Gummer. While Ridley had cited the god of Science to justify his prejudices, Gummer's preference was to call upon the Supreme Being himself. He described vegetarians as 'deeply undemocratic food faddists who want to impose on the rest of us views which come from their own inner psyches' and they became a favourite target of his pseudo-religious pronouncements. 'The Bible tells us that we are masters of the fowls of the air and the beasts of the field and we very properly eat them', Gummer told the nation, mustering all the authority of a man in possession of a direct line to the Almighty.

If there was one thing that Tom couldn't stand it was Bible

bashers. He'd seen enough of the religious fundamentalists on his own side, trying to argue the opposite viewpoint to Gummer by maintaining that Jesus had been a practising vegetarian. You might have thought this an unlikely supposition, given the two fish that had featured quite prominently in the supposed culinary miracle by which the Lord had managed to satisfy the hunger of five thousand people. But the answer was convenient. The fish were in fact seven bunches of grapes, mistakenly included on the menu only because of a shoddy translation!

Even though Tom remained as unconvinced by this wacky little theory as he was by the Minister of Agriculture's biblical interpretation, he could at least excuse it as relatively harmless. His religious allies might be dismissed as a little bonkers, but they were not responsible for government policy. Neither had any of them, like Gummer, fed their young daughter a beefburger in front of the television cameras as part of some ill-fated publicity stunt to show that Mad Cow disease did not pose a public health threat.

By the time the train to Devon is an hour out of London, there's a large enough exodus of commuters to allow him to grab a seat. Yet still there are distractions. A fellow passenger seated a couple of rows in front is having to deal with constant calls on his mobile phone. 'At this rate everybody will be using the bloody things before too long', Tom grumbles to himself. There seem to be more and more things that get on his nerves these days and cell phones have risen to near the top of the list.

He has to admit, however, that tonight's conversations are providing good entertainment. The phone user is evidently receiving calls from his partner, who is upset about something. Evidently, she wants him to tell her that he loves her and he is doing everything he can to appease her anxiety without having to utter those embarrassing words in front of the assembled passengers. They, on the other hand, are all listening attentively, waiting for the moment he succumbs. To everyone's amusement, he is making a complete hash of the difficulty. The harder he tries to keep his voice down and hide his awkwardness, the quieter the rest of the carriage becomes.

'Of course I do'.

'We'll talk about it when I get home'.

'Try not to worry. I'll be at the station in twenty minutes and we can talk about it then'.

'Of course I do.

'Yes, I just said I do.

'I did say that I do.

'No. I didn't mean that. You know I do.'

He tries to wriggle his way around to a conclusion that will quieten her.

'Let's talk about it when I get to the station. Goodbye darling.'

And he presses the button to disconnect. A couple of minutes later the ringing tone resumes and they go through the whole conversation again. This little drama makes a real change from the usual overheard mobile phone conversations – pompous bosses fixing up apparently vital meetings and consulting loudly with secretaries and other subordinates. A few passengers are by now taking real pleasure in the central character's discomfort. Commuters who would not normally dream of communicating with each other are exchanging reserved smiles and engaging in a communal session of *schadenfreude.*

'As if I've got anything to feel superior about when it comes to dealing with women', reflects Tom, chastising himself for joining in with the merriment. After all, the main reason he's on his way to spend a few days with his brother and family in their Devon weekend cottage is to try to keep busy after the break-up with Wendy, nearly four months ago. The separation has caused something of a midlife crisis, arising as it has in his fortieth year.

They had been together for nearly eight years and he had come to take her for granted. She had become increasingly unhappy about the time and energy he put into his work. Wendy had had enough of constant demonstrations and protests. It was time to move on. The biological clock was ticking and she wanted children and a normal family life. He would not listen.

'My work is too important to start a family', he told her.

'I can't be at home this weekend because I have to speak at a demonstration.'

'Northern Weekend want me to appear on their Friday night debate. It's my duty to go.'

Always there would be some vital reason to be away. She put up with it, feeling partly guilty about her dissatisfaction and her desire to weaken his devotion to the great cause. Then she had discovered his brief fling with a supporter from Swansea, who had so admired his work and told him she would do anything to help. It had been over several months before Wendy found out, but it proved to be the final straw. She chucked him out and, difficult though it proved, stubbornly resisted his apologies and pleas for another chance. He'd been miserable ever since, not realising how much he would miss her. All he wanted now was to settle down and play the family man. Unhappy and disillusioned, his precious campaigning hardly seemed to matter that much any more.

By the time Tom stops thinking about Wendy for a while, the mobile phone man has left the train, along with the vast majority of commuters. It isn't until they stop at one of the small towns deep into rural Dorset that he next has company. A large man of roughly his own age, with ruddy complexion and round, friendly face, takes the seat next to him and immediately pulls out what looks like a handful of receipts from his jacket pocket. He gazes intensely at the top one. Intrigued, Tom glances across and spots that it is a ticket for the national lottery, launched only a few months previously. The portly fellow traveller catches his eye.

'Got your numbers for tomorrow night yet?' he enquires.

'No, not yet', Tom replies politely, hiding the fact that he considers himself far too radical to indulge in anything as conventional and popular with the masses. He disapproves on these principles alone, let alone his objection to the hijacking of charities and good causes for such a commercial venture.

'I won £10 three weeks ago', his new acquaintance continues. 'My first three numbers comes up and I says to the missus, "ay, ay, we could be off to the Bahamas next week". Then the next two numbers comes down and – would you believe it? – they're only one away from two of my other numbers. I could have been a millionaire!'

Several other tales of near misses and small victories ensue. Most notably, a second cousin has won several hundred pounds with numbers chosen via a complex mathematical calculation involving wedding anniversaries, family christenings and the date of the Queen's coronation. Tom feels himself losing the will to live. Only a year ago, the worst you were likely to endure from a stranger on a train was a discussion about the weather. Now it seemed that almost the whole nation was dwelling in lottery land, sharing their experiences of bonus balls and rollover jackpots.

Thankfully, the rest of the journey is completed without yielding much more to moan about.

Friday night and Saturday passed. He drank too much and started to become even more morose and nostalgic. As usual when drunk and depressed, his alcohol-fuelled musings took a political turn. He was soon back to a familiar theme – General Election night in May 1979.

'Aah, I remember that night Thatcher was elected. We knew that it was the end of everything worth fighting for…'

Rob and the friends who had joined him in the pub exchanged weary glances. The older brother knew that they were in for a long evening of doom and gloom and that the blame for all Tom's personal despair was about to be laid at the door of the UK's first female prime minister. Sometimes she still served a purpose, did the dear old Iron Lady!

He rose late on the Sunday with a bit of a hangover, played for a while with the two youngest of his four nieces and then started to get a little weepy and miserable again. Rob tried to cheer him up.

'I'm reading this new book, *High Fidelity* by Nick Hornby. I suppose it's about male obsessions really. These blokes are always making lists, most of them about music – a bit like we always used to. You know – your five favourite songs, your five favourite guitar solos and so on. It's really funny.'

'Oh yeah, it sounds interesting,' replied Tom, without too much conviction.

'They don't do their five best protest songs though. What do you think?'

Rob was playing his trump card. He knew that if a combination of music trivia and radical politics wouldn't engage Tom, then nothing would.

It seemed to do the trick.

'*The Times They are A-Changin'* would be number one,' offered the younger Moore definitively, 'and then probably *Blowing In The Wind* and *With God on Our Side*.'

'What about *Desolation Row* and *Oxford Town*?' replied Rob.

'Yes, and I'd have *The Lonesome Death of Hattie Carroll* and *Masters of War* in there, too.'

'And don't forget *It's Alright Ma (I'm Only Bleeding)*.'

After a few more Bob Dylan songs were named and sung, Rob suggested a change of rules.

'OK, seeing as we've only got Dylan songs, let's exclude him. He's too bloody good. What else would you have?'

'Definitely *Meat is Murder* by The Smiths and probably *Glad to be Gay* by Tom Robinson.'

'Mmm,' responded Rob, unimpressed. 'I'd have something by Ewan McColl, or maybe Pete Seeger. I'd probably choose *We Shall Overcome* because I always remember mum singing it on those old CND marches. I'd have to have an anti-racism song in there as well – *Birmingham Sunday* by Richard Farina is my favourite, though I suppose Billie Holliday's *Strange Fruit* must take some beating. Sam Cooke's *A Change Is Gonna Come* would be a contender too.'

'What about anti-war songs? Apart from Dylan, I reckon Elvis Costello's *Shipbuilding* is my favourite', Tom butted in.

'Good choice, good choice', Rob responded, imitating a well-known television presenter. 'I'd go for Buffy St Marie's *Universal Soldier*. Or *I Ain't Gonna' March No More.*'

'Who's that by?'

'Phil Ochs.'

'Never heard of him.'

'Never heard of Phil Ochs? Ignorant boy. God, and I nearly forgot one of the best anti-war songs of the lot – *I'm-Fixin'-To-Die Rag* by Country Joe and The Fish.'

'Have you not listened to anything after 1968, Rob? To think you once accused me of being musically stuck in the past! What about something at least a bit more modern? The Clash or the Sex Pistols?'

'No, I'm afraid that punk stuff is a little too aggressive for me.'

'Well what about the Anti-Nazi League lot – Billy Bragg, for instance? And then there's Bob Marley, or Christy Moore and all those Irish nationalist inspired songs. Or better still, something that lays into Thatcher – *Tramp the Dirt Down* by Elvis Costello. I'd probably have that in my top five.'

'Yes, that's not bad. Peter Gabriel's *Biko* is a good 'un, too. But I still reckon the sixties were best. *I Hate the White Man* by Roy Harper!'

'Roy Harper! Who'd have thought to look at him that my successful big brother is still a pathetic old hippy at heart! You realise we haven't got anything about pollution or environmental destruction in there yet?'

'Ah, the sixties rule again! *Big Yellow Taxi* by a mile. Or what about *What Have They Done To The Rain* or Tom Paxton's *Whose Garden Was This*?'

'I don't know that one either. *Hard Day On The Planet* by Loudon Wainwright?'

'Not in the same league.'

They spent another hour or more debating and enjoying a hearty sing-song. Tom felt cheerier, particularly after a few lusty choruses of Country Joe and the Fish.

'Give me an F. Give me a U. Give me a C. Give me a K. What's that spell? What's that spell?'

When they had finished, he went up to his bedroom to read the local rural Devon rag, *The Weekly Gazette*. Where he lived near London, the regional paper was full of assaults, burglaries, even murders. By contrast, a typical front-page story in the small town of his brother's country retreat concerned a fire that had broken out at a seafront hotel and had barely charred the ceiling of one small room. This week's main headline concerned youths who had been overheard plotting to pelt carnival floats with conkers collected from the local park. The reporter had done her best to give her piece import with a dramatic headline, *Carnival Conspiracy Foiled,* followed by quotes from the two police officers who had bravely confronted the conker-armed youngsters and prevented the terror attack.

Tom smiled and flicked over the pages, failing to find anything other than the readers' letters column to interest him (more complaints about yob culture and deteriorating standards) until he reached another crime report on page thirteen.

VICAR ADMITS SIGN THEFT

Local vicar Reverend Tony Swallow has admitted stealing an advertisement hoarding from outside the local Quickshop Supermarket. The six-foot high sign, carrying the message "We Are Open On Sundays", was taken from the store early last Sunday and was later found outside the main parish church. It was spotted by churchgoers and passing motorists alike.

The Reverend Swallow, 62, has been no stranger to controversy. Four years ago, he enraged some of his parishioners when he organised a coach to a demonstration in London against the Gulf War. More recently, parents at a local school protested after he told sixth- formers that they should strive to become misfits in society by voicing their opposition to the arms trade and exploitation of poor people in the Third World. He has also upset some of his congregation by having one of his ears pierced and describing fox hunting as 'unchristian'. The Reverend said that he had taken the supermarket sign as 'a protest against the legalisation of Sunday trading and the increasing erosion of spiritual values'.

There was a mixed reaction to his protest yesterday. Mother-of-three Pauline Mitford, 32, was concerned that the sign might distract passing motorists. 'Everybody was looking at it, so I think it's a bit silly', she said. But husband Gary, 34, disagreed. 'Fair play to the vicar. He's entitled to make his point if he wants', he argued.

A spokesman for Quickshop refused to comment on the theft but told The Gazette exclusively that the company would not be taking legal action. 'Basically, we're opening on Sundays to provide a service for our customers', he added. 'For many families, it is the only day in the week when they can enjoy the full Quickshop shopping experience.'

Tom went running to his brother.

'Bloody hell, Rob. Have you seen this?' he asked, handing over the paper.

Rob read the story quickly.

'Good for him!'

'Yes, but the thing is I know him, but I had no idea he's moved to Devon. He used to run the CND group when I was in Bristol. and he supported Marie's animal group as well. He always was a bit of a radical.'

'Really? Well it doesn't sound like he's changed very much. Every time I come down here there seems to be some story about him in the local rag. He's always stirring up the natives in one way or another. Why don't you get in touch while you're here?' he added, sensing an opportunity to get his miserable sibling out of the house for an hour or two.

'Yes, I just might do that.'

12

That evening he found the telephone number and gave the vicar a ring. Although they had not been particularly close in the old days, Tony Swallow remembered him immediately and, after a brief chat, invited him round the next day 'to catch up on the last dozen years or more'.

When he arrived at the vicarage, he was greeted warmly. The Reverend was a smallish, stocky man, bald on top with wild wisps of curly grey hair at the back and sides. Something about him reminded Tom of a cuddly bear. He also wore an incongruous, bright stud earring in his left ear.

'I read about the earring – very trendy!'

'I'm glad you like it', answered the Reverend, bellowing out the hearty laugh that characterised the conclusion of most of his sentences.

'Mind you, I'd never have expected you to be making fashion statements, Tony.'

'Probably not, but I thought an old man keeping up with the times might give the school kids something to think about. Not to mention some of my parishioners, who think that a man wearing jewellery must be proof that the Devil is at work. They hate it,' he emphasised with obvious relish, letting rip another loud laugh. 'So for that matter does my wife. And the children are threatening not to visit again until I get rid of it. They say it will frighten my grandchildren!'

More loud laughter.

By profession and inclination the vicar was a good listener, so with Tom needing little encouragement to talk about his woes, the full story of the break-up with Wendy was soon disclosed. Tony Swallow made what he hoped were the right noises.

'I don't know what I can usefully say, Tom, except that I'm very sorry. Of course, I think you've behaved foolishly, but you know that already and you're hardly the first to do so. The flesh is weak and all those awful clichés. And to quote another platitude I'm sure you won't thank me for, time is a great healer. You will get over it, even if me saying so isn't much help right now. I'm very sorry.'

'It's not just Wendy, though' Tom continued. 'Sometimes I think I've been involved in this campaigning lark for too long. Life is passing by and I've never done anything else. I sometimes think that those people who say it's a waste of time and energy have got it about right.'

'You don't really believe that, do you?'

'I don't really know what I believe any more. There are so many opportunities out there in the world, and here am I stuck in the same old groove, giving more or less the same talks I was giving more than ten years ago. The words fly out of my mouth so easily that I hardly think about what I'm saying. Things that once stirred and angered me have practically no emotional impact whatsoever. Sometimes I can hardly bear the sound of my own voice. I describe some of the most vile and wicked atrocities that human beings commit and it hardly seems to move me at all. I know – or at least I like to think I know – that somewhere deep inside I still care about these things, but sometimes I really do start to wonder.'

'I don't like to hear you talk like that, Tom. It saddens me, it really does. Forgive me if I'm being insensitive, but leaving the separation from Wendy aside, you are – how should I put it – at a certain point in your life. Somewhere around the big four-o, I expect? It tends to be a bit of a difficult time for us poor creatures, doesn't it? No doubt you feel your youth slipping away and think it is downhill all the way from here. Well believe me, you're still a spring chicken at forty and it needn't be the end of anything!' added Tony Swallow, laughing out loud again. 'There's still plenty of time for mischief, even for an old man like me.

'Look, I know I'm biased,' he continued, 'but it's my belief that struggling to make the world a kinder and less violent place is a particularly worthwhile thing to do. As you know, I've always been more concerned with human issues such as poverty, fairtrade and CND, yet I also have the greatest respect for people like Marie and yourself, who have chosen to fight for animals first. God knows they need our help. The thing is though Tom, that it seems to me that the best that any of us can do is find a worthy cause we deeply believe in and pursue it as consistently as we can. You chose the path that you wanted to follow and I just wonder whether you would be able to find equal significance elsewhere?'

'Yes, I do understand all that, Tony, but the problem is that it's not only my own life I'm dissatisfied with, I'm so short of patience with everybody else, too. I can't stand the bigotry of some of our supporters. You know the sort – fundamentalists who insist that anybody who doesn't share their outlook 100 per cent is beneath contempt. People who lack the imagination to see that the world is a bit more complex than they can envisage.'

'Aah, yes. As a man of the cloth Tom, I can tell you that I've met a good few fundamentalists like that in my time and I don't need telling that they are a right pain in the neck, God bless 'em!'

Another loud laugh.

'It's my belief,' Reverend Swallow went on, 'that fundamentalism is simply a form of ignorance – albeit the kind that you can partly excuse when it is born out of passion and youth. The point is, though, that it's a human trait. It's certainly not confined to animal rights campaigners or followers of any other cause for that matter. I suspect that every intense belief – whether it is political, religious or ethical – is bound to attract followers who see the world in stark black and white terms and think that they – and only they – have found all the answers. Indeed, if I'm honest, I think that most of us who feel particularly strongly about an issue are guilty of a bit of self-righteousness and intolerance from time to time, don't you? I know I am. Fortunately my wife is very good at taking me down a peg or two whenever I get too much on my puritan high horse!'

'Frankly, I find it hard to believe that anyone could be as self-righteous and closed to other opinions as some of our lot though!' retorted Tom.

'Oh, I wouldn't be so sure of that, Tom. I could introduce you to a few Christian fundamentalists who could give even the most extreme activists a run for their money. But what you've always got to remember is that they *are* a small minority. You should never allow them to sour your opinion of all the quiet and caring people that I'm sure you meet all the time.'

Tom pondered the vicar's words.

'Well, even if you're right', he eventually responded, 'I sometimes wonder whether we're really achieving that much any more. When I first got involved in all this, I really believed that things would change. I wasn't stupid – I didn't think that all cruelty would be banished overnight, but as more and more people became involved, I did think that there would be more radical progress. We just seem to have lost momentum. Young people nowadays are more interested in road protests and anti-globalisation campaigning. Don't get me wrong, I think all this eco-warrior stuff is fantastic, but it's galling that our cause seems to have faded from the public eye as a consequence.'

Tony Swallow looked at him with exaggerated incredulity.

'Tom, now you really are allowing your misery to get the better of you. I've never seen so much about animal rights in the media, much of it positive, too. The public's imagination has really been captured by those live export demonstrations and the death of that poor woman.'

Tom had to admit that the vicar had a point. Members of the public had been galvanised into action as never before. Throughout the previous winter, protests against the live export of cattle and sheep had spread across UK ports – from Shoreham in Sussex to Plymouth, Dover and Coventry airport. When this miserable trade had moved to the tiny Essex port of Brightlingsea, the majority of the local population had turned out onto the narrow streets to turn back the lorries. Then there had been the tragedy at Coventry Airport, where a young woman called Jill Phipps had been fatally injured after falling below a lorry carrying calves bound for continental veal farms. Her sad death had provided fresh impetus to the protests, attracting many people who were new to any kind of campaigning. Every evening, television news had featured the demonstrations, almost always sympathetically. Suddenly, animal protestors were no longer dismissed as sentimental, or as dangerous extremists. It was OK to cry when you caught the eye of a calf about to be sent on a long and unhappy journey overseas. Lying down in front of sheep transporters on the public road was presented as brave and legitimate.

The Reverend beckoned Tom into his office, strewn with files, papers and newspaper cuttings.

'I kept some of this stuff on live exports because I thought it would be useful to show some of the local school kids how standing up for what you believe in can make a real impact,' he explained, searching for his glasses amongst the mess. 'Look at this, for instance. "Far from being the worst amongst us, live export campaigners represent the best of Britain: compassionate, determined and brave". And listen to this one: "the animal rights movement has expanded the very vocabulary of political discourse and our sense of what it is to be human. Jill Phipps was a brave woman, who gave a fierce commitment to a cause whose time has come". They're both articles from national newspapers and there's loads more like that.'

Had these events taken place a few years earlier, Tom Moore would doubtless have been as full of enthusiasm as his host and equally anxious to proclaim them as a potent sign of unstoppable momentum for progress. But his mood was dark, so his view was sceptical. Even though local councils had supported the protests and tried to ban the live export trade from their ports, their efforts had been scuppered by High Court judges.

'All that public support and good publicity didn't get us anywhere though, did it? What was it that judge said? To allow the bans to stand would be to give in to "mob rule" and "unlawful protest". Whatever we do they end up dismissing us as a rabble.'

This remark irritated Tony Swallow.

'If you're looking for great victories all the time, Tom, I suggest you do go and find something else to do. It doesn't often work like that, does it? Campaigning against the status quo is, by nature, a thankless task. It's usually the equivalent of repeatedly slamming your head against a brick wall. I can well understand why many people either give up or turn bitter and disillusioned. And some of us do go at least a little mad', he added, reverting to his chuckling self. 'But I don't see why you should let it happen to you. You're lucky – at least you don't have to maintain belief in a Supreme Being while the world appears to disintegrate around you!

'Two steps forward, one step back – that's the way it has always been with social progress,' he went on. 'If you want to look on the gloomy side – as you clearly do at the moment – I admit that it sometimes looks more like two steps backwards for every single sign of enlightenment. I agree that it does often seem that the human world is essentially unchanging. The Middle-East, Rwanda, the Balkans – these may be today's headline-grabbing examples of brutal persecution and genocide, but there have always been their equivalents and I fear there always will be. Yet aren't there also moments when you just marvel at the endurance of the human spirit and the way that, against all odds, it triumphs over tyranny? When I watched those millions of black South Africans toiling over great distances in intense heat and then queuing patiently for hours just so they could vote for the first time in a democratic election, I don't mind admitting that I cried with joy, Tom. I'll never forget what Mandela said: "The sun will never set on such a glorious human achievement". It's moments like that that make all the effort worthwhile, don't you think? And remember it was little more than ten years ago that we were still struggling to make people boycott South African goods and Maggie Thatcher was condemning Mandela as a terrorist.'

The unhappy Tom didn't know what to say to this. At the time he'd felt much the same about the end of South African apartheid. He and Wendy had visited his brother the weekend after the election to celebrate. But that had been more than a year ago. His personal world had fallen apart since then and he was determined to resist all optimism. Nonetheless, despite himself he found something compelling in Tony Swallow's enthusiasm. He wanted to hear more.

'I know what you're saying Tony, I really do. The trouble is that victories like Mandela's take so long to achieve and don't happen often enough as far as I can see, especially when you're campaigning for something that most people don't look on as particularly important. Most of the time it just feels bloody hopeless.'

'Well, yes, I suspect we all feel like that sometimes. But you just have to remember that it never is "bloody hopeless". Even if I agree that the big successes don't come often enough, there are still plenty of smaller victories to keep us going, aren't there? And that certainly goes for your cause as much as any other. I'm no expert and even I can think of a few.'

'Such as?'

'The ban in this country on veal crates and pig tethers for a start. And students don't have to do dissections at school any more, do they? Besides, you can't always measure success so dramatically. It's about changing long established attitudes as well, isn't it? A little earlier you mentioned the road protesters. Well, the road at Twyford Down was still built, despite all the opposition. Does that mean that all those brave young people who camped out for months have failed? Of course it doesn't. Even though they broke the law, many, many people respect and admire them for what they did. They've opened up a whole new debate about roads, transport and the destruction of the countryside. Who knows where that will lead? I see that the government's now given the go-ahead to build the Newbury bypass and I bet there'll be even bigger demonstrations there. Then, there are those two activists who are being sued by McDonald's. Who would have thought they could keep the big boys in court for more than a year, and get themselves in a position where they feel able to refuse the multinational's offer to settle the case? And what about the campaign I'm involved in to cancel Third World debts? I don't suppose for a minute that they'll all be written off, but we're raising awareness dramatically and it looks like we're going to form a pretty strong alliance that I'm sure will achieve some changes for the better. And I don't see that it's any different with your cause either. It matters to lots of people who wouldn't have known anything about these issues had it not been for campaigners like yourself. Just look at how many vegetarians there are now compared to twenty years ago. Probably millions in this country alone. So while I can accept that progress is often frustratingly slow, it's blatantly untrue to say that it isn't happening.

'Anyway – and I promise I'll shut up for a minute after this point, Tom… I'm afraid I can't get out of the habit of giving sermons!' He paused to laugh again. 'One thing is absolutely for certain, and that's that nothing will ever get done if people stop standing up for the things they believe in.'

Tom hesitated, at a loss for what to say. He felt vaguely tearful.

'That's true, I suppose,' were the only words he could muster.

The conversation turned to more trivial matters.

'Do you ever hear from Marie?' asked the Reverend Swallow.

'I haven't seen or heard from her for years, apart from exchanging Christmas cards. You know she married and had two children? They're probably both at school by now. I think she's gone back to teaching.'

'I knew about the children, but I hadn't realised they'd be that grown up. How quickly the years pass by! I was always very fond of Marie. She was so fearless and clever – a good laugh too.'

'Yes, she certainly was.'

13

It was his brother on the phone.

'Are you watching the news?'

'No. I've only just come in.'

'Well, turn on the telly quick – BBC1!'

'Why'?

'Helen's going to be on.'

'Aunt Helen?'

'Yes. Her case ended today. Must go. Speak to you later.'

'OK. See you.'

The news was full of the usual stuff – an interview with a woman who had just been released from hospital, six weeks after being injured by a huge IRA bomb in a Manchester shopping centre; loyalists rioting in Northern Ireland over attempts to divert the summer Orangeman parades; discussion of a new document from the opposition Labour Party – *New Labour, New Life For Britain* – in which Tony Blair had laid out his plans to revive the nation with a 'stakeholder economy'. The broadcast was nearing the end before the presenter introduced the item Tom had been waiting for.

'At Liverpool Crown Court today, four women were acquitted of conspiracy and criminal damage charges after a jury failed to convict them of breaking into an International Weapons Group factory and vandalising a jet fighter plane earlier this year. They could have faced up to ten years in prison, but this morning they walked free.'

While the newscaster spoke, the screen showed footage of four women, one much older than the others, leaving court and waving to a group of cheering supporters.

'We can speak now to our Defence Correspondent, Justin Denver', added the presenter when the brief film was over. 'Justin, what can you tell us about the case?'

'Well, Michael, I'm standing outside Liverpool Crown Court where, earlier today, four women – 68-year-old Helen Newton; her daughter, Sophie Newton, aged 39; 36-year-old Sara Mulligan and 24–year-old Debbie Sinclair – walked free through that door you can see behind me, after being acquitted of all charges in what was, in many ways, an extraordinary case. The four women admitted in court that in January this year they had broken into an International Arms Group weapons factory, armed with household hammers. They had used these to damage and put out of action a fighter jet which they claimed was about to be sold to the Indonesian government and used to support the illegal occupation of East Timor and the persecution of that country's native people. Indeed, not only did the women admit to the attack, they actually telephoned the police from within the aircraft hangar immediately after they had damaged the plane, telling them what they had done, why they had done it and where they could be found. Police arrived soon afterwards and the four were arrested and charged. Yet despite the undisputed evidence, the jury failed to convict all four defendants on charges of criminal damage and conspiracy to cause criminal damage.'

'This can't be very good news for the government, Justin. What are they saying about today's verdict?'

'Well, Michael, no government minister was available for comment when I tried to speak to them earlier today, so officially we don't know what their response will be. But what I can tell you is this: I spoke to two senior backbenchers, both close to the Prime Minister, and they told me that they were very concerned that this will be seen as yet another blow to flagging government morale. With the opposition Labour Party making much of its commitment to an ethical foreign policy, one MP told me that links to a brutal regime like Suharto's Indonesia may well add to the sense of an administration that is somehow without principle and steeped in sleaze.'

'Thanks Justin. And there'll be more on that story later this evening, over on *Newsnight* on BBC2.'

The *Newsnight* piece included an interview with the four women in which they thanked the jury for accepting that their action had been a duty rather than a crime. Invoking the Genocide Act, they had claimed to use only reasonable force in order to prevent crimes by the Indonesian government against the East Timor people. The interview was followed by an anger-stirring report on how 200,000 people – one third of East Timor's population – had died since 1975, and how the jets supplied by British companies had been deployed for ground attack, despite government claims that they were only used for training.

When the programme was over, Tom punched the air with delight before he rang Rob back.

'What fucking heroes, eh?'

'Fantastic, isn't it?' replied Rob.

'All that information about East Timor would never have been on the national news if they hadn't done that.'

'I know. It's brilliant. Makes you feel proud to know them, doesn't it?'

'It certainly does. I just hope that I'm as committed and full of energy as Helen when I get to her age.'

'That'll be a tall order' his brother joked. 'I'm afraid there aren't too many Helens in this world.'

14

Posing as a food journalist researching an article on modern food technology, he moved dreamily around the poultry processing plant. He had already seen the worst – a seemingly endless procession of live birds hung upside down on a steadily moving line that took them towards their deaths; the automatic slaughter machine that grabbed their necks and guided them towards the electric throat cutter; the first steps in the swift evisceration process – bleeding trough, boiling water tank and de-feathering machine. The experience had left him dazed with repulsion. Now he had moved on to the other side of the factory, where lines of women dressed in neat white uniforms and hats were working flat out, removing various bits of dead chicken as the conveyor moved relentlessly from the slaughter room towards the end of a process that would soon see them weighed and packaged in cellophane, ready for despatch to the butcher and supermarket. It took probably less than an hour to transform a wing-flapping, squawking chicken into a processed carcase.

The work looked revolting. It was freezing cold. The massive room stank. The conveyor belt clattered noisily. The workers had to shout to make themselves heard above the din of machinery as they squeezed entrails from necks, stuck their hands into slit stomachs to remove giblets and chopped off unwanted feet.

'How many we got today, Sue?'

'24,000.'

'Standard rate then – 3,000 an hour.'

'That should keep us busy', joked Sue, making the best of the joyless task.

It made him feel sick inside, but he kept up the pretence, sounding fascinated by the factory manager's obvious pride in the speed and efficiency with which new technological innovations could produce 'further processed' products – chicken slices for sandwiches, curries and casseroles.

'So little is wasted – and that includes time as well as the bird', he announced. 'Productivity is everything here.'

In the evening, Tom soaked long in the bath, trying to scrub away the stench and misery of it all. He kept thinking about Geoff the manager and what he had said. He had joined the company at seventeen and worked his way up to middle management. He worked long hours and wore a permanently harassed expression. He seemed a decent sort of bloke – in his mid thirties with a friendly, pleasant face and two kids at home who he hoped would do better at school than he had and maybe go to university. 'They're not thick like their Dad', he had said. He had assured Tom that he had little to do with the slaughter side of operations since his promotion, but that anyway there were stringent health and animal welfare standards enforced throughout the factory. Environmental health officers and vets were always on hand to check. Moreover, the company took its responsibilities seriously and was constantly striving for further improvements.

Geoff appeared to believe what he was saying. In a way this

made it worse, not being able to dismiss the bloke as some unfeeling sadist. The only conclusion that Tom could draw was that one of them must be mad, for theirs was so much more than just a difference of opinion. Seen through the campaigner's eyes, any attempt to apply the concept of animal welfare to processes so grotesque was a glaring distortion of what his eyes and ears had witnessed. It was not that the manager was being deliberately dishonest: it was rather that he seemed to inhabit a world of total fantasy and denial – a world that he shared with the vast majority of his fellow citizens. In almost every similar-sized town there was some equally barbaric enterprise where some species or other was being bred, tortured, degraded or butchered, invariably hidden well away from public gaze and always governed by the reassuring platitudes of 'strict controls' or 'high standards of welfare'.

The more he thought about it, the clearer it became. Perhaps there were worse things than killing factories for animals? In the great scheme of human evil, even he couldn't really compare it with some of the atrocities that people had suffered. Unlike human genocide, animal abuse was not based upon hatred or envy of the oppressed. He thought of his Chilean university friend, Miguel, and all that he and billions like him around the world had suffered and lost through the centuries. He thought of the merciless barbarism that Pol Pot's regime had inflicted upon the Cambodian people. And he thought of the Nazis, too. It was not that he believed that chickens were capable of the depths of terror and despair that human victims of tyranny must experience, but nonetheless the comparison would not go away. After all, a concentration camp was exactly what came to mind when he thought about Sunny Farm Chickens. It was something about the scale of the killing, its cold efficiency and utter indifference to the lives of the slaughtered. He knew, of course, that the world would scoff at such a comparison. It was dangerous to make, offensive to many. Yet he was not alone in thinking like this. He recalled what that Jewish novelist had said: for animals it was an 'eternal Treblinka'.* Sunny Farm Chickens might not be Auschwitz, but it remained something vile and unnecessary, as were all those other factory farms and vivisection laboratories where creatures were routinely despatched at the whim of their oppressors. Without them the world would be a better place. Trying to put an end to such misery might not be everyone's idea of an important cause, but it was his cause. It was what he did and what he knew about. It mattered to him. Was that what Tony Swallow had meant when he had suggested that you had to create a role in life that gave you some significance? Find a message that counted for you and go on repeating it, doggedly? Was that perhaps the best that any of us could hope for?

15

It was two months before the millennium and Tom was working late in the office. Partly, he had been trying to catch up with correspondence, but he was also enjoying one of those spasmodic bursts of enthusiasm for work that were nowadays far less common that they once had been. He felt energised in particular by events at the weekend in London, where Peter Tatchell and three colleagues had intercepted President Robert Mugabe's motorcade and attempted a citizen's arrest during the Zimbabwean president's shopping trip to London. Tatchell had run out into the road as the vehicles left the hotel, opened the door of Mugabe's limousine, grabbed him by the arm, accused his regime of 'murder, torture, detention without trial, and the abuse of gay human rights' and told the President that he was 'under arrest for torture'. The police were called, but rather than detaining Mugabe, they had assisted him in getting away

---

* Isaac Bashevis Singer in *The Letter Writer* from *The Séance and Other Stories*.

to continue his shopping and instead, violently arrested the four campaigners. Tatchell & co were held in custody for seven hours and were later charged with criminal damage, assault and breach of the peace. (Charges that were eventually dropped).

Over the years, Peter Tatchell had established himself as one of Tom's modern-day heroes, even if the high-profile campaigner's courage and indefatigable spirit left him with a growing sense of inadequacy. Threats, arrests, intimidation and physical violence – Tatchell had endured them all during numerous campaigns that stretched back over decades to initiatives against capital punishment and the Vietnam War and for land rights for Aborigines in his native Australia. How did he keep going in the face of such hostility? Anti-apartheid, gay rights, women's rights, peace and liberation for the Palestinians in the Middle East and for the Kurds in Iraq, racial equality, religious freedom, racial harmony and, more recently (and to Tom's delight), animal protection – he had stood up unflinchingly for these and so many other causes that Tom considered important. Oh well. It was no good wasting your time feeling unworthy by comparison. You just had to do your best, that's all. As his brother had said about Aunt Helen, the trouble was that there just weren't enough Peter Tatchells in the world. 'More's the pity', thought Tom. 'If there were, then there might also be fewer President Mugabes'.

He wasn't expecting the office phone to ring so late in the evening but answered instinctively rather than waiting for the ansaphone message to kick in.

'Is that Tom Moore?' asked the male voice, quietly.

'Speaking.'

'I think I've some information that might be very useful to you.'

'Can I ask what kind of information?'

'I'd rather not talk about it on the phone. Can we meet?'

'Well, I suppose so. But I'd like some idea of what it's about first?'

'It's about Brian Dalton. It could be very bad news for him.'

Tom's interest was aroused. Professor Dalton, the animal experimenter he most loathed and reviled! The man he had several times confronted on television and radio and had never managed to land a solid blow upon. Dalton, who was one of that group of scientists who always presented themselves as innocent victims of a vicious witch-hunt by extremists, when all they wanted to do was to dedicate their lives to curing killer diseases. Worse still, the last couple of years had seen the Professor achieve minor celebrity status as the presenter of a TV series that attempted to popularise science. *Science Made Simple* had addressed sophisticated issues such as gene mapping and the nature of pain. It had glorified the role played by animal researchers in medical advances. Tom would give anything to get back at him. It was personal.

It wasn't until the telephone conversation with Harry Murray – as the caller identified himself – was over, that Tom realised he'd been a bit hasty in agreeing to meet. It was the mention of Dalton that had led him to a rash decision. Nowadays he was normally a bit more wary. He'd had enough of this kind of thing before: supporters who had some pie-in-the-sky, top-secret idea that demanded cloak-and-dagger discussions. Last time some bright spark had had a brainwave that involved persuading the surviving Beatles to reform for a fundraising effort. Easy as that! More crazy still, some crackpot had told him to fly a plane over the centre of London and laser-beam a message that 'vivisection is evil' across Oxford Circus. No doubt Harry Murray had some similar hare-brained scheme. Tom's heart sank at the thought of having to go through with the meeting.

Despite the boost that Peter Tatchell's recent endeavours had provided, his enthusiasm for work remained fragile. These days it ebbed and flowed, as did the desire to do something fresh and exciting. Twice this year he had been introduced at talks as a 'veteran campaigner'. Christ, he knew he was getting on a bit, but there was no need to rub it in! The compliments he received no longer flattered him – or perhaps it was just that he no longer received enough of them.

Despite these periodic bouts of disenchantment, he soldiered on. Partly it was because he wasn't brave enough to do anything else, but he tried to attribute higher motives to his decision. All that knowledge and experience he had gained. Surely this was irreplaceable? These enthusiastic youngsters with their naïve certainty about the way forward: what did they really know about anything? It needed someone with his tried and tested judgement to guide the ship. If he sometimes demonstrated a lack of enthusiasm, it was down to frustration at lack of progress or the depressing state of the wider world. Only rarely did the thought occur to him that he was beginning to sound exactly as he had come to remember his father.

Harry Murray turned out to be nothing like Tom had imagined. He arrived for the evening meeting in the SAFE office in an expensive dark blue suit and carrying a combination lock briefcase. He was a large man with receding, black curly hair and a dome-shaped head. Tom reckoned he was probably only in his mid-thirties, though he looked older. He claimed to be working on behalf of university colleagues.

It soon emerged that he was not the predicted fantasist and did indeed possess genuinely damaging information about Brian Dalton. There were half a dozen photographs of the Professor with an attractive young woman about twenty years old. They seemed to have been taken at a formal party. She was wearing a long red evening dress and he a lounge suit. The most intimate showed him kissing the woman on the cheek – though the couple's expressions and body language hinted at greater intimacy.

'Are you trying to tell me he's having an affair with her?' asked

Tom.

'Yes, he is.'

'Who is she?'

'One of his students. Her name is Billie Slater. She's not the first.'

'Really?' exclaimed Tom. 'Randy old bugger! I never suspected him of having an eye for his female students.'

'Oh, he puts it around a bit, does Brian.'

Tom studied the photos carefully.

'I grant you they suggest a story that might cause him embarrassment', he eventually concluded. 'But I can't see that there's any real proof of any hanky-panky here.'

'I agree,' Murray replied. 'But there is when taken alongside these.'

The visitor handed over several photocopies of letters. They consisted of correspondence between Dalton and the student. Some left little to the imagination. 'That was a sizzler of a shag last night' began one missive from the Professor. Her letters were considerably less crude and expressed desperate unhappiness about his wife and family and that she could not see more of him. Tom laughed in amazement.

'Bloody hell! Are these genuine? Where did they come from?'

'Oh, they're genuine all right. And there's more. I'm not at liberty to tell you my source though. Suffice to say that it isn't only you animal rights people who would like to see Brian Dalton taken down a peg or two. Apart from several jilted ex-students, he's got plenty of enemies in the academic world as well. People think he's been a bit too ruthless in pursuing his ambition and there's a lot of bitterness over his television career. Academics don't like colleagues who become media personalities, particularly when they're seen to be dumbing down their subject. There's a lot of envy, of course. The irony is that this sort of indiscretion becomes so much more threatening to him now that he's something of a celebrity. I suspect one or two newspapers will be very interested.'

'So why are you offering this to me?'

'Because your organisation clearly has an interest in bringing Dalton some negative publicity and my colleagues don't want to be seen to be involved. There's nothing more to it than that. If you decide to use the material, there'll be no charge and the only condition is that you insist that it has been sent anonymously through the post – which it will be – and that you have no idea of the source.'

'Can I ask another question?'

'Go ahead.'

'Does his wife know?'

'Not as far as I know, though to be honest you'd think she must suspect something after all these years. Perhaps she chooses not to.'

The meeting ended with an agreement that Tom would take a week to discuss the matter with his associates before giving Murray a final answer. The campaigner felt mostly elated. 'This'll serve Bastard Brian right', was his predominant reaction. He could imagine the newspaper headline now – *The Extra-Curricular Activities of The Nookie Professor!* What a laugh! For sure he would have preferred revelations more specific to Dalton's research – some actual proof of cruelty or negligence in the laboratory – but in the absence of any of that, this would have to do. At least the scientist would be getting what he deserved.

He couldn't sleep for excitement. Yet as the waking hours dragged on, a few doubts started to seep in. What if it were some kind of set-up? He'd better check carefully. And even if it wasn't, he began to wonder whether there might be something a bit sordid about exposing this loathsome man to the almost equally loathsome tabloid press? What about the pain it would cause to his wife and children? Weren't they as much innocent victims as the cats and mice he was so keen to protect? He weighed it all up and concluded that public exposure would, after all, be the correct course of action. Nevertheless, just to put his mind at ease, he would discuss it with a few trusted confidants before reaching a final decision.

The first person he chose was Reverend Tony Swallow. They had kept in touch quite regularly since their meeting more than four years ago and there was nobody whose opinion he valued more deeply. The certainty of the vicar's response surprised him.

'I'd be very careful if I were you, Tom. In fact, I don't think you should touch it with a barge-pole.'

'Why on earth not?'

'Well, I'm sorry to quote the Good Book at a non-believer like you, but Christ's "let he that is without sin amongst you cast the first stone" comes firmly to mind. Remember when you first came round to the vicarage and you were so unhappy about breaking up with Wendy? You admitted to me that you'd had an affair and that it caused a lot of unhappiness when she found out. Would you wish to inflict the same pain upon others?'

'But this is different.'

'How do you reach that conclusion?' Swallow replied, plainly irritated by his friend's attitude.

'For a start, we're talking about a man who has spent years claiming that a few nutcases who threatened him and sent poisonous letters through the post have scarred his family life. He's used their supposed suffering ruthlessly to divert attention from the misery he causes to animals. Yet it turns out that he is perfectly prepared to cheat on his wife and children – quite regularly, so I'm informed. He's a hypocrite as well as an animal abuser.'

'I see your argument Tom, but I'm afraid I don't agree with it at all. Even if we accept a degree of hypocrisy in Dalton's behaviour, overall I don't see too much relation between his private affairs and his work. I mean, if his private life were completely beyond criticism would it make any difference whatsoever to his abilities as a scientist? Or make his treatment of those poor creatures any more or less justified? Personally, I don't think so. I think we confuse the public and the private too readily.'

'Yes, but the point is that Dalton's so-called public life is a secret. Finding out exactly what he actually gets up to in the laboratory has proved impossible. He's slimy and evasive. Here's the first chance we have to get some sort of justice.'

'Would it really be justice? He's broken no laws. He's only following the path that society teaches researchers to take. Should you really be that personal? Ruining his life is hardly going to save any animals or advance the case against vivisection, is it?'

'Well, actually I think it might. For a start, he'll be so busy dealing with all the flack – family troubles and probably disciplinary action at work – that he's not likely to find much time for his research. And it also helps us to create a public perception of these people as fundamentally dishonest. George Bernard Shaw said that "he who dares to vivisect will not hesitate to lie about it". This kind of backs that up.'

The fact that Tony Swallow didn't answer immediately made Tom feel that he was winning the argument. Instead, the vicar switched tack.

'Look, you know I agree that these experiments are a moral crime, even if they're not illegal. I'd like to see them banned nearly as much as you would. Neither am I here to defend Dalton for cheating on his wife. After all, I'm a vicar! I believe in the sanctity of marriage. Yet I still don't see it as a valid reason to create all that misery – not only for him, but for his wife and children as well. What have they done to deserve having their names dragged through the mud? And what about this student and her family? Why should they be put through all that? Two wrongs don't make a right, Tom. The end doesn't always justify the means.'

'Don't you think his wife and children deserve to know? They've been lied to and cheated on.'

'Yes, maybe they do. But I don't think it's your business to tell them. And it certainly isn't the job of the gutter press to turn it into an exhibition for public titillation.'

Shortly afterwards, the conversation closed. Although they ended on polite terms, they could sense each other's annoyance. Forthright condemnation was not what Tom had been hoping for or expecting. As for the Reverend Swallow, he was disappointed with what he considered his friend's lack of imaginative sympathy.

The following afternoon Tom decided it was time to discuss the Dalton business with some of his campaign team. There was a bright and dynamic young man named Dan, who had joined SAFE straight from university and was fast becoming one of its most valuable members of staff, plus a dedicated, quiet and unassuming woman of similar age named Katy. She had been active in a local group before getting her job. Tom outlined the story, carefully avoiding certain details in case he decided not to go ahead. It was Dan who reacted first.

'Bloody brilliant! That'll teach the little shit.'

'You don't think there's anything a bit dubious about putting him through all that for something that has nothing to do with his work?' asked Tom, opting to play devil's advocate.

'You're joking, aren't you? Whatever pain he suffers is nothing compared to what he's inflicted on animals. He deserves everything he gets and more.'

'OK, let's accept for a moment that he does. What about his family? Do they deserve everything they get? Aren't they innocent victims as well?' He was beginning to sound just like Tony Swallow!

'They shouldn't have anything to do with him. They know what he does for a living.'

Tom found this a bit extreme.

'Hold on, Dan. Even if you blame his wife by association – which, if you ask me is a bit harsh – you can hardly blame his children as well. They didn't have a lot of say in choosing their father, did they? Next you'll be blaming the family dog for living with him!'

'All right – point taken. So maybe it isn't entirely their fault. I can't see that that's any reason to protect them though. Perhaps they'll come to their senses and get rid of the bastard. I mean if he were a rapist you wouldn't say that it should be kept secret because it might affect his family life, would you? Well, what he does to animals is just as bad as far as I'm concerned, so I can't see any reason not to expose him.'

'Just a minute', said Tom. 'Let's think this through. Whether you like it or not there is a difference between a rapist and Dalton. One's breaking the law and the other isn't. While we might find what he does vile and unnecessary, that's not the view of the world we live in. It's impossible for a rapist to think he's doing something acceptable – unless he's completely mad – but it's quite feasible that Dalton actually believes his work is for the greater good of humanity.'

'You know that's bullshit, Tom. You're the one who's published details of those experiments. What sort of bastard burns the feet of mice or severs the tongues of cats? And what good is that supposed to be to people? I'm sorry Tom, but we're not here to show sympathy to fuckheads like that – if you'll excuse my language.'

Tom smiled at his youthful colleague's conviction and certainty.

'I think I've got a fair idea of your opinion then, Dan! What about you Katy? You're very quiet. What do you think?'

'On the whole, I think I agree with Dan', she answered hesitantly.

'I do feel a bit sorry for his wife and children, but I also feel for the students he abused – as well as the animals of course. He's used his position to take advantage of what were probably impressionable and vulnerable young women. He's treated them as callously as he treats those animals, so I don't see why he shouldn't pay for it.'

'Mmm, thanks for that, Katy. It's interesting to have a feminist perspective, though I don't know how we can be certain that the students were vulnerable and abused.' He never could quite shake off a last vestige of superiority when it came to this feminist business.

'So what are you going to do?' interrupted Dan, aggressively.

'I'm going to think about it for a while. Meanwhile thank you both for your input and it goes without saying that this remains top secret.'

'I really don't believe this,' fumed Dan as he walked away. 'I still can't see what there is to think about. Nail the bastard, that's what I say.'

Tom rang Harry Murray a couple of days later with his decision. As soon as he received all the information in the post he would telephone newspaper contacts and try to interest them in an exclusive exposé of the television scientist. All went more or less to plan. Photographs and copies of letters arrived in his office and the third newspaper he contacted – a New Labour sympathising, medium-selling tabloid – was keen on the story. There were three or four meetings with journalists, checking the details. He was then assured that the editor wanted 'to go big with this one'. Tom, for his part, urged the reporter to include information on Brian Dalton's abuse of animals – that was the key issue.

On the evening before the day of publication, he felt the same kind of adrenalin rush he had once regularly experienced about campaigns. He could hardly wait to read the article. Surprisingly he slept deeply, so much so that he was late rising the next morning. He dressed hurriedly and rushed out to the newsagent, opening up the paper and scanning the pages almost before he was out of the door. His initial reaction was one of disappointment. The front page was given over to a different scandal concerning four Premiership footballers who had indulged in a group sex orgy with two models. Several inside pages were also taken up with the lurid detail. This was followed by another 'exclusive' on a married Tory MP who had been caught by a sting operation, offering to pay a reporter posing as a rent boy for gay sex. The middle four pages offered an unexpected break from sexual matters, featuring instead a thinly disguised plug for the government's Millennium Dome project and offering readers a chance to win free tickets when the delayed exhibition eventually opened. The Dome was described as 'the world's greatest exploration of who we are and where we are going' and the report went on to lavish praise on the promised array of clever gadgets and technology. This irritated Tom immensely. For him the initiative was a waste of valuable public funds and he was equally disapproving of a list of sponsors that included arms manufacturers, burger barons, car manufacturers and others from the world of corporate business. It was nothing more than a testament to the hubris of a Prime Minister already too concerned with leaving behind some tangible legacy. 'God help us if that's who we are and where we're going', he muttered to himself.

He eventually reached the Dalton exposé he had been looking for on page 23. It was shorter than he had hoped and read as follows:

BONKING BOFFIN!

Lecherous lecturer's love-nest lab

TV brainbox Brian Dalton, 45, had steamy sessions with at least THREE sexy science students, it was revealed last night. The randy researcher – presenter of BBC's Science Made Simple series – boasted in letters of his hot hanky-panky behind the Bunsen burners with brunette beauty Billie Slater, 19.

Father of two Dalton has been the target of animal rights extremists and has even endured death threats for his experiments on pain in cats and mice. But it is his life as a love rat rather than his work with lab rats that seems set to threaten the perky professor's twenty-four year marriage. Friends say that his wife Christine is 'very upset and angry' and that she and the couple's teenage children are staying with her family in Sussex. Dalton could also face action from university authorities over his torrid tutorials with busty Billie and two other students.

'This gives a new meaning to the concept of scientific exploration', said a close colleague last night.

There was no sign of Dalton at his Cambridgeshire home yesterday. Billie Slater was also unavailable for comment and was thought to be staying with her parents at their home near Worcester.

Despite the initial exhilaration of seeing the story in print, Tom felt a further tinge of unease at the nature of the revelations and the pain he knew they would cause. The lack of any meaningful reference to Dalton's work also frustrated him. But as the day wore on and word spread about the source of the article, a number of fellow workers and supporters telephoned to say how good it was to see the researcher get his come-uppance. This made him feel better. He had done the right thing after all.

In the evening, he got a call from ex-partner Wendy. She had heard through a friend and demanded to know whether he had had anything to do with the Dalton story. When he owned up, she reacted angrily, shouting down the phone that he was 'a disgusting fucking hypocrite' before slamming down the receiver.

Part 4 – The hour that the ship comes in

16

He was staying on his own in his brother's weekend cottage in Devon, spending a few days walking along the coast. It was February 2005, the week before the ban on hunting was due to be enforced. Down in the heart of hunting country, the local media was treating the ban almost as if it were as life-threatening as the invasion of Iraq or the tsunami. All sorts of local folk were enjoying their moment of fame in the media spotlight, gravely pronouncing on the imminent disaster for country dwellers. 'To expect hounds to chase a sock is enough to reduce a grown man to tears', the wife of one hunt master had solemnly and eccentrically declared, clearly less than enthralled at the prospect of drag hunting only. One woman, crying in front of the cameras, claimed she'd never be able to see her friends again, while another protested that she was being deprived of 'quality time' with her children. Blacksmiths, pub owners, hunt staff and clothing manufacturers – all appeared with tragic stories of how they would be condemned to the dole queue once hunting was outlawed.

'I can't believe some of the news reporting down here', Tom said to Tony Swallow when he visited his old friend one morning. 'They even ran a news item claiming a hunting ban could be devastating news for the South-West's doily industry! I kid you not. Apparently, no more hunting means no more hunt scenes and eventually no more doilies!'

'Good gracious – the Bishop's wife will be devastated!' roared the Reverend. 'Is nothing sacred to you "antis"? I must say I'm not too surprised though, Tom. I'm afraid that with a few notable exceptions, our local media tends not to be too incisive when it comes to anything controversial like hunting. They don't want to rock the boat. Too many local bigwigs involved in it all.'

'I'm sure that's true, Tony. But it's hardly an excuse for letting these people spout all this garbage about job losses without pointing out that the idea is to stop animals being killed, not to prevent people dressing up in silly clothes, keeping packs of dogs or chasing a scent. And don't you just love the idea that pubs are going to be put out of business, as if everyone is going to give up drinking because the hunt can no longer slaughter wildlife?'

'Ridiculous it may be, Tom. But I'm afraid that hunting is a real obsession for those involved in it, particularly down here. Some people have a passion for all kinds of good causes; this lot have a passion for chasing animals across the countryside. It's sad but it's true. I've got some otherwise quite reasonable parishioners who consider the ban to be the most vicious assault on human rights that Britain has ever seen.'

'Well they should bloody well get a life', answered Tom, feeling not an iota of sympathy.

17

Thursday 24 February 2005
18 Salisbury Road
Plymouth
Devon
PL8 4WJ

Dear Tom,
Long time no see. I hope you still remember me! The last few days have made me think lots about my old animal rights and hunt

saboteur colleagues (not that you were much use as a sab!), so I thought I would drop you a line. Remember how we always used to say we'd celebrate with a big party and a bottle of champagne when hunting was banned? Well, the day has finally arrived and yet I didn't feel like cracking open the bottle at all. Of course, I do think that the ban is fantastic news – the trouble is that you know these fanatics aren't finished. They'll do anything to carry on hunting. They think it's their 'right'.

I returned to England from India almost six months ago and have been along to a few of the local anti-hunt group meetings. First time I've been involved in any animal campaigning for ages. A group of us arranged to go to one of the big hunt meets on Dartmoor last Saturday, on the first day that the ban came into force. You should have been there, Tom. It was a hoot! There were microphones and television cameras everywhere, not to mention hundreds of hunters. I've never seen so many plush off-road vehicles or horseboxes. It was all a bit scary really. Fortunately, there were far too many police and media about for there to be any trouble. Besides, the hunting folk were too caught up in the momentousness of the moment to worry too much about us lot. Union Jacks were flying at half-mast and some of the crowd were close to tears, poor things! I was stood fairly close to one of those public school types – you know, those men with booming voices that suggest every word they utter must be completely fascinating to the rest of civilisation. Before the rally, he was going on about some 'first class' and 'challenging' grouse shooting on the Yorkshire moors, but by the end he was quite subdued. 'I'm not normally an emotional sort', I heard him say, 'but I must confess I felt myself welling up a couple of times back there'. This was in response to a couple of speeches claiming that this country would defeat the hunt ban in the same way that it had overcome the Norman conquest, Hitler and BSE! Apparently, they see themselves as defenders of British democracy in the tradition of

Oliver Cromwell! Talk about delusions of grandeur, eh?

God, what a weird bunch they are! It's such an unholy alliance, Tom: The rich and privileged united with the rural underclass in a fanatical love of killing wildlife. I bet they inwardly despise one another.

You're probably wondering what I'm doing in Plymouth? Well, I went out to teach in India three years ago, soon after my divorce went through. I taught at the International School in Delhi, which was really for ex-pats and the locally well-off. But I did do a bit with the anti-globalisation movement out there – partly because people like me can't live happily without getting involved in some form of campaigning and partly out of guilt, I suppose, because I was teaching children from families who have benefited fantastically from the opening up of the free market. New technologies and multinational companies have created a lot of wealth and millionaires out in India, but there's been a hell of a price to pay among the poor. Men, women and children all work horribly long hours in what are known as 'export processing zones' – basically sweatshops – and are paid peanuts. Small farmers have also suffered, forced to abandon their traditional methods and industrialise. It's all taking place in the name of free trade and it's all supposed to be about choice, though actually it's always those with money, power and technology that make the rules, set the agenda and take the profits. It seems to me that whenever you hear about globalisation creating greater wealth and opportunity, you can also be pretty sure that there'll be plenty at the bottom of the heap left worse off and with no choice whatsoever. I reckon somebody ought to start a campaign against choice!

I came back in the summer and have taken a temporary job at a comprehensive here, covering for a woman on maternity leave. It's far harder work than teaching in India, I can tell you! My contract lasts until the end of the summer term and I'm not sure what I'm going to do after that. I might go back or maybe

I'll take a permanent teaching job over here. India was a great experience for the kids, but I think Debbie, my youngest, needs a more settled life now. She is fifteen and though she's great at making new friends, I think she'd like to stay at the same school until she finishes. Emma is going to take time out before going off to university.

What about you Tom? I hope this finds you. I know you were still with SAFE a few months ago and I'm just presuming you're still there. I don't know how you've kept going all this time. I always had you down for going off and becoming a boring academic somewhere, long ago.

Guess what? I saw an old clip of you on telly a few Saturday nights ago. It was on a programme called *TV's Naughtiest Nightmares from Hell.* There was a studio audience and somebody got angry and attacked the bloke sitting next to you. It looked like that Dave Howard, who always used to be a spokesman for the militants. You should have seen the shocked look on your face when the two of them were scrapping on the floor! You must remember it?

It would be good to meet up some time. Hope you are well and happy.
Love
Marie x

Tom felt elated to receive the letter. He read quickly through, more immediately interested in the single kiss at the end than the content. What was its significance? Obviously, it was a sign of affection, but did it mean anything more? Three or four kisses would certainly indicate romantic interest; no kisses and he wouldn't even have had reason to think about it. Why had Marie mentioned her divorce? Was she sending a message that she was free and single? Aah, Marie… how he had adored her! And to think she had been in the Westcountry at the same time as he had been there on his walking holiday. If only he'd known!

He brought himself up sharp. How ridiculous he was being! When would he ever grow up? Fancy reaching almost fifty years of age and still dreaming like a teenager, desperately searching for signs of amorous intent and analysing every word and gesture from the object of his affection! Did it never go away, this Old Adam?

18

It was Marie's idea to meet for lunch halfway, in a smallish Wiltshire market town accessible to them both by train. A teaching colleague had told her about a 'marvellous' restaurant, much praised in newspaper food reviews, where she was sure they would cook something special for vegans. So it was that they found themselves greeting one another for the first time in getting on for twenty years in the surroundings of the award-winning *Bogart's Bistro*. It consisted of a long, thin room with roughly fifteen heavy oak tables of different sizes, tastefully stripped wooden floors and a decorative Victorian fireplace. The mauve and white walls were adorned with several large framed reproductions of 1940s movie posters. It felt a little bit too fashionable for his liking, but he didn't complain because he thought that Marie's taste might well have changed over the years.

It was nearly two o'clock by the time they arrived and only two other tables were still occupied. They had hardly had chance to exchange a few words when the waitress – an elegantly dressed, slim young woman with short curly blonde hair – approached with two menus so detailed that they looked more like monthly magazines. Rose – as she introduced herself – was the partner of 'Chef' and had a friendly yet authoritative manner, marred only by a slight hint of superciliousness.

'No problem at all', she responded reassuringly when they explained that the restaurant had been recommended and that they were both vegans.

As soon as she ran through the list of starters, however, it emerged that there might well be a problem after all. The carpaccio of beef in truffle oil and the aromatic sausage in tomato jus were clearly out of bounds, but the waitress expressed surprise when the crab bisque and sautéed squid were also rejected.

'Oh, I didn't realise that you weren't allowed to eat seafood either', she announced, slightly disdainfully they thought.

'We are allowed to eat it, but we choose not to,' corrected Marie, firmly.

They decided the best bet was to move straight on to the main course.

'Might I suggest the sesame filo pastry parcels?'

Rose was soon in full swing, describing the pastry ingredients and cooking method in pedantic detail. Tom felt a great sense of relief when she had finished.

'To accompany, how about our special potatoes cooked in hay and infused with Chef's homemade ketchup?' Rose continued.

'Hay!' exclaimed Marie in surprise, realising as soon as she had done so that she might have made the near-fatal mistake of inviting further explanation.

'Yes,' responded Rose, smiling proudly. 'You can read about them in the menu. It's based on a Heston Blumenthal recipe. Why don't I leave you a moment to take a look?'

They dutifully obeyed. It appeared that the potato dish demanded a torturously slow cooking process that included singeing the hay with a blowtorch and then heating and freezing chipped potatoes repeatedly to ensure a perfect golden brown finish. At the end of the process, they were injected by syringe with a choice of either Chef's organic ketchup or an equally exquisite house Gentleman's Relish.

The relish proved too much for Tom. He was already struggling to keep a straight face and was now forced to pretend he had a coughing fit in order to suppress a bout of giggles. Marie was aware of his discomfort and feeling mischievous.

'Is the hay organic?' she asked when Rose returned to take their order.

Tom shook with laughter, covering his face to hide his embarrassment. The other customers stared across as he emitted an involuntary snort. Rose pretended not to notice. The irony of Marie's question was lost on her.

'Yes, of course. It's obtained from a local Soil Association approved farm.'

With great difficulty, Tom managed to hold himself together. He hastily agreed to Rose's selection of salads – watercress and shredded beetroot in ginger and lime dressing for Marie and rocket and pine nut in pomegranate vinaigrette for him – to accompany the pastry parcels and potatoes cooked in hay.

When she had gone, he eventually managed to calm down, his eyes aching from tears of laughter.

'Tom!' exclaimed Marie in mock disgust.

'Sorry, I'm not really used to this sort of thing.'

'Do you think I am?'

'Well, to be honest, yes, I thought that you might be. It was you who suggested this place.'

'Good God, no. Sorry, I had no idea that the woman who told me about it is a bit of a pretentious food snob. She's obviously got more money than sense as well. Did you notice the prices?'

'It's hardly surprising, is it? Not when you consider the labour costs. It took us about three hours to read how to make the chips and tomato sauce – sorry, I mean the Gentleman's Relish infused potatoes – let alone to prepare and cook them. We could be here forever.'

They came to an agreement not to order any wine, mainly so that they could avoid Rose talking them through the list. It proved a wise decision. Even ordering two glasses of water required what seemed like an inquisition. Still or sparkling? Chilled or semi-chilled? With or without ice? Garnished with slices of organic kiwi or sharon fruit?

'God, out in parts of India there are people who have literally nothing, Tom', Marie began as soon as Rose was safely out of sight again. 'They have to walk miles to collect any water, let alone have fifteen choices of how to drink it. I can't help finding this obsession with choice a bit distasteful. Everybody over here seems to think that choice is the same thing as freedom, which it's not. Fifty types of water, fifty brands of margarine, fifty flavours of crisps – what good is it to anybody? And it's not just the trivial things either. Parents want the right to choose their kids' school, the government wants us to have the choice of which hospital we go to, people who can't conceive want the right to choose free fertility treatment. Infinite choice is viewed as some God-given right. Yet I sometimes think that the more of it we have, the more we seem to want. Why can't we just accept how incredibly wealthy and privileged most of us are and be satisfied?'

'You've obviously given this choice question a great deal of thought, Marie. I remember you mentioned it in the letter you sent me after the hunt ban. I think I see what you're getting at, but I'm not sure how far I really agree though. Surely people have to struggle for greater opportunities? Otherwise, things just stay the way they have always been and it's only the rich that enjoy all the privileges. I think it's a good thing that people fight to improve their lot and to get their slice of the cake.'

'No, no, you've misunderstood me completely. What you're talking about are communal values. Of course I agree with equal choice and better opportunities for all. Yet why do we have to have the right as individuals to choose any school for our kids? Or to perpetuate our own genes when we can't have children naturally? At the very least, I don't see why the state should pay for it all. Surely, the socially responsible answer is to make sure that the local school is good enough for everybody and that all the orphans in the world have a home. It's all of this hankering after what everybody else has got that annoys me – if the bloke down the road has a big car, then I've got the right to have one too. It creates a kind of frenzy of envy.'

The conversation was cut short by the reappearance of Rose with their meal. As a man who valued quantity as much as quality, Tom's first reaction was one of disappointment at what he considered meagre portions. There were two small 'parcels', a handful of chips and about ten rocket leaves with half a dozen nuts, covered in a teaspoonful of dressing. While he had to admit that it tasted pretty good, he still felt cheated.

'What do you think?' asked Marie.

'Well it's quite nice for a glorified pasty with an unusual filling, plus a few chips with too much ketchup and not enough vinegar for my liking. Oh sorry, I nearly forgot to mention the few lettuce leaves. Don't eat them all at once!'

'It's nouvelle cuisine – I think it's meant to be minimalist.'

'Minimalist? I call it a tight-fisted load of old bollocks.'

'Oh well' sighed Marie, 'it's an experience if nothing else.'

Left in peace again, they took each other through the last twenty years of their lives. For Marie it had been marriage, divorce, bringing up two children, teaching, a couple of years working for an NGO on debt cancellation in the lead-up to the Jubilee 2000 initiative and voluntary work, mostly for peace and environmental campaigns. Tom was surprised how little she had had to do with animal issues.

'You used to be so passionate about it'.

'Oh, I still am, otherwise I wouldn't have got involved in the hunting campaign again. Besides, once you're aware of the horror, there can be no going back. You can never lose that. But I couldn't stand any more of "the movement".'

'What do you mean, "the movement"?' he replied, imitating

her inverted comma hand gesture.

'Well, the self-righteousness for one thing. When I was young and completely immersed in it all, I also used to believe we were the chosen people, full of special compassion and sensitivity in an uncaring world. But I suppose having children changed all that for me. I met other mothers at playgroups and nurseries who had no interest in the things that I cared passionately about and I started to realise that some of them are just as good as the people on "my side". And I also began to see that we had things in common that I hadn't appreciated. Above all, most wanted the best for their children and some were prepared to make fairly heroic sacrifices to get it. I think that was the thing that struck me most deeply and it sort of changed my perspective a bit.'

'In what way?'

'Well, I stopped seeing the world as "them and us" for a start. I didn't want to be part of any group that thought it was intrinsically better than another. Ever since, I've always kept on the fringes of the campaigns I've been involved with, because I've found that they're all a bit prone to the same faults really.'

'So did you bring your children up as veggies?'

'Oh, don't be so ridiculous, Tom. Of course I did. But I think I know where you're coming from and yes, in some ways I admit that I did find it difficult to strike a balance between my own strongly held beliefs and those of the world outside. I wanted the girls to mix well and have a normal social life, while another part of me just wanted them to dare to be different. It's so fucking horrible out there that in some ways I wanted to protect them from it all.'

'You wanted them to have choice then?' asked Tom, a little triumphantly. He thought she was all over the place with this choice business. Could you really equate parents wanting to conceive their own children with the products on supermarket shelves?

'No. I wanted them to be open-minded', she replied, annoyed by his male insistence on trying to have the last word. 'It was inevitable that I would be influencing them with what really mattered to me, but ultimately I wanted them to make up their own minds. I'd seen too many parents who think of themselves as 'alternative', drumming their minority views into kids when they're too young, like a religion. I was determined to avoid that.'

'And do you think you succeeded?'

'Mostly, I hope – though you know what they say about parents.'

'What's that?'

'"All parents are the wrong parents" – have you not heard that before? Emma and Debs seem fairly balanced and caring though. I'm pretty proud of them.'

Marie had not got much further when the predatory Rose reappeared to collect the empty plates.

'Let me tell you about the desserts', she began, her tone inferring that she was inviting them into a realm of culinary bliss that only the insane could refuse.

'We've got this fantastic summer pudding. Chef uses a lovely cinnamon bread and he moistens it in buffalo milk. It offsets the tartness of the cranberries and bilberries beautifully.'

'We don't drink buffalo's milk', interrupted Marie, increasingly irritated.

It turned out that the only dish suitable was peaches poached in Cointreau. Tom didn't much fancy this and certainly didn't want to pay the ridiculously inflated price. At the same time he didn't want to cut short his conversation with Marie. So while Chef went to work on the peaches, they got back to talking. Marie turned again to her disillusionment with the cause that had dominated her youth.

'Maybe it was just that I was young and naïve, but in my day it all seemed much more innocent and peaceful. As the years went by, more and more people were ready to justify violence. It all just started to get a bit nasty.'

'I don't know whether that's true, Marie. People always tend to look back to when they were young and imagine things were much better. Were they really that different though? Your lot used to terrify me when they'd smash up that factory farming equipment.'

'I know what you're saying, but it **was** different. We were idealists. We were like the eco-warriors nowadays, destroying fields of GM crops. People were on our side. It wasn't until a few years later that the animal cause started to attract a bunch of people who wanted to be pseudo-terrorists.'

'Oh, come off it, Marie. The idea that the animal rights movement is nearly as dangerous as the IRA was mostly a media invention, wasn't it? It was hardly terrorism.'

'It might have been hyped up by the media – I don't dispute that. Nevertheless there were some nasty things done, one or two nasty people doing them and a lot of others who should know better willing to defend them. And there still are.'

The conversation was interrupted again by the emergence from the kitchen of Rose and the poached peaches. It was immediately clear that as a means of extending the conversation, the dessert was likely to prove a dismal failure. Each small plate consisted of half a peach covered in a little liquid and artistically surrounded by half a strawberry and a slice of kiwi fruit.

'Enjoy!' commanded the waitress.

They both took tiny bites to make it last longer.

'It seems to me that nothing has changed that much', Tom resumed. 'Twenty years ago the Animal Liberation Army was supposed to be like the IRA and now it's presented as the biggest terrorist threat after Al'Qaeda. In those days it was mostly Dave Howard who made the wild claims and now it's a few other loudmouths who fuel the media by making outrageous statements. The newspapers lap it up and before you know it, the world is apparently faced with a "terror threat" to rival suicide bombers. Yet if you include the attacks on hunt sabs, there's actually far more violence committed against protesters than by them. To this day, nobody has been seriously hurt by the so-called terrorists, while anti-hunt campaigners end up in hospital every other week – as you once did yourself.'

'That's not the point, Tom – true as it may be. Like I said before, there are still some pretty indefensible things being done – hurling bricks through people's windows, threatening and intimidating people and their families. It's horrible and I don't want to have anything to do with it. All that hatred: all that characterising anybody who disagrees with you as 'scum'. It's fascism and I find it offensive.'

'This is a real turn-up for the books! I never thought the day would come when I'd be defending the ALA against you, Marie, and it's not that I wholly disagree. It's just the lack of perspective that annoys me. Threats and intimidation are pretty despicable – but they're the kind of thing that happens on hundreds of dump housing estates every weekend, as is arson for that matter. As for actual physical violence, there's been nothing to touch the sort of thing you see in city centres every drunken Saturday night. None of it's exactly the equivalent of hijacking planes and flying them into the Twin Towers, is it?'

'No, I'll grant you that.'

By this time their plates were empty again. Rose returned, catching the talk of terrorism and looking slightly perturbed. She quickly regained her composure and presented further possibilities for extending the meal.

'Can I offer you guys coffee? We've Americano, mocha, cappuccino, latte or …'

'Two black please', interrupted Marie, deliberately taking a stand against choice and sophistication.

'Two Americano. Certainly.'

They were then faced with a further choice: a strong, full-bodied fairtrade Columbian; a mellower and fruitier organic Italian; or the Brazilian house blend with 'full and nutty flavour'. Predictably, they both went for the fairtrade.

'What about a topping with that?' enquired Rose. 'We've spicy ginger, mint, chocolate or cinnamon.'

'Look,' continued Marie after they had refused the waitress's latest offer, 'I'm no different to anyone else. When I see what they do to animals, I immediately feel full of anger and loathing for those who do it. Somehow though, you have to separate hatred of the act from personal abuse. You have to rise above the idea that you can justify threatening and harassing those who don't share your views. After all, most of the cruelty is sanctioned by the world we live in.'

'I agree with you entirely – in theory at least. In practice, what worries me is that when you look at any campaigns for social progress, success is hardly ever achieved by lawful and peaceful methods alone, is it? Name me one! I do sometimes wonder whether the nastiness is unavoidable.'

'A necessary evil, you mean? I don't buy that, Tom. Apart from anything else, targeting individuals and their families shows a terrible lack of empathy and imagination.'

Tom thought about Brian Dalton and shuffled uncomfortably.

'Well, maybe the problem is that people with too much imagination and empathy can never take decisive action? They're too worried about examining all the consequences of everything they do. Perhaps there are times when it does take a single-minded, blind fury to change things? "The best lack all conviction/ The worst are full of passionate intensity" and all that.'

'Still full of literary quotes, eh Tom? Whose is that one?'

'W.B. Yeats – the Irish poet. He was writing about the Irish nationalists, nearly 100 years ago'.'

'Yes all right, I know who he is and what he was writing about, thank you very much. Well, let me tell you that I disagree heartily with both W. B. Yeats and Tom Moore on that point. I have to believe that you can fight tooth and nail for change and still set an example by being peaceful and caring.'

'That's exactly what I used to say to you all those years ago, Marie', he replied, a little bit boastfully. 'Yet even if you're right about some of the militant brigade, I do think it's really important not to condemn the whole movement just because there are a few extremists out there. I've also met some wonderful people who, quite frankly, I do think are better than almost everybody else I've come across. Just because the press isn't interested in them, it doesn't mean that you need to forget their existence.'

'That's fair enough, Tom. But I think you should also recognise that there are members of the so-called enemy who, if you got to know them well, may turn out to be every bit as caring in other ways. Even if I don't like what they do, it doesn't necessarily make me a better person.'

'Well what about your letter? You were hardly very complimentary about the hunt followers, were you? Are you now claiming that apart from the love of killing wildlife, deep down there are wonderful and compassionate human beings just waiting to get out?'

She hesitated.

'Well, actually I do think it's quite feasible that some of them may be good people in some areas of their life, yes. I grant you it's pretty hard to imagine though!' she added, giggling.

'Mmm. Quite frankly, I think you can go too far with this liberal "everybody's good really" argument. What about the Hitlers and Pinochets of this world?'

'That's not fair, Tom. We're talking about ordinary people living in a democracy, not fascist dictators.'

'All right, well what about arms dealers and people traffickers then?'

'Mmm – you've found a couple of pretty good examples there, I must admit! But look, all I'm really trying to say is that the majority of us are neither all good nor all bad and it's important to recognise that fact.'

'As always, I sort of agree with you, Marie. Except that I can't help but feel that some ideas and values are just intrinsically more worthy than others. It must always be better to be kind than cruel. And whatever you say about the dangers of belonging to any particular campaign, you have to do what you can to make sure that kindness wins out as much as is possible. I can't see how you can achieve that without people getting together to protest against injustice.'

'OK, those sure are mighty fine sentiments, Tom', she quipped. 'I'll certainly drink a toast to that little speech – at least I would do if I hadn't finished my coffee!'

They had to go. The time had flown by and they had been so busy discussing their shared interests and putting the world to rights that they had hardly scratched the surface when it came to catching up on their personal lives.

Tom offered to pay the bill, gritting his teeth to avoid showing how much the high prices hurt. He wasn't sorry that she insisted on paying half and didn't argue too convincingly against it. They both agreed that they had enjoyed their reunion and that it would be good to get together again before too long. Marie would get in touch when she finally decided where her future lay.

19

July 7, 2005. Like most of the nation, Rob and Tom Moore were glued to the early evening television news. Britain's first suicide bombers had struck in London and the extended coverage was trying to communicate the day's momentous events in as much detail as a popular broadcast would allow. They'd shown the shattered tube trains and bus, the blood-spattered injured and the distraught friends and relatives of those who were missing. They'd interviewed witnesses and told stories of heroic rescue efforts by fire crews, underground staff and passers-by. They'd speculated on who might be responsible for the atrocities. Then the Prime Minister appeared, having flown down to London from a much-publicised meeting of the G8 world leaders in Scotland. Before the bombings, the summit had been the headline story of the week, following on as it did from the previous weekend's massive *Live 8* music concert and other large-scale protests in support of the *Make Poverty History* campaign. Could the apparently sympathetic Tony Blair persuade President Bush to put US dollars behind the initiative to end world hunger? That had been the burning news issue. To date there had been no public response from the American President, whose most newsworthy contribution to the summit had been to fall off his bicycle after crashing into a security guard. While Bush was unhurt, the victim had apparently been taken off to hospital.

But now Blair had other concerns. Wearing his most solemn and statesmanlike expression, he exuded defiance. Terrorism could never defeat the spirit of the British people, he asserted. The heroic qualities that had shone through that day's tragic events would prevail.

Until this point the brothers had watched the news broadcast in grim silence, but the appearance of the Prime Minister proved too much for Rob.

'God, that man's a fucking arsehole!' he exclaimed.

Such vehemence surprised Tom. As the years passed by, he had come to expect more measured responses from his materially successful big brother.

'"The spirit of the British people" – what rubbish!' Rob continued. 'Does he really think that people behave any differently when a bomb goes off in Madrid or Palestine? A crisis like that brings out the best in some people – that's just a universal human truth. It's nothing to do with being British.'

'Yes, and I notice he's not so keen to talk about his own role in the bombings', added Tom. 'We all know this wouldn't have happened if it hadn't been for the invasion of Iraq.'

Disregarding his own foul-mouthed outburst, Rob felt duty bound to temper what he considered his younger brother's rash and extreme statement.

'You can't say it wouldn't have happened, Tom, and you can't entirely blame Blair for other people's violence either. I agree though that everybody other than him and his cronies know that the Iraq war has made us much more susceptible to attacks.'

'Well, that's very big of you, Rob. Thanks for that.' replied the younger, sarcastically. 'Whatever you say, I do blame Blair and Bush – totally.'

What was it about Rob that always made Tom want to react so uncompromisingly? He wasn't often like that with other people. Somehow it was the roles they usually slipped into with each other. The older brother considered that the activist phase was something to be grown out of. From his more mature perspective, it was his duty to put the younger sibling in his place. Tom, by contrast, felt a constant urge to provoke his elder brother out of his lapse into conventionality.

Rob – as normal – eventually looked to say something amusing and dispel any bad feeling that might develop.

'I expect Blair has been working 24/7 on Al'Qaeda ever since 9/11. Do you think they'll start calling this 7/7?'

'It's not funny, Rob.'

They soon drifted back to pontificating.

'The big lie', offered Rob 'was to react to the Twin Towers as if it was some unique event in the history of humanity – all that crap about the world and the rules will never be the same. Why?

History is littered with examples of brutal terrorism in which the innocent suffer and die. The scale might have been pretty dramatic but that's about the only thing that was new about it.'

'And the fact that it was committed on the soil of the world's only superpower', Tom interrupted.

'Yes, there's that, too. But that was no reason for Blair to join in with the warmongering, was it? I mean, look at Chile. Over the years, as many people were killed as a result of Pinochet's military coup as in New York. Yet nobody argued that the killing of those innocent people suddenly turned the world into a new place, demanding indiscriminate bombings and torture, did they?'

'Well, the big difference was that America was the Osama Bin Laden of that particular atrocity, wasn't it? It was them that orchestrated the terror.'

'Exactly. Yet as soon as they become the victim rather than the perpetrator there's this ridiculous bully-like overreaction – "shock and awe" and all that disgusting violence. It can only make things worse.'

They were interrupted by the sudden return home of Rob's partner Georgie with Alice, their three-year-old daughter.

'Daddy, Daddy!' the child yelled, running into Rob's arms.

'Can we have sushi for tea?'

'No, not tonight darling,' he replied. 'Uncle Tom is staying and he doesn't like sushi.'

The little girl looked daggers at Tom and burst into tears, overtired and hungry after her late excursion. Soon her loud sobs drowned out the continuing television coverage of the day's horrific events.

'But I want sushi, Daddy!' she demanded, stamping her little foot in defiance.

'No darling, I've told you, not tonight. Look, if you go and ask mummy really nicely, I'm sure she'll make you some penne pasta. That's also your favourite, isn't it?'

Alice's sobs reduced in volume and frequency while she weighed up this option. A moment of contemplation followed, after which she concluded that the pasta alternative was acceptable and raced off to find her mum.

'Mummy, Dad says I can have penne pasta!' she yelled as she left the room. Crisis averted, the brothers returned to watching interviews with shocked and grieving commuters.

Although they partly loved to discuss politics and current affairs together, Rob and Tom had also become wary of such issues. While there was always plenty to agree upon, eventually a note of tension was always likely to creep in. Rob tended to be a little bit on the defensive about his prosperous life – holiday home, regular exotic trips abroad, his own boat – and his comparative refusal to uphold the family's dissenting spirit. Tom made him feel a bit guilty about his own priorities. This unease had grown stronger since the children by his first marriage had grown up – the youngest was sixteen now – and the divorce. Second wife Georgie was a well-known children's author, much admired for the social realism she brought to her fiction, but while they both espoused solid left-wing values, these were expressed more in 'pillars of the local community' type activities – school governors and trustees of a nearby community centre – rather than political activism. On Iraq, however, he felt on safer ground, having come out of demonstration retirement to join the million or more who had marched through London on the eve of the invasion.

Sibling rivalry in the Moore family manifested itself in unusual ways. In many respects Rob considered his life infinitely richer than his brother's. The younger had missed out on the things that were most dear to him, particularly children. Tom also annoyed him. When was he ever going to grow out of his student protest mentality? But he also experienced pangs of envy over his lack of ties and a grudging admiration for that dogged campaigning spirit. He had to admit that it had made him think about issues he might otherwise have ignored. For sure, some of this animal and vegan stuff was going a bit far, yet even in this his brother had had some influence. Rob had greatly reduced his meat intake and, where feasible, he and Georgie ensured that what they did eat was obtained from organic or free-range sources. If it hadn't been for the rest of his family, he liked to think that he might possibly have become a vegetarian himself.

As for Tom, he felt similarly ambivalent about Rob's lot. He was exasperated by big brother's failure to embrace all of the same values. How could he know what went on in slaughterhouses and still eat meat? How could he drive around in a big car and travel on so many aeroplanes when global warming threatened us all? In other ways though, he continued to look up to him. Rob was all right: he liked him. Deep down their differences were not that great. A bit of him was also jealous of the family life and easy-going success.

Later in the evening they were on familiar and safer ground, chatting away about their family and shared childhood. Some of the old photograph albums were brought out and there, amongst the snapshots of holidays and domesticity, were several from their protesting past. A grainy, creased and yellowing black-and-white picture from the Aldermaston anti-nuclear march showed their youthful mother pushing a bemused looking Tom in a pushchair. Rob, grinning broadly, stood beside them. An enlarged photograph, clearly purchased from the local newspaper, featured their parents together with Aunt Helen and a couple of other campaigners who the brothers did not recognise. They were standing beside two posters of starving African children and a homemade banner that carried the message – *Support the Biafran Children – Kids Give Up Sweets For A Week*. Tom, serious and proud, was standing at the front alongside three other children, one of whom was Helen's younger daughter, Sophie. Rob was not there. A little later they came across a colour photo of the older boy, clearly marked summer 1968 on the back. He was at a protest against Enoch Powell, not long after the politician's anti-immigration speech had fuelled racial tensions across the country.

'God, look at the length of your hair, you horrible dirty hippy!'

'Yeah man, looking pretty good at the back, wasn't it? The shirt is rather fetching, too, don't you think?'

It was a bright, multi-coloured, flowery shirt, predominantly purple.

'Look how young mum looks in this one!' exclaimed Tom, picking up the Aldermaston picture again. 'It's still hard to believe that your own mother could once have been that young and attractive.'

'Yes, it is,' responded Rob, quietly.

It was he who introduced a more critical note to the nostalgia.

'Fat lot of good it did giving up sweets for a week. I read in an article the other day that three million children faced starvation in the three years of the Nigeria-Biafra conflict.'

Tom leapt to the protesters' defence.

'I don't agree with that at all. That was probably the first time that large numbers of people in rich countries started to worry about the Third World and Africa. Think of all those acts of generosity towards people from far-away places it has inspired since. Surely that's been worthwhile?'

'I can't see that all the generosity in the world has made a great deal of difference. What lessons have been learned from those children's suffering? None whatsoever. Civil war, tyrants, corruption and famine – there's more of it than ever before as far as I can see – especially in Africa.'

'Probably that's true', the younger conceded, 'but if it hadn't been for campaigners, things would have been a lot worse. Look at the money and awareness that Band Aid raised, for instance, let alone all the less publicised pressure groups and charities that beaver away from day to day. They must have saved and improved the lives of millions. And what about the Jubilee 2000 initiative to cancel Third World debt? You can't say that hasn't had any impact. The very fact that it is being discussed at the G8 summit is a fantastic achievement.'

'Oh, I grant you that every few years a particular crisis hits the headlines – Ethiopia in the 1980s and Rwanda a decade later. Now it appears to be Sudan. A few pop stars, comedians and other celebrities get all self-righteous about it and stimulate a wave of fundraising and protest. Meanwhile, all the basket cases too numerous to mention – Congo, Ivory Coast and Somalia for a start – fail to strike the publicity jackpot and people go on dying in their hundreds of thousands. The only thing you can be certain about is that there will be plenty of conflict, corruption and misery for the arms dealers to get rich pickings out of.'

Tom recognised the grim truth in what his brother was saying. How could he not? Was there anything on earth more despicable than arms dealing? Nonetheless, he was not going to accept this negativity without a fight. It was his duty to fly the protester's flag. Moreover, this was a symbolic battle in which both were seeking to justify their very existence. He opted for a more personal approach.

'Well, what about South Africa? Look how anti-apartheid campaigners like you were vilified. Look at the stick you all took over trying to stop the South African rugby tour.'

'Yes, trying to stop a rugby international certainly wasn't cricket', said Rob, affecting an upper-class English accent. '"How dare you disrupt such a great bastion of the British sporting establishment?"' he mocked, beginning to regret that he'd brought politics back into the conversation.

'Oh, you're so witty Rob', responded Tom, not amused and determined to make his point. 'Everyone condemned Mandela as a terrorist, yet now he is probably the most admired man in the world. Nobody back then could have foreseen that South Africa would ever be free of apartheid.'

'Yes, and left to an epidemic of AIDS and different kinds of political corruption.'

'Bollocks, Rob! Even you must accept that the defeat of apartheid was a great triumph, whatever the problems South Africa faces now. You should be chuffed with the part you played.'

It still made Tom felt proud to think of his brother running onto the pitch at Twickenham, all those decades ago. He had long reinstated the victory over apartheid and Mandela's policy of truth and reconciliation as an inspirational example, vital to maintaining his fragile faith in the possibility of human progress.

'Well, I suppose you're right', Rob surprisingly accepted. 'Anything has got to be better than those racist bastards. But I still don't really know how much all that campaigning had to do with it. The political pressure from around the world just grew too intense for the apartheid regime to survive.'

'Precisely. And who created the political pressure in the first place? Maybe the anti-apartheid campaigns wouldn't have brought down the South African government on their own – I'll grant you that. Without them though, the politicians and business world would probably have ignored the whole issue.'

'I suppose what it does show', continued Rob, absorbed in his own train of thought rather than his brother's reply, 'is that you can never really know how history will come to judge you. I mean, do you remember how Dad and everyone else used to rant and rail against Harold Wilson's Labour government in the sixties? It was only concerned with television and image; it was obsessed with science and technology; it had sold out to big business and betrayed the ordinary working man. Yet in retrospect, some of its achievements look pretty impressive. Abortion and homosexuality legalised, the first anti-racist legislation enforced, capital punishment abolished.'

'And neither did Wilson send our troops out to support a mad American war – unlike Blair', added Tom.

'No, that's absolutely right. And to think how we used to attack him on those anti-Vietnam marches because of the speeches he made in defence of the war. We hated him. It's only in retrospect that we've learnt how difficult his position was. He had to be seen to support the US because we were so indebted financially and we now know that he resisted pressure to send troops pretty heroically.'

'So what are you saying, Rob? If history can change our judgement, does that mean that in forty years time we might be congratulating Blair on the invasion of Iraq?'

'Well speaking personally, I expect to be dead or at least past caring! But seriously, I suppose it is still possible that everything might work out fine. Hardly likely though, is it? I would have thought that the war will almost certainly continue to be seen as a disaster. But you know, in some ways that's a shame, because I'm sure the government has done some good things.'

'Oh yes, like what?' Tom snapped back. He had come to dislike Blair almost as much as he had despised Thatcher.

'Like the minimum wage and Northern Ireland for example. And what about your hunting ban?'

'You're suddenly sounding rather upbeat about New Labour and progress in the world, Rob,' said Tom, biting his lip to refrain from going off on a rant about how it had been the backbenchers who had got the Hunting Act passed, despite Blair having changed his mind and decided not to push for a ban.

'Oh no, I don't think anybody can accuse me of being upbeat, little brother. It doesn't seem to me that New Labour has achieved that much – not when you consider all the hype that surrounded its election anyway. I just look at all the political optimism of my youth and feel that it amounted to next to nothing. I mean, look at Dylan. Didn't he allow *The Times They Are A Changin'* to be used as the soundtrack for a jeans commercial?'

'It was an advert for the Montreal Bank actually. Apparently, he's promoted Starbucks as well.'

'Well, I reckon that just about says it all.'

'Bloody hell, Rob, sometimes you sound just like Dad. It's a good job that not everybody is as disillusioned as you are, you grumpy old sod. Look at Aunt Helen. She must be nearly eighty by now and she's still going strong – running the local CND group, holding weekly pacifist candlelit vigils, promoting universal vegetarianism, a leading member of the Cuban Solidarity Group – still believing in the underlying goodness of humanity and that everything will be put right if only we can achieve the perfect socialist state.'

'Ah yes, but we all know that Helen's a complete crank', replied Rob dismissively, though smiling fondly at the thought of his favourite Aunt's naïve and unquenchable idealism.

'And we all know what a crank is,' interrupted Tom, triumphantly.

'An important part of an engine that causes revolutions!' the two brothers shouted out in unison, laughing as they did so at the recollection of one of their father's favourite expressions.

Appendix – author's note

When I began planning this book, the intention was to write a non-fictional account of protest movements in the UK over the last fifty years. I am not entirely certain how it metamorphosed into the novel cum drama-documentary it turned out to be, other than that it seemed a far more interesting and appropriate way of telling the story I really wanted to tell. The final version mixes factual accounts of historical incidents – Peter Tatchell's attempt to arrest President Mugabe, the murder of Victor Java and so on – with fictional characters placed in real events and other episodes that are a complete invention. I can only trust that this combination of fact and fiction does not leave the reader in any confusion over what is historically accurate and what is imagined.

For the first part of the book, I'm grateful to Maisie Carter and Joy Coombes for their recollections of the early days of CND, particularly the Aldermaston marches, (and to Joy for so much more). *The CND Story*, edited by John Minnion and Philip Bolsover, also proved helpful. *BBC News* archives, freely available on the internet, were a rich source of background material on any number of issues, ranging from the history of Trafalgar Square as a centre of protest to the Chilean military coup. Thanks also to John Salvatore for his memories of the anti-apartheid movement in the late 1960s.

The animal rights section (and, to a lesser extent, the chapter that deals with Tom's university days) is based much more upon personal experience of a campaign I have been heavily involved with for more than thirty years. A more imaginative writer would probably, I think, have externalised that experience and placed Tom Moore, Septimus the Severe, Marie Westwood and company in another campaigning world. My attempts to do so failed dismally and I was left with no satisfactory alternative to setting the book in an environment I know well. My hope is that those who have dedicated their time to other protest movements will recognise similar human strengths, weaknesses and idiosyncrasies to those displayed by my own cast of characters. Some of the incidents described in this section are also based upon actual events, including, bizarrely, a television chat show that ended up with an animal activist being physically attacked by a defender of the fur trade. Nonetheless, my radically altered version is set in a different place at a different time and none of the fictional characters in this or any other part of the book are representations of real people.

My thanks to Andrew Tyler for allowing me to quote from his groundbreaking and powerful article, *Slaughterhouse Tales*, first published in *The Independent* on March 13 1989. The original idea was to reproduce the 3,000 words in full, but somehow it didn't quite fit naturally into the final version. Those who would like to read more can, however, still find it through an internet search. It's well worth the effort.

The titles of the four different sections are all derived from Bob Dylan songs, *The Times They Are A Changin'* (obviously), *Blind Willie McTell*, *Senor (Tales of Yankee Power)* and *When the Ship Comes In*.

The D. H. Lawrence quotation ('And as the white cock calls in the doorway ...') is from the essay *Aristocracy*, in *Reflections On The Death Of A Porcupine*, first published in *Phoenix 11, Uncollected, Unpublished and Other Prose Works (1968)*.

The scene where Aunt Helen is on trial for disabling a military aircraft at the time of the Indonesian government's suppression of East Timor is based on the courageous protest by Joanna Wilson, Lotta Kronlid, Andrea Needham and Angie Zelter, who, in January 1996 and as members of the Seeds of Hope (Ploughshares Movement), carried out a similar initiative (with a similar outcome in court) at British Aerospace's factory at Warton, Lancashire.

I owe the maxim from which I took my title – 'a crank is an important part of an engine that causes revolutions' – to the writings of the late E. F. Schumacher.

Thanks to Adrian Howe for showing faith in the book.

I am also indebted to close friends and colleagues from the past who have shared experiences and influenced my thinking, and without whom, 'in spite of time's derision', it would have been impossible to write *Cranks & Revolutions*.

If I thought the book could do them justice, I would dedicate it to all those never-say-die campaigning pensioners, who, in their different ways, are the inspiration for Aunt Helen, Elizabeth Plant and the Reverend Tony Swallow.

Above all, my gratitude is due to Sharon Howe for her generous spirit and her unstinting support for the project. Her proofreading skills and incisive comments on the many draft manuscripts were also invaluable.